IMMORTAL DEATH

THE IMOGEN GRAY SERIES BOOK FIVE

LAURETTA HIGNETT

CHAPTER 1

"*M*on dieu, what have you done, *pauvre conne?*"
I barely even noticed the tiny, gruff voice swearing at me in French. It was a squeak on the wind, a nothing sound, easily dismissed. There was no one else around anyway; not a soul in the town square apart from us, so maybe it was a fragment of my fractured mind. My conscience, perhaps. The ghost of all my poor choices.

I chuckled softly. The voice chose a bad time to try and make itself heard. Right now, right at this very second, despite all the earth-shattering events that were probably about to unfold, I couldn't bring myself to care about anything except for the gorgeous hard man underneath me.

The ground shook; a deep, subtle, ominous rumble. I could hear the Ancient's screams echo through the dimensions, piercing every single realm with his furious cry. Every other time in my long, long history, that deep scream of outrage, and that rumbling of the earth would signify the beginning of my worst nightmare. It meant a terrifying chase, a cold-sweat flight for safety, three days of running or he'd catch me. That sound should have reduced me to blind, gibbering terror.

This time though, I didn't give a fuck. I was still straddling my lover on a park bench in the town square, with a glistening sheen of sweat on my skin from our lovemaking. There was an impenetrable pocket dimension fixed around the portal. I was safe.

I tipped back my head and laughed, watching gold-red sparkles trail from my hands as I waved them through the air. My skin was glowing. "I've never noticed this before," I said wonderingly, twinkling my fingers in the darkness. "I've never appreciated my full powers. I never got the chance to play with them. I was always too busy running." I brushed a glowing red-gold fingertip over Rafael's lips. They parted softly; his eyes were so dark, still drenched in lust, watching me with an expression of wonder on his face.

I knew what he felt like. Being with him, wholly, completely, was everything I ever hoped it would be and more.

I giggled lightly, hearing my voice trill prettily like a windchime. Oh, it was definitely *more*. I'd been avoiding trying to use my full powers my whole life. I squashed them down deep inside of me. Every time I was forced to pull them out, that mysterious, ancient powerful creature would blaze into our reality in a fit of murderous outrage. He'd hunt me, find me and rip me into tiny pieces.

And every single time the Ancient did that to me, I would regenerate from one of those tiny pieces he tore me into. Sometimes it took *decades* to fully heal. The whole time I recovered, I was in torturous, agonising physical pain.

It was the worst thing about my existence, the cruel irony of my curse. I had a full arsenal of power at my disposal and I couldn't ever use it. There were so many times in my long, long history that I gave in to whatever asshole was harassing

2

me, because if I used my full powers to fight them off, the Ancient would do much, much worse.

I didn't know who the Ancient was, or why he hated me so much. Nobody knew. I'd run down every lead and investigated every powerful creature I'd ever heard of, and nothing had come up. He hadn't been seen on Earth before, not by anyone. He didn't match any description of any other mythical creature. His powers were god-like, and he didn't seem to care about anything at all apart from doing his best to destroy every tiny part of my body.

I'd even considered the idea that he might be the Creator itself, a facet of the Creator, maybe, a jealous manifestation of some sort, annoyed that I'd blundered onto this green earth when I wasn't supposed to be here. I could only guess he despised me for what I was, because there was no one like me on Earth. Half human, half star.

I'd gone my whole life stuffing down the star part, because it brought me nothing but pain.

Not anymore.

"I remember the first time I did this," I murmured in Rafael's ear. "The first time I'd used my full power, I'd fallen into a creek and I was scared. I was with my aunt, and she couldn't get to me. I reached deep inside myself and pulled at the power I could feel at my core, and I leapt straight out of the water like a crocodile. My aunt was terrified." I giggled. "She ran into the grasslands screaming. It took me a whole day to convince her I was fine. Of course," I added, grimacing, "the Ancient found me the day after that, and ripped me apart. I watched him coming, a great beast made up of thousands of eyes and enormous wings. I must have had the dumbest look of wonder on my face."

I didn't remember much after that.

The memories were fuzzy; it was a long time ago. Two-hundred and fifty, maybe three-hundred thousand years ago.

I was immortal. The only true immortal on Earth, in fact. No matter what I did, I couldn't die.

Believe me, I tried. I'd tried everything. Apart from the usual practical methods anyone would use to induce death, like beheading or throwing myself into lava pits, I'd tried sorcery, witchcraft, demonology, even invoking various gods and goddesses, every time hoping that one of them would be able to end my curse for me.

Nothing worked. Every time I was hurt, I regenerated – sometimes from a speck of dust.

It was beyond intolerable. I'd spent millenia as a suicidal person who couldn't kill themselves. I doubt there was a more miserable person alive than me.

Not *now*, though. Not anymore.

I'd come to Emerald Valley on a mission. I was here to find the one person who knew how I could become mortal, but I'd found much more than that. I'd found a lover, my Vampire King, Rafael – someone who inexplicably loved me for the car-crash of a person that I was. I'd found a sister in Marigold, the sweet, loveable witch who would do anything for me. I'd found a grumpy sister-in-law in her wife, Backman. I'd found a hilarious curmudgeonly granddad-type in Father Benson, whom I'd just laid to rest. And I'd found my kid.

Or rather, he'd found me. I rescued Leroy, he rescued me right back, and I loved him with all my heart. I'd never been prouder of anything in my entire life. For the first time ever, I had people to love, who loved me in return – not for my immortality, or my strength, or what I could do for them. They loved me for me, and I loved them right back.

And, also for the first time ever, I wasn't in a hurry to die. In Emerald Valley, I'd found life.

The only thing I *hadn't* found yet was my father. He was the only one who knew what I was.

My father had been human in the end, completely human, in fact. But he'd been something else when I was born, something unknown. Something not of this world.

A star, apparently. A creature so rare and obscure, only the most ancient fae could recognize my scent. It was a faerie queen who told me that I am part-star. She didn't have the language to explain herself more clearly and was slightly bemused about my apparent parentage. Apparently, the stars, as she knew them, did not come to Earth. Ever.

To confuse things even further, the demons I'd just fought were convinced I was one of them. According to them, my essence felt the same. Since the demon Haagenti had mentioned it, I was rolling a theory around in my head that my father had been some sort of ancient, benevolent demon god, or something like that.

I couldn't be sure, and I might not ever find out. By the time I'd been old enough to form proper memories, my father had been completely, entirely, wholly human, and he'd died, just like humans did.

He'd been reborn, too. Over the course of the last few hundred-thousand years, I'd met him again and again, always reincarnated in a new body, but still the same soul I'd known. He still had that same curiosity and love for humanity that was so uniquely him. He *loved* being human. On the rare occasion I managed to find him again, I demanded that he tell me what I needed to do to become human like he did, so I could die.

His answer was always the same. *Live.*

Kinda a slap in the face for someone who only wanted to die.

Ironically enough, it was what Benson had said to me as he was dying in my arms. I had to *live*. The thought occurred to me that he might have been my dad, but it didn't feel quite right. In all our lives together, my father was always protecting me, always guiding me, regardless of what body he wore. Benson, by contrast, always got me into trouble. He had more of a 'naughty best friend' energy to him.

My father was here somewhere, though. I just didn't know who he was. The witch who scryed for him told me that he wouldn't be in town when I arrived, but he would be back, and soon. I'd checked out every single man in the Valley, but came up with nothing. Granted, my mission to find my dad kept getting interrupted by evil bastards trying to destroy the world. I'd find him eventually, though.

I'd come to Emerald Valley to find my father, and I'd found so much more here. I'd saved the world on a few different occasions, in fact. I'd come here to find out how to die, and instead, I'd learned how to live. And now, with my full powers flaming inside me, my vision heightened, and my senses on fire, I was more alive than I ever had been. I wasn't in any hurry to place myself on the mortal coil and shuffle off it. Not when I had friends who loved me, family who adored me, and Rafael underneath me.

The earth shook again, a gentle, rolling tremor. Rafael's brow had furrowed slightly; he was worried. I curled myself around him, holding him tighter, reluctant to let him go.

"It's okay," I whispered. "The Ancient can't touch me. The pocket dimension is warded especially for him, I made sure of that. He won't be able to get out." My eyes narrowed. "For the first time in history, I'll have him exactly where I want him."

In an instant, I'd gone from floaty, horny bliss, to snarling vengeance. I bared my teeth, growling softly. "What I wouldn't give to get into that pocket dimension and rip him apart. Give him a taste of his own medicine." Revenge. Bloody, tortuous revenge. I wanted it so bad it made me gnash my teeth.

The ground rumbled underneath us again. Not so subtle this time. He was coming.

"Imogen," Rafael murmured. "We must prepare, just in case. He is unknown. I fear for your safety."

His lips were so close to my ear, the vibration from his words tingled down my neck and into my breasts. I arched my back and moaned again, in a bizarre abrupt volte-face. I wasn't angry anymore, I was just horny.

I bit my lip and ground myself against Rafael, unable to concentrate, helpless in the river of lust that surged through me. He shifted underneath me, sending jolts of pleasure right through my body.

I rubbed my bottom lip along his jawline, moaning softly. It was so hard to concentrate on anything right now, not while I was glowing golden, saturated in my full star powers, consumed with thoughts and feelings and sensation, experiencing the entire spectrum of human, and, apparently, star emotions at the same time. I let my head loll back and I moaned, arching against my lover.

The ground shook again. Above us, I sensed rather than saw the portal pulse. The invisible pocket dimension wrapped around it shimmered once, a rippling lavender glow in the darkness.

Suddenly, a scream rent the air, ripping through my eardrums; a scream of such pain and misery and outrage I felt it smash into the depths of my soul.

"*Imogen*." Rafael swooped me to one side and stood up, placing me on my feet next to him.

I bared my teeth and laughed. "It's okay. Let him come." I curled my hands into claws as battle-lust gripped me again. Oh, all these feelings, my emotions were heightened, everything was so intense. "Let him come," I growled again.

The portal pulsed again. The earth beneath my feet trembled, and–

A vicious jolt rocked the earth as a mighty force hit the ground in front of me. I was knocked off my feet, my hands sandwiched over my ears as the Ancient's scream ripped through our Earthly dimension.

He was here.

CHAPTER 2

*S*uddenly, there was only silence. The town square was deathly still.

I got to my feet slowly, hauling Rafael up with me. I chuckled. "We've got him."

He inspected the blank space in front of us. "How can you be sure, my love? There is nothing here."

"I can *feel* him," I whispered, holding my hands out to where the pocket dimension would be. "I know he is in there. He's watching me." I smiled and held up my hand, letting my star powers light up the space in front of me, an eerie red-gold glow. "I can feel his pain."

I heard a note of gloating in my voice. "He's furious, outraged, completely tortured by my presence." I laughed out loud again. "It's *delectable*."

Rafael pulled me closer, watching my face carefully. "Imogen..." He tilted his head slightly, concern coloring his features. "Are you okay?"

"Of course I am. I've never been better. I've got my life-long nemesis stuck in a tiny pocket dimension. He's in a cage.

He can't get me." I flexed my fingers, cracked my knuckles, and scowled. "I want to beat the shit out of him."

"Hmm." Rafael wrapped his arm around me, and I melted into him. God, he was perfection; all hard muscles and smooth skin, so firm, the memory of him inside me... I pulled him back down, practically throwing him back on the park bench, jumped on top and straddled him, desperate to feel his bare skin on me again.

My head whipped back to the invisible pocket dimension. I wanted to tear the flesh off the Ancient.

Rafael was so hard underneath me... I growled, and rubbed myself up against him.

"Argh!" I shouted out loud. "This is too much!"

"My love." Rafael stroked a finger down my cheek and I dissolved into him. "You are like a newborn vampire, so full of lust and hunger and heightened emotions. You cannot focus. I understand."

I laughed. "I guess I am a bit like that. All this... this..." I held up my hands, mesmerized at the glow running over my skin. "This *power*. It's insane. I can't concentrate. I want to tear the Ancient apart and I want to love every single inch of your skin, and I want to rip open the vending machine back in the pub and shove every single packet of Doritos in my mouth at once..."

"It's okay," Rafael murmured. He put both hands on either side of my cheeks, and held my gaze. "You'll get used to it. And if you can't, you can dial down your powers, can you not?"

"Yes, but I don't want to," I growled. My menace was considerably reduced by the fact that Rafael was squishing my cheeks between my hands. "I don't ever want to dial my powers down again. I've been hiding my candle underneath a bushel for far too long."

He smiled. "And you are glorious," he said to my squished-up face. "A goddess."

A high-pitched but gravelly voice grunted right next to us. "Non, she is a *stupide salope*. What in the blazes have you done, harlot?"

"Shit!" I shot up and off Rafael's lap, landing beside the park bench, frantically adjusting what was left of my clothes.

My bra had somehow disintegrated. I held the tatters of my blouse closed with one hand, and shimmied my skirt down with the other, while Raf adjusted his suit and buttoned his jacket, covering his bare chest. "Who said that?" Both of us looked frantically around for the voice that had spoken.

No one was here.

The town square was completely devoid of life. I met Rafael's eyes and frowned. He was confused, too.

With my star powers blazing through me I could almost feel everything alive within a hundred square radius. I could sense all the mourners singing and wiping tears from their eyes in the pub behind us; the young Belgian couple in the bakery over on Main Street, firing up their ovens, even the people in the houses beyond that, sleeping peacefully. One young mother sat up, blinking, confused, woken by the slight tremor beneath the ground.

It wasn't the Ancient who had spoken. He was silent and invisible, stuck in the pocket dimension in front of me. I could feel him, incoherent with rage, ready to explode.

"Rafael," I whispered. "What was that?"

"Me, you blistering buffoon," the little gravelly voice said, from right beside me.

I swiveled around, and blinked.

A stone gargoyle sat there beside the park bench, barely the size of a small dog. Carved out of solid rock, crouching down, with a grotesque, overly muscular frame, a heavy ridged brow, wide mouth open, and huge fangs bared. It was tiny, and made out of rock. It wasn't animated, and it definitely wasn't moving now.

The statue had been next to the park bench when I stumbled out of Benson's wake, looking for somewhere to puke. I'd dismissed it as a new addition to the town square; a random, slightly intimidating artwork of some sort. This town was full of rich eccentric artists, so I didn't give it a thought. Plus, I was very drunk, and not really paying attention. It wasn't alive, so I didn't worry about it.

It wasn't alive now, either. But the voice had to have come from somewhere…

I edged closer, staring at the gargoyle intently. The fangs were a bit much. I reached out with a finger, and tapped on the rock.

It snapped. "My God, woman. Keep your fingers to yourself! As if you haven't done enough already!"

I fell back on my ass, and blinked. "Christ on a bike!"

The gargoyle unfroze again and sneered at me. "Oh, surprised, are we? *Imbécile*. What did you think I was doing here?"

I sat up, and dusted off my palms. "I thought you were someone's weird craft project, actually. Something not worthy of notice, obviously."

"Bitch," the gargoyle snapped his claw-tipped fingers at me. "You should be trembling in fear."

"At what?" I let out a bark of laughter. "At you? I've done shits bigger than you, sweetheart."

"My love." Rafael leaned down, extended his hand, and helped me to my feet. He met my eyes. "It is a *gargoyle*."

"I'm not blind, Raf. I know what he is."

I kept my words light, because it was almost impossible

for me to concentrate on anything right now. The fear swimming in my lover's eyes was throwing a bucket of cold water all over my libido. There was a gargoyle, right here. Right next to me.

Apparently, it was bad news. The worst kind, in fact.

Gargoyles have been carved all throughout time by great master carvers and used to adorn great buildings and mighty cathedrals. Their creators spun great stories around these sculptures – their purpose was to guard against the gravest danger. Most humans don't realize how magical they are, and it would come as a surprise to these master carvers that the thing they created for a purpose could actually be *used* for that purpose.

These great artists that created gargoyles did it with an intention: To guard against danger. So, when the gravest danger approaches, the inanimate rock could be inhabited by a guardian spirit – a spirit guide that had been through several hundred incarnations and had a good knack of knowing when the shit was about to hit the fan. These spirit guides found it easy to use a gargoyle as a vessel to carry them towards the danger so they could sound a warning.

I'd met several in my lifetime. They were always bad news. This one could have chosen a more intimidating vessel, though; he was only the size of a corgi.

I peered down at the little thing. "Where did you come from?"

He unfroze in that unsettling way of his, and snapped his fangs at me. "My name is Viscount Claude Clément Deschamps," he announced grandly, tossing his stone head. "You may call me the Viscount."

Wanker. "Hmmm. No. I'll call you Claude."

"I was called to manifest about an hour ago, so I found the closest vessel to this location," he said, jabbing a claw towards the portal. "I manifested in this sculpture, on the side of the little church, over there." He rubbed his hands over his ridiculously muscled torso. "The six-pack is a bit much, I'll admit. I like the fangs, though."

"You've been there for a whole hour?"

He nodded.

"You've been, erm, watching us?"

He curled his lip. "If you're wondering if I enjoyed watching you two make love on this park bench, the answer is no. You rut like animals. It is disgusting. You should probably not bite her again," he nodded at Rafael. "Not unless you want to turn her."

Only humans could be turned into vampires. There were precise steps to trigger the Vamp Metamorphosis, and it didn't work for everyone, even if you got all the steps right. First, you need to be completely human. It didn't work on shifters or anyone with even a drop of fae blood. Then, you needed to be bitten three times by an ancient vampire – and they had to be *old*, so they'd have enough of the right pathogens to trigger the genes to activate. Then, you needed to be drained of most of your own blood, and you'd have to drink the ancient vampire's blood. Lots of it. Enough to put the ancient vampire's life in danger, in fact.

The Metamorphosis wasn't something that ever happened accidentally, and it would never happen to me. I wasn't human, to start with. Rafael was probably ancient enough to have the right pathogens, but I would never put his life in danger by draining his own blood. It was a good thing, too, because I liked it when he bit me. I was looking forward to more of that in the future.

I rolled my eyes. "Do those little stone bumps you call eyes actually work, Claude? Can you actually see me?"

He snorted. "I wish I couldn't. That outfit is hideous. I

understand you were attending a funeral. Do you have no respect for the dead?"

"I mean, can you see that I'm not human?" My skin was still glowing golden. I waved my hand, showing him the red-gold sparkles that followed in the night air.

He made a rude noise. "Pah. I can see, but I don't care. Your humanity can be turned up and down like a dial." He ran his gaze over me, assessing every single inch, his expression distasteful. "Whatever you are, you are still human enough to be turned Vampire if you're not careful."

"Okay. Speaking of dials, can you dial back the French sassiness?"

"*Non.*" He glared at me. "The Source compels me here to guard this spot. You want me, you take me as I am."

"Who said anyone wanted you?" I muttered under my breath. "Okay." I waved my hand carelessly. I couldn't let a tiny ugly little gargoyle get to me. "So what are you doing here, Claude?"

He rolled his eyes again. "*Putain de sa mère la pute!* Are you some sort of moron? What do you think I am doing here, *pouffiasse?*"

A low growl came from Rafael. "Watch yourself, Viscount," he said, wrapping an arm around me so I was slightly behind him. "You may be here for a worthy purpose, but if you insult my mate one more time, I will wrench your spirit out of that stone vessel and banish you back to the astral plane. Then, the destruction of this Earth will be on both of our heads."

I turned to stare at Rafael. "Destruction of Earth? Dramatic much?"

The gargoyle ran his eyes over Rafael. "You are prettier than she is, so I will hold my tongue. You seem smarter, too. She seems unable to grasp the gravity of the situation." He unfroze, and leapt to his feet, perching on the edge of the park bench he could meet our eyes. "Whatever has just come through this portal has triggered the apocalypse," he declared.

I rolled my eyes. "I hate to rain on your parade, Claude, but the thing that has just come through the portal has been on Earth many times. In fact, he was only here a few months ago. He's the bane of my existence, actually." I gritted my teeth. "Now I've got him trapped, and I finally get to find out why he's been hunting me. He's not going to destroy the Earth. His only beef is with me. He's an ancient powerful creature, yes, but he's shown no interest in taking over the Earthly realm."

"Oh, it's all about you, is it? It is not *what* he is. It is what he will *do*. And I hate to break it to you, sweetie," he sneered at me. "He's not trapped."

I arched an eyebrow. "Yes, he is. He can't get out."

"He can go back up through the portal," Claude pointed out. "He has not done that yet. He is still on this plane of existence."

I clenched my fists. I didn't want him to go back. I finally had him where I wanted him. "Well, I still can't see the danger. He can't stay on the earthly plane longer than three days. It seems to be a rule of our dimension for him. So even if I *can't* open the pocket dimension and beat the shit out of him, and even if he *doesn't* leave through the portal, we just have to wait a few days and he'll go."

The gargoyle looked up towards the invisible portal, hanging just above the statue of Sir Humphrey. "He's not going to leave," he said darkly. "Catastrophic events have been put in motion. The heavens weep."

I turned to Rafael. He looked worried, but confused, like me. I faced the gargoyle again. "Can you be a little more specific, buddy?"

"You think of yourself as the spider who has caught the

16

fly. *Non.* You've caught a bird, and he will shake the whole web apart."

"Hmmm. No. Too obscure."

The gargoyle huffed out a breath. *"Casse-couilles,"* he muttered under his breath. "I cannot tell the future. I have been called here because whatever is in that pocket dimension is set to destroy the world. I am here as a portent, a sign, a warning, perhaps. I will possibly witness the apocalypse."

"Hmm. Sounds grim."

The earth beneath our feet shook; I stumbled slightly. Rafael took my arm. We both glanced at each other, wide-eyed.

The gargoyle looked at me smugly. "See?"

The supercilious expression on his face was too much; my senses were still too heightened. "You little shit." I stepped forward and slapped him across the face.

He reared back, shocked. "Did you... did you just slap me?"

"You're French, aren't you? I thought it was appropriate."

His stone eyes flew wide. *"Fils de chien,"* he swore. He leapt at my face, claws out.

I managed to grab his arms before he dug his claws into my cheeks, but wow, he was strong! I flew back, landing on the wet grass, and he scrabbled his legs on top of me. Straining, I pushed him back. He extended his leathery wings, popping them out wide, each with a tiny claw on the end, and started jabbing me with them, hitting my hip, then my thigh.

"Take that, bitch! And that!" He poked little holes in my skin like a sewing machine, right up and down my sides. I squealed in outrage.

Rafael reached down and grabbed him by the neck, straining to pull him off me. Claude spun around, snapping at him with his fangs. "Stay out of this, *enfoiré!*"

17

It was like being attacked by a very strong, foul-mouthed poodle. He wriggled around and clamped himself onto Rafael's head, smothering his face with his ridiculously defined pecs and abs.

I scrambled off the ground and yanked at his wings. "Get off my boyfriend, you tiny French wanker!"

"What the hell is going on here?" The ground shook again, this time with thundering footsteps. Backman loped towards us, Marigold trailing right behind her. They skidded to a halt in front of us.

Backman's mouth dropped open. "Holy smokes. Is that a gargoyle?"

I fisted Claude by the neck, hauled him off Rafael and punched him in the mouth. "Yes." I punched him again. "Your powers of observation are excellent."

"Imogen." Marigold peered around Backman's broad shoulders. "Why is there a gargoyle here?"

Claude clamped his fangs down on my finger, severing it at the knuckle, and wriggled out of my grasp. "Ow!" I screamed. "Goddamnit!"

He flew up on his stone wings, landed on top of the statue of Sir Humphrey, and glared down at us haughtily.

I growled up at him. "You bit my finger off!"

"It's already growing back. Don't be a baby."

I snarled and lunged towards him again. Rafael held me back by the tattered remains of my shirt. "My love," he said. "I don't think we will accomplish much by brawling with a gargoyle."

"No, but stomping his head off will certainly make me feel better."

"It's a waste of time," he murmured in my ear. Rafael's hands on my body distracted me from my bloodlust again. I huffed out a slow breath. He was right. I didn't even know if it was possible to do any damage to that damned stony bastard.

I tore my eyes away from the gargoyle and instead watched my index finger grow back. First, a whitish bone bloomed like a mushroom out of the stump, and was quickly covered by fat, muscle and finally skin. It was mesmerizing. I'd never seen myself heal that fast before.

Backman planted her feet and put her hands on her hips. "What's going on?"

The gargoyle sneered down at me. "Why don't you tell *them* what you've done, Immortal?"

"I haven't done anything!"

"Imogen," Marigold breathed out, looking at me. "You're glowing!"

I waved a hand through the air, trailing red-gold sparks. "Cool, huh?"

"It is *not* cool. Your friend is bringing about the apocalypse."

"That's a bit dramatic, Claude."

Backman cleared her throat. "He is a gargoyle. Obviously something has gone seriously wrong."

"There's something in the pocket dimension," Marigold mumbled. "The silent alarm went off." She looked at me. "Imogen, what have you done?"

"What have *I* done? I've done nothing!"

"Only a spot of public indecency, that's what," the gargoyle muttered. "Indecent exposure, lewd behavior…" He shuddered. "I'll never get that sight out of my brain."

I picked up my severed finger off the ground and threw it at him. "Shush, you."

"You better tell us now, little drill bug." Backman crossed her arms over her chest.

"Fine. Look, it's no big deal. But apparently, making love to Rafael was the trigger I needed to bring out my full star powers, and, of course, the Ancient has come through the portal."

Marigold's eyes popped. "He's here?"

I nodded.

On cue, the ground rumbled softly under our feet again.

Suddenly, anger flooded through me. I couldn't wait to tear him apart. Every memory of the pain he'd inflicted on me came rushing back, and I wanted to rip and smash him to pieces. "Get Leroy," I snarled. "Get this pocket dimension open so I can punch this asshole in the face."

Rafael tucked me under his arm and faced Backman. "She's a little overwhelmed by her full powers," he said to her.

"I'm not. I'm getting used to it, I swear. I've never had the chance to play with them before." My finger had grown back. I clicked them together and watched a sprinkle of red-gold sparkles drift into the air.

"My love, I hate to point this out, but we're in trouble. There's a gargoyle standing guard in front of a trapped, ancient powerful supernatural creature."

"This is bad news," Backman rumbled, nodding.

Claude snapped his wings. "Finally, someone takes me seriously!"

"Guardian," Backman said to him formally. "Can you tell us what the danger is? Do you know what to expect?"

"I cannot see ahead," he said stiffly. "I can only tell you that the creature will rip this world apart to have its vengeance."

"He's that powerful?"

"Not him." Claude thumbed his nose at me. "Her. Both of them actually. They're going to tear this world apart."

There was a moment of silence.

Marigold looked at me. "If you dial down your powers, will he go away?"

"I don't want him to go away," I said, baring my teeth,

suddenly overwhelmed with the need to face my tormentor directly. "Someone go and get Leroy."

Marigold would need him to help break open the pocket dimension. My kid was a very talented witch. If Marigold wouldn't do it, Leroy could probably do it all by himself.

Distracted again, I wondered where he was. Normally he was first on the scene whenever something terrible came through the portal. More often than not, it was his fault it came through in the first place.

He always fixed his mistakes, though. I should probably do the same.

I forced myself to concentrate. Where was Leroy? He was probably at home, in bed. He'd been at Father Benson's wake with me, and he'd left around nine to cycle home with some of the older kids from the Outdoor Education Center. I hadn't heard from him, but the kid was almost fourteen years old and had enough witchy firepower to bring down a small city.

I didn't worry about him. I worried about whatever idiot would try and hurt him. He was probably on his bike, pedaling furiously towards the town square right now.

"He'll be here soon, I'm sure," I said out loud. "You can go ahead and start to open up the pocket dimension, Marigold."

She ground her jaw. "No." One of her hands drifted down and rested on her belly.

For a second, I'd forgotten she was pregnant. A flood of emotion hit me, heightened by my new star powers, and I could almost feel her fear.

The world might end. She'd never get to hold her babies.

She planted her feet, defiant. "No, I'm not opening this pocket dimension, Imogen, are you mad? This is the creature that's been ripping you apart for hundreds of thousands of years. If I let him out, what do you think he's going to do?

Slap you in the face and go home? He'll rip you apart again! And worse, he'll rip all of us apart!"

"Not *now*," I said, clenching my fists. "I've got my full power now, Marigold. I can fight him. Not just me, but you and Backman and Rafael. We can all fight him."

Leroy would help, too, but I wouldn't let him. He was still just a kid. We'd need him to open up the pocket dimension, but I'd send him away as soon as it was open. I turned and looked down the street, half expecting to see him on his bike, but the street was empty. Where was he, anyway?

"This is madness," Backman muttered, pinching the bridge of her nose. "We don't even know what the Ancient is."

Claude snapped his wings. "I know what he is. The Destroyer. The Destroyer of the World."

I made a rude noise. All he ever wanted to do was destroy *me*, not the world. He was trapped. This was my chance to get back at him; it was probably the only chance I'd ever have.

And they were holding me back.

Anger surged through me. Pure, petulant outrage. I stepped towards Marigold, my eyes sparking. "You should be helping me," I growled. "I've helped *you*. I've saved you all before, many times. I've sacrificed myself. I've lost body parts for you people!"

Backman stepped in front of her wife and leveled a hard stare at me. "Back up, little drill bug. Before you do something stupid. Control yourself."

I growled back at her. Behind her, Marigold's eyes turned ruby red; her fingers curled over. A red glow bloomed in her fists.

I looked at her and laughed. "You're standing in a glasshouse and throwing fists of gravel in the air, Barbara.

You should be talking to your half-demon wife, there. She's got as much control of herself as I have."

The intensity in Backman's eyes exploded. "She's *pregnant*."

A rush of cold air blew over my skin. I froze. Oh, God, what was I doing? Backman was my friend. Marigold, somehow was more than that. My sister.

Rafael pulled me to his body and wrapped an arm around me. "Marigold," he said. "Can you open the glimmer window? We will be able to at least see the Ancient. We could talk with him. Reason with him, perhaps."

"He isn't reasonable, Rafael," I said darkly. "You can't reason with that kind of rage."

"Perhaps." Rafael ran his thumb down the side of my cheek, and I melted into him, my anger temporarily forgotten. "But we should try, at least."

Backman turned around, and cradled Marigold's face in her hands. Instantly the ruby glow disappeared, her clear blue eyes gazed back at her wife. "Babe," Backman rumbled. "Can you open the glimmer window?"

She nodded. "I can. I don't think I need Leroy for this."

We all backed away.

Marigold stepped forward, raising her hands in the air, closed her eyes, and started to chant in a low, deep tone. Her words grew in resonance, echoing around the dark town square, vibrating with power. The air in front of her shimmered, a glowing lavender wall appeared in front of her. Slowly, it faded, leaving a square outline hanging in mid-air.

Marigold opened her eyes, and gasped. Her skin went deathly pale. Quick as a whip, Backman wrapped a hand around her waist and pulled her backwards into her arms.

Adrenaline flooded my system; I felt like I could explode at any second. Rafael held me back. I let him, even though I wanted to smash my way through the window and rip the Ancient's head off.

"Is it secure, Marigold?" Rafael's voice was a whisper on the wind.

She nodded, staring at the window dumbly.

I edged forward, and looked inside the pocket dimension.

There was a monster in there.

The creature was twelve foot tall, and took up the whole space inside of the pocket dimension. I'd only ever gotten glimpses of him before, while he was screaming through the air, maddened with rage, just before he caught me and ripped me into bloody tiny shreds.

His appearance hit me like a ton of bricks. His body was made up of four enormous golden rings, shimmering and shining in an eerie, otherworldly way – a living, breathing metal, and completely covered with thousands of eyes, all blinking and peering in different directions. The noise it made raised gooseflesh all over my body; an unnatural, malevolent hum.

I froze in front of the glimmer window, suddenly terrified. This was my own personal monster; my torturer, my constant tormentor. This was the nightmare under my bed.

A warm, heavy hand fell on my shoulder, reassuring me. Another cooler, slim hand slid into my own palm. Backman and Marigold stood beside me, giving me courage.

I stared at the creature. Several long moments passed.

Finally, I opened my mouth. I couldn't find the words to say, though. There was only one question. "Why?" I croaked.

The wheels moved; spinning, the eyes blinking and narrowing, widening, collapsing in on themselves. The rings became two, then one, then the golden circle morphed into a tall shape, the shining living metal taking on a new texture.

Finally, a man stood there in the glimmer window. A man-like figure, anyway. Eight foot tall, perfectly muscled, rippling and tensing with unfathomable power. He was stripped bare to the waist, with long golden hair and the face of a perfect young god; a young Odin, or a Poseidon, perhaps, although no living artist would be able to render his magnificence on any earthly medium. His eyes glowed white, piercing me, ripping through my flesh and examining my soul.

I gaped at him; he was more terrifying now than he had been as a many-eyed ring monster.

He tilted his head up and glared at me with those powerful eyes. His lips fell open; I flinched back involuntarily.

I felt a squeeze on my waist. Rafael still had his arms around me. His touch gave me comfort. I took a deep, shuddering breath. *I could do this.*

The weight of the moment felt almost unbearable. I'd been waiting for this for hundreds of thousands of years.

I lifted my chin, hoping for defiance. "Why?"

The perfect face stared back at me. "You *dare* ask why?"

The force of his words blistered through me, and I gasped. Next to me, Backman flinched and put her hands over her ears. Mortals weren't supposed to hear his voice. I could tell.

I bit my lip, tasting blood. The pain helped me focus. "Yeah, I dare. Why? Who are you?"

"Who am I?" The Ancient gathered himself up, growing taller, more menacing, his voice dripping with outrage. "How dare you?"

"How dare I?" My mouth dropped open. Blistering-hot pinpricks of anger pierced the fog of terror that surrounded me. "How dare I? What the hell does that mean?"

"You dare ask who I am, when you have been torturing me for thousands of years?"

"Me? I've been torturing *you?* Are you fucking kidding

me?" My eyes sparked; I could see the reflection in the glimmer window; red-gold embers twinkling in the night air. Power surged down to my fingertips. "What the hell do you mean, I've been torturing *you?*"

The Ancient leaned forward slightly, menacingly. "You torture me," he growled, the words vibrating straight through the pocket dimension and into my soul. "You attempt to destroy me, over and over again."

Oh, this is a joke. It must be a joke. I squared my shoulders. "Okay, now I *know* you're insane, because you are the one that rips me into tiny little pieces over and over again! Do you even know how much it hurts to grow back my body parts?" Outrage was beginning to overwhelm me; I began to shake. How dare he?

He scoffed. "Physical pain. Physical pain is nothing. Nothing compared to what you do to me."

"What do I do to you?"

He leaned closer; white eyes sparking. "You crush my hope."

"I crush your *hope?*" My voice reached ear-splitting levels. "I crush your hope, so you decide to crush me into tiny pieces? You try to destroy me?"

"You cannot be destroyed as you are now." His face was cold, uncaring. "Physical pain is nothing. It means nothing. It is gone in a flash. My torment endures."

"A flash? It takes me decades to regrow my body after you try to annihilate me!" I threw my hands up, my fury exploding like a grenade. The force of my anger caused Rafael and Backman to stumble away.

"Imogen," Marigold said warningly. I glanced over my shoulder. She had taken a few steps back and braced herself, her eyes glinting with ruby. "Calm down."

I whirled around again to face the Ancient. "I will not calm down. How dare this motherfucker stand there and tell me that I'm the one torturing *him?*"

"This is not doing any good, love," Rafael said. "Please, back away."

The glow around me expanded; I clenched my fists. "No. No, none of you have any idea what he has done to me. I've been running scared my whole immortal life, Rafael! That fear taints everything, it destroys everything!"

He tugged at me again, trying to pull me away from the glimmer window. "You're not scared now."

"Damned right I'm not! Because I'm going to rip this window open and shove his pretty head up his own ass!"

A tiny fireball hit me in the back. "Imogen! Back up!"

I whirled around and snarled at Marigold. "I will not!" My fists curled into claws, a searing heat flamed on my palm, I tossed a fireball back at her.

Quicker than I'd ever seen before, Backman exploded into a huge mass of fur and fangs and swatted the fireball away. She planted herself in front of Marigold, reared up and roared at me; sharp teeth pulled back from her muzzle.

I looked down at my hands, shocked. "Why do I have the same powers as Marigold?" I hadn't even tried to form a fireball. It was instinctual; ingrained in my being. I'd never felt that before.

Behind me, the Ancient made an arrogant noise deep in his throat. "She is from the same stock, you imbecile. A tiny sliver of the light, lost to the endless darkness."

I turned to face him again. "Imbecile?" My voice trembled with rage. "You've been chasing me for countless millennia, because I somehow mysteriously hurt your feelings." I poured as much scorn as I could into my words. "I don't care how strong you are. I'm going to open up this pocket dimension and rip you a new asshole." I snapped at Marigold behind me. "Get this pocket dimension open."

"No," Marigold snarled back. "I'm not having you risk

yourself just for your vengeance, Imogen. You need to talk it out, you need to start to understand each other."

"He's a monster, Marigold! Monsters have to be destroyed!"

"*He* is the Destroyer," Claude muttered. He froze again, poised on top of the plinth next to the statue of Sir Humphrey.

"I can't open it myself, anyway." Marigold shook her head stubbornly. "Even if I wanted to, I can't. I need Leroy to help me take it down. It's keyed to him, too."

Leroy. "Where is he?" I cocked my head. "He should be here by now."

Marigold frowned, and glanced down towards Main Street. "He would have heard the silent alarm. Normally, he'd be first on the scene."

"That's what I thought, too." Slowly, deliberately, I turned my back on the Ancient and patted my pockets, looking for my phone. It was almost easy to ignore everything else right now; worry for Leroy was starting to leach into every overwhelming emotion I had.

My clothes were in tatters. I bent down, looking underneath the park bench where Rafael and I had made love, looking for my phone. There it was, lying on the grass underneath the bench seat. I knelt down and scooped it up in my hands, and jabbed a finger on the screen.

I frowned. "It's dead."

"Mine too." Rafael held his phone up in his hands. "I wonder why?"

Claude, up on his perch next to Sir Humphrey, unfroze and peered down at us, a look of pure disgust on his ugly fanged face. "There was a mini electro-magnetic pulse when her unearthly powers came out. During her orgasm," he added, sneering. "God knows I'm never going to be able to wipe that sight out of my brain."

I cringed. "Maybe don't look next time?"

"Next time you decide to get it on in public, I'm going to call the police, that's what I'm going to do," the gargoyle muttered. "Besides, I was compelled to be here. I didn't know you were going to get freaky on the park bench."

I heaved out a sigh. "Backman, can you call Leroy?" I asked, turning to face her.

The bear growled back at me.

"Oh, right. You have no thumbs. Never mind."

Marigold sighed. "I'll call him. I'm not opening this portal, though. He won't do it either, and you know it."

I pinched the bridge of my nose. She was right, he wouldn't do it, I knew that. I was starting to see sense, anyway. Opening up the portal just so I could kick the Ancient's ass probably wasn't a good idea. "Just call him, please."

She frowned down at her phone. "His phone is off."

"It's off?" A chill ran through me. "He never turns his phone off." I shot a worried glance at Rafael.

"Let's run to your cabin," he said, taking my hand. For once, his strong, firm grip didn't reassure me.

I nodded, and glanced over at Marigold and the giant bear beside her.

"Go," said Marigold, nodding. "I'll shut the glimmer window."

I ground my teeth, a sudden flare of anger surging back again. "He could leave."

"He could. He can leave at any time. He could have gone by now, too."

"I will guard the Destroyer," Claude declared.

I rolled my eyes. "Oh yeah? What are you going to do, prick him with your little wing-claws? Flex your abs at him? Swear at him in French?"

Claude deliberately turned away from me and clamped

his lips together. "Slut," he murmured from the corner of his mouth.

"I heard that."

There was no fire in my voice anymore. I was too worried about my kid. I had to go and find Leroy.

"Go," Marigold curled her hands into Backman's fur. "Find him."

I nodded, took Rafael by the hands and ran.

CHAPTER 3

e didn't speak as we ran. We didn't even take the roads; instead, we ran as the crow flies, straight up the south side of the valley through the woods, headed towards my cabin. My powers still surged within me; I had no reason to tamp them down. I held myself back, though. I didn't want to let go of Rafael's hands. We blazed through the forest around the valley, heading straight up to my home.

It took almost no time at all. At the same time, it felt like it took years to climb the valley. My fear for Leroy weighed me down, slowing time.

It got even worse when I started to smell the smoke.

At first, I dismissed it as common hearth smoke; some old soul around here had lit a fire. Then, as the cloud thickened, and the other houses thinned out, my heart leapt into my throat.

It was coming from the direction of my cabin.

I shot Rafael a look and tugged him forward. Together, we smashed through the trees almost to the top of the ridge where my cabin sat. I gasped.

It lay in ruins; a black, smoldering shell.

I couldn't even speak. The whole cabin had been completely destroyed. The thick logs that made up the sides of it were crumbled, reduced to charcoal, scattered around a scorched clearing. Melted puddles of plastic were dotted through the charred mess; unidentifiable. The blaze that did this would have been catastrophic.

"I don't understand," I breathed out. "How did we not see this? How did we hear nothing?" My voice shook. "Leroy? Leroy?"

Rafael darted around the clearing quickly and shot back to me. "His bicycle is not here," he said softly. "There is no recent scent of him on the driveway. He didn't make it back to the cabin."

"He—He didn't go home?" My chest was aching, I rubbed it, trying to clear the pain. The panic was hurting me. Hurting *so* bad. "Where is he, then? Where is he, Raf?"

Rafael shook his head and clamped his hands on my cheeks, holding me together. "He is not here." He held my gaze, forcing me to understand him. "He was not here. He did not cycle back up here after the wake. But something happened here," he said in a low tone. "It smells of magic. Someone has unleashed a spell on this place, incinerating your cabin to ashes under a blanket of protection. We should have sensed this," he growled. "My security should have seen it. A blaze of this intensity should have lit up the night sky."

"I don't understand," I whimpered. "Where is he then?"

"We must go back."

A noise hit my ears; the sound of two sets of feet running through the forest. Rafael pushed me behind him and moved into a crouch, snarling.

"My King!" Sonja blazed out of the forest into the smoldering clearing, with her muscled-up mate Brick beside her.

"I have been trying to call you. We all have been. Alpha and Bravo teams are frantically searching for you."

"Sonja." We faced the oncoming vamps. "I am fine."

The king's right-hand woman had an expression of pure relief written all over her face. "Your phone has been off for the past hour. Not even the locator worked. The electrical systems in the whole valley are fried. Even our security systems were offline for a small time."

"I know. It is okay, Sonja."

She stepped forward, unable to help herself, and touched his outstretched hand. Rafael was her god, and she worshiped the ground he walked on. Satisfied he was real and unharmed, a tiny bit of tension eased out of her. Which didn't say much, considering she was the stiffest vampire I'd ever seen in my life. "Where have you been?"

"It doesn't matter," I cut in rudely. "Do you know what happened here, Sonja?"

She glanced at me. "I do not know. Brick and I were on the patio of the Country Club, and suddenly I could smell smoke. I checked the security footage, and I could see it drifting up into the sky." She shook her head. "I do not understand how this could have happened, my lord. We should have seen the flames."

I grabbed her by the shoulders. "Have you seen Leroy? Did you see him anywhere?"

She shook her head. "I left the wake shortly after he did, no more than two hours ago. He left with Brandon, Sebastian and Darla." She pulled out her phone, opened an app and zoomed through some security footage. "This is from Main Street," she said, angling the phone so I could see. "He is here, outside the bar, collecting his bicycle with Darla. You are both still inside at the wake at this point." The time-stamp said 10.03pm. She changed windows. "Here he is cycling down past the cafe, headed towards the lake. And here," she changed windows again. "There is a camera at the crossing." She pointed. "You can see him here, taking the south road towards your cabin. The shifter children went east, towards the Outdoor Education Center. They were headed home."

"Leroy didn't make it home." My voice shook again. I grabbed Sonja's arms. "He's not here, is he? Please tell me he's not here."

Sonja's glassy eyes touched me, heavy, for once, with empathy. She shook her head. "The scent of him is here, but it is old. He did not make it home."

Rafael inhaled deeply, tasting the air around us. "He cycled towards home two hours ago. It would take him twenty minutes to get back to the cabin. This place was destroyed by magic, so it is impossible to tell how long it has been burning for."

"The Ancient came through one hour ago," I said. "Could he have done this?" A rage gripped me; I clenched my fists, skin glowing.

"Whoa." Brick zipped in beside me. He'd taken off to do a loop of the cabin, nose to the ground like a bloodhound. "Did you level up, Imogen? You're glowing like a fifteen-year-old kid at her quinceañera."

"Something like that," I choked on my snarl of frustration, wanting to tear off my own skin. What the hell was the use of all this power if I *couldn't find my kid?*

"He's not here," Brick declared. "Also, I found this." He held up a hefty wooden box. "It was buried in the ashes."

My heart hitched a beat at his words – he found something? Then, it stuttered, clenching painfully. The Ancient was right. Hope *was* painful.

I looked. "That's Leroy's spellbox." I stepped forward and flipped the lid. Inside was a handful of very old grimoires, ancient texts of power, as well as some rare herbs. I flipped it closed and examined the ornate carving on the lid. "It's not burnt."

"It smells of magic," Sonja wrinkled her nose. "He warded it so it would not be destroyed in a fire."

I nodded. "It makes sense." The cabin was almost burnt down only a few days ago by a demon, and a valuable grimoire was almost destroyed. Leroy must have put all his precious books and materials in this spellbox and warded it, just in case it was in danger again. I clutched my chest. "Oh, God, where is he?"

Rafael turned back to me, a spare phone to his ear. "He is not at the Outdoor Education Center. Debbie has not seen him. The older shifter children made it back to the Center just before half-ten."

I took a shallow breath. Leroy should have made it back to the cabin by then, too, but he wasn't here. And the cabin was completely destroyed.

Rafael held my stare. "Let's backtrack down the road. He may have simply fallen off his bike and smashed his phone, and is injured somewhere."

I nodded, and took Rafael's hand. *Please God, let it just be a broken leg and a smashed phone...*

Someone destroyed our cabin, though. Two hours ago, Leroy left me, cycled up the valley and disappeared. At some point not long after that our cabin was magically incinerated and covered up so we didn't see it. At the same time, Rafael and I made love on the park bench in the town square, and the Ancient came through to our world.

My head spun out of control. The Ancient couldn't have done this… Or could he? Did *he* do something to Leroy?

The Ancient was trapped, though. I couldn't see him until the glimmer window was activated, but I felt him the whole time he was there. And if he wasn't trapped, his first and only priority was always ripping me to pieces.

But where was Leroy?

We ran down the long driveway and out onto the winding road that ran around the upper level of the valley a little, then down towards the town. I let Rafael take the lead, even though I felt like I could fly. Anxious energy flooded through me, shaking me to pieces.

Halfway down the valley, Rafael flinched, and suddenly slid to a halt on the blacktop.

I froze. Sonja and Brick zoomed to a complete stop behind me, immediately fanning out, scouting the area around us.

"He was here," Rafael murmured, moving into a crouch. "His scent clings to this road. This was as far as he came when he was cycling home."

Brick crashed through the thick bushes off the road, and came bounding back instantly, twigs and leaves jammed in his hair. He lifted his hands in the air. "I've got his bike," he announced, obviously trying very hard to keep the triumph out of his voice in deference to my utter, utter panic.

The sight of his bike destroyed me. "Goddamnit!" I screamed. "Where is he, Rafael?"

Sonja moved like a ghost through the trees to my right. She drifted out, her clothes impeccable. "There is no trace of his scent anywhere around here. He did not move off the road."

"His bike did, though," Brick sniffed the handles like a dog. "There are new scents on this. One strong, a human smell, with a feminine-smelling perfume. She touched the handlebars. And another one, a male, I think. My nose is not as good as a wolf, but I know my aftershaves. Someone pulled Leroy off his bike and tossed it into the forest. Or, the male talked him into getting into a car with them, and the female tossed his bike into the forest."

"He wouldn't let that happen." I shook my head. "He loves

that damn bike. Someone took him. How did they manage to do it?" I clenched my fists. "The kid is boobytrapped to hell. I don't understand!"

Rafael's jaw tensed again. He was thinking furiously. "You're right. If someone were attacking him, he would never come quietly," he said. "He would fight. There is no sign of a disturbance anywhere around here."

"They incapacitated him somehow, and they went on to the cabin and blew it up," I said. "They put a spell on him, or something."

Brick shook his head. "The female smell on the handlebars is strong; there's no magic smell on it at all. I don't know about the male smell, it's too faint, but there was no magic here."

Rafael lifted his head suddenly, inhaling deeply. He shot off the road and into the bushes and came out holding Leroy's phone.

"There's no trace of any other scent on it," he said softly, holding it out to me. "No one else touched it. Leroy threw this into the bushes himself."

I squeezed my eyes shut. Out of all the nightmares I'd ever had in my long, long life, this was the worst. Leroy was gone, and I didn't know where he was.

That kid was my whole heart. He was the one who made me whole again, after thousands of years of living as a wraith of a person. He forced me to experience the full spectrum of humanity – the highs, the lows, the good and the bad.

I had to get him back.

I paced back and forth thinking furiously. "I can do this," I muttered. "I've done it before. I can find him." I cracked my knuckles. "Last time I needed to locate someone, I blackmailed a blood witch to get exact coordinates and beat her to death afterwards," I muttered. "I'll get Marigold to do a spell."

Sonja let out the tiniest scoff. "No, the last time you tried to locate someone, you asked Marigold to do a spell and she called a greater demon who almost succeeded in pulling the rest of Hell through the portal, too." She softened her expression. "And I hate to point this out, but you still haven't found your papa."

I frowned. "Okay, maybe using Marigold is off the table."

"That might be best," Rafael agreed.

I exhaled heavily. "Fine. No magic. Just good old-fashioned detective work." I ground my jaw. "Here's what we know so far. Whoever took Leroy managed to do it without a fight, which means they either tricked him, or he wanted to go with them. They picked him up in a vehicle of some sort, and I think it's safe to conclude they drove up to the cabin and destroyed that, too." I took a deep breath. "We just need to find that vehicle."

"There has not been much traffic through the town. Most cars we will be able to recognize. There may be some guests from the funeral, but we should be able to narrow it down." Sonja agreed. Her phone buzzed; she glanced down at it. "Sire, you have an urgent petition from one of your subjects in D.C."

"Not now," Rafael held up one hand. "Delegate it, if you can."

She nodded. Despite my anguish, my ears pricked up. There was a vengeance demon running around D.C, causing absolute chaos amongst the supernatural community, tearing apart the odd vampire or two. It would have been much worse, except the vamps she destroyed all turned out to be rogues with an evil agenda.

But because it was entirely my fault she was there, I sandwiched my mouth closed. I hadn't gotten around to telling Rafael about Sandy and the banana yet.

I wrenched my attention back to the road. "Do you have cameras around here?"

"None here," Sonja said. "We have them on the cross-roads, and on top of the ridge. We should be able to find this vehicle."

"Let's go, then."

* * *

WE RAN WEST, straight to the country club, and burst into the security room. Sonja had phoned ahead. Boris from the Bravo team had already pulled up every conceivable view of the town in the timeframe that Leroy had disappeared.

I leaned forward, watching the screens. "See, here," Boris said in his thick accent, pointing at the first of five screens. "Your child leaves the bar, and mounts his bicycle." I followed Leroy on the screen, cycling down the street, the hollow in my heart aching badly. Boris pointed at the screen again. "He reaches the crossroads up from the lake, and he leaves his friends to follow the south road. The shifter children head east."

I watched Leroy cycle up the road, pushing hard down on the pedals as he slowly climbed the hill. Cycling up and down the valley had given him some serious muscles. He wasn't the pale, skinny tortured kid I'd picked up just out of L.A. anymore. He still had the angelic good looks, but now, he was starting to look like the cutest member in a boy band. He was a powerhouse of a witch, too, a natural, with innate psychic powers born from a childhood of torment, now enhanced by an obsession with witchcraft. He'd learned so much. Whoever had grabbed him must have known what they were taking.

Rafael, sensing my distress, squeezed my hand. I took a shallow breath and concentrated on the footage.

Boris pointed to the third screen. "We see him here, in one of the mini-cams in the trees, as he travels up the south road. It is halfway to your cabin, just before the turn off to the west ridge road." It was just a brief glimpse, but you could see him pushing hard, heading up the hill on his bike. "That is the last time we see him." He pointed to the fourth screen. "Now. Look here."

The footage on the fourth screen showed a view from the top of the ridge, looking down on the valley. "Your cabin is here," Boris pointed to the bottom left of the screen.

I squinted. "I can't see it through the trees."

"Just watch." He tapped the keyboard, and the trees waved wildly, the footage sped up. "Twenty minutes after we see Leroy biking up towards your cabin, we see this."

The trees stopped waving, the footage resuming at normal speed. I watched the screen carefully. Suddenly, there was a bright flare where my cabin stood, like a floodlight had been turned on in the trees. Instantly it was extinguished.

"That's the cabin exploding into flames," Boris explained. "The incineration was magically smothered, somehow. Whoever destroyed the cabin did not want anyone to notice it."

"The bastards that grabbed Leroy did it," I said. "They grabbed him, and they went up and blew up our cabin."

"No."

I glared at Boris. "No?"

"Look." He pointed at the screen. "Two minutes after the explosion was smothered, we see this." I watched carefully. Two faint lights peeked between the trees heading up towards my cabin. Headlights, heading up my driveway. I saw glimpses of the headlights pausing, then reversing, and heading back down the driveway.

"I've checked the footage, and there is no sight of anything around your cabin before the explosion," Boris said. "The vehicle approached the cabin *after* it was incinerated."

I frowned. "That makes no sense."

"Indeed."

"If those headlights belonged to the car that picked up Leroy, that means that they took their time grabbing him, too," I said, thinking furiously. "Twenty minutes from grabbing him, to driving up to my cabin. It would only take two minutes to drive from the spot he was taken."

Sonja shifted on her feet. "Maybe he was speaking to them."

"Or maybe they were bespelling him."

"There was no scent of magic, Imogen," Rafael murmured.

I groaned. "I just don't get it. It doesn't make sense. Someone stopped Leroy on his bike, threw him in their car, chucked his bike in the bushes, then Leroy threw his *own phone* away out the window, and drove up to our cabin, but it was already in flames? It makes no sense." I slapped the desk in front of me. A chunk of timber broke off and hit the ground. Boris turned to me, eyes wide.

"Sorry," I muttered. I took a deep breath, forcing my panic down. "Can you go back to this shot?" I pointed to the third camera. "Can you see any cars head up the south road?"

"It is already done, *uragan*. There are twelve cars that head up that road. Remember that the south road is a main thoroughfare towards this Country Club, so there is more traffic to sift through."

"Show me the cars," I demanded.

Boris rewound the footage on the third tree camera, and showed me every car that drove by, one by one. The night vision wasn't fantastic and we certainly couldn't make out license plates, but we could see the shape and colors as they zoomed past.

Sonja leaned over me, checking each car as it drove past. "That one belongs to the Danish Prince," she pointed. "And that one is Kruskov's." She curled her lip, tapping the screen as a giant stretch Hummer went past. "That monstrosity belongs to the Sheik. So trashy." Another black sedan flew by, and she frowned. "I don't know that one."

Boris made a note.

Another limo zoomed across the screen. "That is Eddie Cheng's," Sonja said. "And that Lamborghini that follows, I think belongs to his mistress."

"His mistress-man," Brick chipped in. He winked at me. "Cynthia is a beard. Her stylist Gordon is Eddie Chang's lover."

I nodded. Any other day, I'd be frothing over the gossip that one of China's leading movie superstars was in the closet, but I was too desperate for information on Leroy.

One by one, we watched the cars drive past on the south road. In the end, we had three we couldn't immediately identify. The black sedan, a ratty brown station-wagon, and what I suspected was a Porsche. It was going too fast for anyone to see properly.

"I'm crossing the Porsche off the list," I muttered. "It will be one of your wanker guests, trying to get a cheap thrill." I nodded at Boris and tapped the paper in front of me. One mystery black sedan, one mystery ratty brown station-wagon. "Do you think you could look through the cameras in town to see if you can spot either of these cars?"

"I am on it."

Sonja sat down next to him and started scrolling through the footage of Main Street.

Boris cleared his throat awkwardly. "My King... there is another problem."

"There are many problems, Boris," Rafael said wearily. "What is it now?"

"This." Boris tapped another screen. Not footage, but some weird spiky graphs, updating in what looked like real time. "The seismic activity in the Valley is... alarming. There are little tremors, centered right in the middle of town. They are irregular in timing, but very slowly escalating in intensity."

I groaned. "That fucker."

"It's okay Boris. We know what that is." Rafael put his hand on my shoulder and rubbed me with his thumb. "We will handle the Ancient in time," he said to me.

I put my head in my hands. "He could leave at any time. He could go back through the portal and just leave," I groaned. "He clearly isn't, though. He's not going to go until he punishes me. And I don't want him to go, either. I need to find out what he is and why he's doing this to me. I've only got three days before he's forced out of this dimension, but I need to find Leroy. He's my first priority." I glanced at Boris. "What does the rate of escalation look like over three days, Boris?"

He tapped on his keyboard, plugging in the numbers. "If the tremors continue at this rate of escalation... we're looking at a magnitude four in three days."

"That's not so bad." I lived through Toba. To be fair, nobody else did. But a couple of mag four tremors wouldn't do too much damage.

I shrugged. "We can put the little problem of the trapped, ancient mysterious supernatural creature causing earthquakes in town in the 'to do' pile."

"I have something," Sonja declared. She pointed to her screen. The camera was in the middle of Main Street, pointing down towards the town square. Just peeking out from behind the church, I could see the back end of the ratty brown station wagon.

I leaned forwards eagerly. "What time is this?"

"The timestamp is just after three in the afternoon. I think it was a funeral attendee." She tapped a button, fast-forwarding the footage. Some of the cars left the car park, but the station wagon stayed there. Night fell on the screen, and the wagon didn't move. "It's a damn creepy vehicle," I muttered. "If Leroy was going to be grabbed by anyone, it would be someone with a car like that."

Sonja zoomed through the evening until movement appeared next to the car. She rewound slightly, and left the tape to play. We watched the screen carefully as a woman with a huge bush of orange hair staggered up the footpath with a wiry figure on her shoulder in a fireman's lift. She opened the back of the station wagon and threw him in the back.

I slumped in my chair. "That's Carol from up the valley. She's got a new boyfriend, some tiny accountant from Cedar Hills. That must be his car. He got very drunk at the wake." I sighed. "I remember seeing her carry him out. They left just after Leroy."

"They still could have picked Leroy up," Boris said.

Sonja had her phone sandwiched to her ear. "They did not," she said. "Carol is still awake, tending to her drunk boyfriend. They passed Leroy on the way up the hill and offered a lift, which he declined." She murmured quiet thanks into her phone and cut the call off. Another message pinged through. "My King, your petitioner in D.C. is asking for an urgent audience again."

"Find out what he wants," Rafael told her.

"He cannot talk on the phone." Sonja frowned down on the screen. "He said it was sensitive. He will call back again when he can."

I tuned her out, staring at the screens in front of me. There were so many cameras, too many cars, and far too many hours to cover. Boris, his eyes darting backwards and forwards, zoomed through all the footage. Going back to square one, he took screenshots of the mystery black sedan, the flash of a silver Porsche, the Lamborghini, and several other of the cars, and fixed them on one of the screens. "I don't want to discount anything," he said gruffly.

Brick left the security room and checked out each of the car's owners in the country club. My heart squeezed. If only Leroy were here, in the country club, eating ice cream with some Arab Sheik or a movie star. He wasn't, though. He wouldn't disappear and not tell me where he was going. He would never throw his own phone into the forest, get into a stranger's car voluntarily, and let them toss his precious bike away.

Time ticked by. I jiggled my legs up and down restlessly. The sky outside started to lighten, and I felt the earth quiver underneath me a few more times. Boris was right, the tremors were getting more intense. The urge to run down to the town square and shake the Ancient by the neck grew stronger.

But I couldn't do that, either. We needed Leroy to help take the pocket dimension down. Since he was missing, there was no way to break it open.

Hours passed. Rafael brought food; I didn't eat it. I glued my eyeballs to the screens, examining each car, checking everything carefully, terrified I'd miss something and I'd never see Leroy again.

The vampires talked quietly amongst themselves. At some point, Brick excused himself to go to bed. He was still a relatively young vampire, and the urge to sleep when the sun rose was still strong in him.

Sonja split her time between her phone and the computer screens. "My King, the petitioner from D.C. is with Home-land Security," she murmured to him. "He has something urgent to discuss with you."

"Not now," Rafael said. He was next to me, rolling slowly through footage of the west end of Main Street. "There!"

I jolted. "What? Where?"

45

"The black sedan," he said. He pointed. "That's it, can you see? The back end of it is parked just there."

It was just a glimpse, but it was clear enough. The mystery black sedan was in a parking space just beyond the garden center. "It's parked right outside–"

The ground beneath us trembled. Rafael paused.

I ignored it. I ground my teeth. "The police station," I growled. "It's parked right outside the police station."

CHAPTER 4

$\mathcal{W}$e drove down the valley into town in a convoy of Rafael's armored Maserati. My heart thudded in my chest, sounding so loud in my ears. The black sedan was clearly parked right in front of the police station. At worst, we'd be able to find visuals of who was driving the mystery car. At best, we'll find them there, at the station.

We might find Leroy at the station, too. The hope was like torture, like a nail in my clothes constantly rubbing against my skin.

My phone rang. Debbie, the camp mother from the Outdoor Education Center. "Imogen?"

"What is it, Deb? Is it Leroy? Is he there?"

"No." She sounded worried. "I still haven't seen him. I'm sorry."

Damn it. "What is it, then?"

"It's Brandon," she said. "He didn't come for breakfast. He's not in his room. No one knows where he is. It looks like he might have snuck out at some point early this morning."

I inhaled sharply. "Shit."

"What's going on, Imogen?" Debbie's voice was strained.

"Something's happening. Leroy's missing, now Brandon. And what's with all the earthquakes?

"I don't know. It's all connected somehow, Debbie. Look, I'll find Brandon, okay? He might be looking for me." The poor wolf still wasn't quite over his insane crush yet, so there was a chance he was trying to find me right now. I'd accidentally triggered some sort of mystic werewolf mating ritual by offering him the throat of his enemy, and he'd been stalking me ever since.

Respectfully stalking me, if I was being fair. I'd hoped that now his leg had grown back it would flush out the old, unwanted energy, but he had still been shadowing me like a lovesick puppy every chance he got.

A thought occurred to me, and I frowned. "What are the chances that he snuck out and blew up my cabin?"

Debbie gasped. "What?"

"Someone blew up my cabin around ten-thirty last night," I told her. "I know it's not his usual stalkery behavior, but *someone* blew it up."

"No. It couldn't have been Brandon. Him, Darla and Sebastian all came home just before that time. I made sure they were all in bed. Cassandra did a bed-check at midnight; they were all asleep."

I ground my teeth. None of this made any sense at all. I sighed, trying to keep a lid on my frustration. "I'll keep an eye out for him, okay?" Mentally, I put Brandon on the list of Things I Needed To Worry About. The list was getting very long.

"I'll organize a fur run with all the kids today, okay? We'll do a sweep right around the ridges. I'll get the wolves to focus on finding both Brandon and Leroy's scent. I'll tell them it's a game, or something." Her voice sounded strained. Nothing was worse than losing a kid. *Nothing.*

"Thanks." I gazed out the window as we drove into town,

narrowing my eyes towards the town square. I could see the statue of Sir Humphrey, shining in the morning sun, with Claude frozen by his feet, his little muscular chest thrust out. Just behind that was the pocket dimension, with the Ancient sitting inside, invisible, shaking the town slowly to pieces. "And I'll–"

I clamped my mouth closed and frowned. I slammed on the breaks. The Maserati slid to a halt in the middle of the road. Sonja was in the car behind me. For a second, I hoped she'd slam into me just so I could smash something and relieve some of the pressure building inside of me, but unfortunately, her reflexes were excellent.

I sighed. "Actually, Debbie, just focus on Leroy, please. I've just found Brandon."

"You what?"

I pulled the car over. "He's in the town square. I can see him now," I said, looking through the windscreen.

"What is he doing there?"

"I have no idea. He's just sitting on the grass, staring into space." I parked the car. "I'll find out what he's up to. And I'll send him home, okay?"

"Okay."

I hung up, got out of the car and marched over towards the grassy square. Instantly, Rafael was beside me, shadowing me, guarding me.

Brandon sat cross-legged on the wet grass, staring into nothingness. For a moment alarm flared inside of me. "Brandon? What are you doing here, honey?"

He tore his eyes away, and focused on me. "I don't know," he said, frowning. "I woke up this morning and felt… a weird pull. A pull towards you," he said, misery flooding his expression. He shook his head. "I'm sorry, Imogen, but this feeling isn't going away. This… obsession. I thought it might go away when my leg grew back, but I'm still feeling it. I have to be close to you."

Rafael tensed beside me.

"Oh, sweetheart," I sighed. "It's okay. It will fade."

He bit his lip. "It hasn't."

Something still wasn't making sense. "But… if you were drawn to me… Why are you here?"

He looked up at me. "I don't know. I thought you were here, I guess." He smiled. "And you are."

God, he was gorgeous. Perfect, tanned skin, cheekbones for days, a chiseled jawline, ridiculously buff swimmer's body. Now that the arrogant smirk had been wiped off his face by the humility of his magical unreciprocated crush, his smile lit up the morning brighter than the rising sun. If it wasn't for Rafael – and the fact that Brandon was too young for me by over two-hundred thousand years – I'd be all over him like white on rice.

He swept his hand, gesturing at the grass. "You're here. Maybe I knew you were coming." His attention pulled away for a split second; he frowned towards the statue. "It's weird," he murmured. "I can feel something else here, too."

I shot Rafael a quick look. "That's because there *is* something here. Something in the pocket dimension."

"Ah." Brandon's gaze focused back on the empty air in front of him. "That must be it."

I turned around, pulling Rafael in closer. "Do you think the Ancient is doing something to him? Pulling him in magically, somehow?"

"I don't know." Rafael frowned. "Anything is possible."

"Maybe Leroy is in there, with him. With the Ancient." I couldn't stop my voice from trembling. "I didn't really look inside when I spoke to him earlier. We should check." I turned to Sonja. "Can you go and see if Marigold is at her store?" It was early, but Marigold was diligent.

She nodded and disappeared. Almost immediately, she returned with both Marigold and Backman swaggering behind her. Backman was wearing the tiniest bra and hotpants set I'd ever seen before in my life. Her face was bright red; her muscles bulged.

I leered at her. "Did I interrupt your Pilates session?"

"I'm going to let you have that one, little drill bug, since you're delicate right now," she growled back. "I was about to break my deadlift record." She flexed her huge biceps. "All this anguish is doing wonders for my P.B. records. I seem to have a lot of energy to expend lately."

"Have you found Leroy?" Marigold yawned hugely. "Oh. Hi, Brandon."

He waved back absently, still staring into space. It was a little eerie. I should probably be worried about him, but I didn't have any extra capacity for worry right now.

"No, we haven't found him. Can you open the glimmer window?"

She blinked, and stared at me. "Why? Are you going to antagonize the Ancient again?"

"I want to see if Leroy is in there."

Her face fell. "He's not in there, Imogen. I'm sorry. He's alive, though."

"I know." I clenched my fists. "I can feel it." He was definitely still alive. I don't know how I knew, but I did.

"I did a basic scry for him last night," Marigold said. "He's not anywhere close to Emerald Valley anymore. Maybe not even in the state. He's not here."

"Neither is the pocket dimension."

She paused. "That's a good point."

"I know." The ground trembled again, and I winced. "I should probably see if I can get the Ancient to stop doing that, too."

Backman cocked her head. "The earthquakes?"

51

There was a sharp thud as Claude the Gargoyle jumped down from the plinth where he had been frozen next to Sir Humphrey. I jolted slightly. I'd forgotten about him. When he froze, he looked just like a stone carving; absolutely lifeless.

"The quakes will destroy the earth!" Claude declared in his high-pitched, gravelly voice. He strutted around the plinth and thrust his little muscled chest out as he walked past Brandon, still cross-legged on the ground. Brandon barely noticed him. "This world will fall," Claude boomed. "The end of everything will be here, right at this very spot. The world will crumble into dust."

I frowned down at him. "I'm sorry, what? The quakes? I thought you said that it was the Ancient who will destroy the earth?"

"Yes, *tête de noeud*, he will. You will. You *both* will. It is obvious now."

I pursed my lips. "You're not big on details, are you? Seriously, what are you even here for?"

He put his clawed fists on his hips and snapped his wings behind him. "*La porte* is right there." He jabbed a finger upwards. "If this creature you have trapped keeps shaking the earth he stands on, the valley will start to crumble onto itself. The basin will fill." He sneered at me. "We are below sea level right here, moron. Not only will this town be destroyed by rockfall, but the portal will be buried. The flow of energy will not have time to adjust itself. The telluric field will be interrupted."

A chill ran over my skin. I stared at Rafael.

Marigold gasped. "The field will fall."

"Yes." The gargoyle nodded solemnly. "If the creature causes a devastating earthquake here, burying the portal and disrupting the telluric field, the earth will be flooded by all the creatures of the realms above and below. There will be no protective layer to keep them out of our realm."

"It will be chaos," Marigold whispered. "Poltergeists might come through from the lower astral plane and wreak havoc. Spirits, archetypes, demigods desperate for worship… they'll all flood in and demand attention."

Holy shit.

Backman took a sharp breath in and shook her head, her lips bloodless. "If the fae get wind that our realm is vulnerable, they could swoop in with their armies and take what they like. The Dark Elves have had their eye on our world for eons. We'd be swamped."

There was a long moment of horrified silence, as the gravity of the situation sunk in. Claude had been right. This *could* mean the end of the world.

"The Ancient can leave at any time," I mumbled. "He can go back through the portal and go home."

"He's not going, though," the gargoyle shrugged. "Is he?"

I put my head in my hands and mumbled into my palms. "We can't let him out. We need Leroy to break the pocket dimension. We don't know where Leroy is." I let out a sob. "This just gets worse and worse."

A soft hand touched my shoulder. "I'll open the window," Marigold said. "See if you can talk to him. It's worth a shot."

I nodded. She put out her arms just over her head and started chanting. Soon, the lavender wall shimmered and cleared into a cut-out window in reality.

I moved so I could see inside, and I kept everyone else well away. No good would come from the Ancient seeing my family here beside me. It would only give him more targets to destroy. I braced myself and peered into the pocket dimension.

The Ancient stood there, facing me, bare-chested, wearing a shimmering white simple wrap around his waist. He still wore the face of a young god.

He stared back at me. The contempt in his eyes was almost physically blistering.

Quickly, I glanced around the rest of the pocket dimension. Nothing else was in there. My shoulders slumped slightly; more hope crushed. The disappointment was far worse than physical pain. He'd been right about that.

I blinked back tears, and tore my gaze back to the Ancient. He lifted his chin haughtily. The ground rumbled beneath my feet.

"Why are you doing this?" I asked.

"You stole from me." His voice rasped against my ears like sandpaper on my most delicate flesh.

"I did not."

"You did. You took my beloved away."

I quickly glanced behind me and met Rafael's eyes. He frowned, and shook his head.

"Unless you're talking about my boyfriend over there, you're sorely mistaken." I raised an eyebrow. "And if it *is* him you're talking about, I'll fight you for him."

The Ancient curled his lip in derision. "Not him."

"Leroy, then."

The creature frowned. "Who?"

"My kid. Do you have him?"

He crossed his arms over his chest, perfect muscles bulging. "I do not care for mortals." The lip curled again. "They disgust me. Just like you disgust me."

"Okay then. That's a little mean, but I guess it's an improvement considering you usually go straight to the ripping-me-apart stage." I stared at him. "Do you know where he is?"

"Your human child is nothing to me." He tilted his perfect head. "Although I will help you find him if you give me Sariel."

I frowned. "Who is Sariel?"

"My beloved," he growled. "You stole him."

"Uh, no. I didn't steal anyone."

"You stole him, and I want him back. Give me Sariel back."

I took a breath, and shot a look behind me. Rafael stood closest, eyes blazing, ready to pull me back into his arms at a moment's notice. Marigold, a tinge of red in her eyes, and Backman, almost indecent in her tiny bra and booty shorts, muscles popping everywhere. They would fight for me. They gave me courage.

I turned back to face the Ancient. "Is that what this is all about? Why you have been hunting me for my entire life?" I raised my eyebrows. "You somehow think I stole your beloved Sariel?"

"I *know* you did." The creature's eyes blazed white. "Give him back to me."

I shot another look behind me, and mouthed at Marigold: *Who the fuck is Sariel?*

She shrugged. *No idea.*

This made no sense. I'd never heard of Sariel before, not in any meaningful way, in any case. All names had been used a thousand times before, so it was likely that at some point in history, I'd met someone called Sariel. Probably several times, in fact.

But I knew for sure that I'd never *stolen* anyone called Sariel. I wasn't in the habit of stealing people. Quickly, I rummaged through my worst memories, replaying some of the shittiest things I'd ever done. There was a lot, so I took a few moments. There were a lot of murders, the occasional mad bit of genocide back in the early days of human history where my madness got the best of me. I never enslaved anyone, though. I never kidnapped anyone.

And I was sure I never stole anyone by the name of Sariel.

It didn't really matter anyway. The Ancient thought I did, and I doubted I could convince him otherwise.

I took a deep breath. "So... if I manage to find this Sariel and give him back to you... you'll stop hunting me?"

"No," he growled. "You are an abomination."

"Well." I pursed my lips. "No deal, I guess."

The ground rumbled. A trace of the most arrogant smirk in the world touched the Ancient's lips.

I stepped closer, suddenly furious. "You can leave at any time, you know. You don't have to stay stuck here in this pocket dimension just so you can threaten me. I don't know who Sariel is."

He let out a bark of laughter so bitter I could taste it on my tongue. "*Liar.*"

The ground shook again. "You'll destroy this world if you keep doing that, you know."

Did I imagine the hesitation in his eyes? The slight trace of fear? It was gone before I could examine it properly.

He clenched his jaw. "Maybe this world deserves to crumble into dust. You mortals do not deserve it."

"I'm not a mortal."

Suddenly, he jumped forward, an inch from my face. Pure white teeth snapped, his eyes blazed white. "You are an abomination," he snarled. "No one should have what you have. No one should have *everything*."

I reared back, shocked at the passion that blazed from him. "Okay, I'm seriously confused. You think I have everything?" A bitter chuckle huffed from my lips. "I've been trying to end my life for the past few hundred thousand years."

"You have Sariel."

Frustration poured out of me like lava; I punched the glimmer window as hard as I could, howling in rage. "I don't have your fucking Sariel! I don't know what you want! All I want is for you to leave me alone so I can find a way to *die in peace!*"

Someone behind me gasped.

He backed off slowly, glaring at me. "Get me Sariel," he said, his tone so low it vibrated through my feet. "Bring Sariel back to me, and I will leave this world intact." Slowly, he moved his muscular shoulders around, and he turned his back on me.

CHAPTER 5

I strode down Main Street, seething. "How fucking dare he? How dare he?" I waved my arms in the air as I walked. "He thinks *I'm* the abomination? I don't even know what the hell he is!"

Rafael walked beside me. "You've never heard of a Sariel before?"

"Never." I shook my head vehemently. "I have no idea what he's talking about. The creature is obviously deranged. There's no reason why he has it in for me, or why he keeps torturing me. He's just some fucking demon who has fixated on me for my entire existence, obviously."

Sonja walked beside me, her long legs pushing her gracefully along while I stomped next to her. She tapped her phone, eyes fixed to the screen. "There are thousands of entries for people named Sariel, all throughout history."

"And I can't recall one person named Sariel that I've ever had anything to do with," I spat out through my teeth. Frustration overwhelmed me; I was ready to explode. "I don't have time for this," I clenched my fists, blisteringly aware that my hands were still glowing. "I have to find Leroy."

"Perhaps Officer Stephens will know who the black sedan belonged to," Rafael said.

"If he's even there," I said. "And he won't be. He never is." Emerald Valley was down to only one local cop – Officer Stephens, who preferred to cruise around the roads circling the Valley instead of venturing into the town itself. Most of the time the station was unmanned, their calls were redirected to Cedar Hills. "We might have to perform a little felony to break into their closed-circuit surveillance footage."

"The door will be locked, anyway," Sonja said. "Even if Officer Stephens is there. We may need to call him to come in if he is out. New station guidelines show they have to keep the main bolt on the door and let people in when they buzz."

"Is that right?" I stomped up the steps of the police station and kicked the door in.

The bolt exploded; the heavy metal door tore off its hinges and clattered to the ground. I turned and grinned at Sonja, and stepped inside.

The station was tiny; just one room with a reception counter in the entrance way which blocked the little office space behind it. Two desks stacked with computers and piled-up stationery sat there, with locked filing cabinets across one wall, and a tiny jail cell at the rear.

The station wasn't empty.

There was an officer sitting at the desk, frozen, his eyes bulging in fright. His uniform was rumpled; his ruddy white face rapidly getting paler. I chuckled coldly, and strolled towards him. "Well, well, well. Look who we have here."

Officer Gary Harmann flinched, then leapt to his feet, clenching his fists. He mouthed wordlessly, his face quivered as a lifetime of arrogant bullying clashed with his most recent traumatic escapades.

I wandered over slowly, picked up an office chair, sat down, and spun myself around in a circle for good measure.

"Officer Harmann," I cooed. "I would say it's good to see you again, but I'd be lying. I guess I could say it's good to see you as a *human* again, I suppose."

A faerie queen had turned Harmann into a pig a couple of months ago. Last I'd seen of him, he was galloping off into the woods on stubby little pink legs. I did vaguely wonder what had happened to him from time to time, but he didn't deserve any of my pity. Harmann had racially profiled me, harassed me, and had arrested me several times. He was the worst kind of bully.

His eyes darkened in anger. He was terrified of me, but he hated me. I wondered which emotion would win out.

Apparently, his hatred was too strong. "You," he hissed, jabbing a shaking finger at me. "You evil *bitch.*"

I shrugged carelessly. "That's me."

"You turned me into a pig!"

"No, that wasn't me, actually. I don't have that kind of magic. You got on the wrong side of a powerful Fae queen. That's on you, sweetheart."

He shuddered slightly at the mention of magic. "I spent eight weeks naked in the woods, eating garbage," he hissed at me. "All because of you."

"You probably shouldn't have harassed me so much," I said brightly. "It was a classic case of 'fuck around and find out,' huh? Well, you found out."

"You broke out of my jail cell!"

"You arrested me with fabricated evidence. Again, that's on you."

His fists trembled; he clenched them so hard his knuckles went white. "You're a criminal. The worst kind of criminal. You have no respect."

"Respect?" I cocked my head. "You think I should have had respect for *you?*" I huffed out a laugh. "Why?"

"I'm the law!"

I fixed him with a heavy stare, leaned forward, and lowered my voice. "You harassed me because you didn't like the color of my skin. You convinced yourself that I was some sort of criminal because you are *racist*, and you made up evidence to arrest me. You stuck your nose in where it didn't belong, and you found out what happens when idiots do that."

There was a pause. Harmann took a breath in through his teeth, calming himself. His fists flexed, and unclenched. Hatred burned in his eyes, but a smirk lifted a corner of his lips. "I was right, though, wasn't I? It's not profiling if you're right. You *are* a criminal."

The change in attitude put me on guard. "I'm no criminal."

He let out a bark of laughter. A smug expression crawled onto his face. "Turns out, you are. I was right all along. I was right to arrest you." He chuckled again. "And your little reign of terror is going to be over very soon."

"What are you talking about?"

He smirked. "You're a murderer."

"No, I'm not."

Sonja coughed behind me. I ignored her.

Harmann tipped his head back and laughed out loud. "Yes, you are. I've seen the evidence myself. I've seen footage of you, running away from a grisly crime scene. More than one, in fact." He glanced up at Sonja and Rafael behind me. "Did you know she's a serial killer? Did you know that?"

Rafael cleared his throat elegantly. "And where did you see this footage that you speak of, Officer Harmann?"

The cop glared back at him. All his arrogance and entitlement had come rushing back. "That ain't your concern. You have no power here, Di Stasio. All your money won't buy her way out of trouble." He sniffed. "You should cut her loose. She's about to go down in the worst way. You don't want your business tainted by an association to a psychopath like her."

"A psychopath, am I?" I said silkily. I plastered a smile on my face and rose slowly to my feet. "Maybe I should show you what a *psychopath* I am."

Rafael grabbed my arm and pulled me back. "*Amore*, wait."

"Seriously, Raf, he deserves to swallow his own teeth."

"Yes, I know." A smile touched his beautiful lips. He leaned his head closer to mine; I inhaled him greedily. It calmed me. "We need information," he murmured.

I took a deep breath. He was right. I needed to find Leroy. There were answers here, I knew that.

I shot Harmann another look. His conceited, smug expression made me want to shove his head up his own ass, which I was sure I could do if Rafael would let me. Trying to get answers out of this cop would be tricky unless I tortured him, and there was a chance I might get carried away.

I huffed out a sigh. "You better question him, then." I turned around and dumped myself unceremoniously back onto the office chair.

"*Si*." Rafael turned to Harmann and faced him directly. "You said you've seen footage of Imogen at multiple crime scenes. Who showed you that footage?"

Harmann spat at his feet. "Fuck you, you dirty wop. I don't answer to your kind, I don't care who you are."

I almost laughed. Harmann was so racist that he thought the worst thing about Rafael was that he was *Italian*. My fiancé had fantastic impulse control, though. He simply took another step closer and focused his gaze on Harmann. "I will ask again," he said softly, the words weighted with layers of vampiric compulsion. "Who showed you footage of Imogen at a crime scene?"

Harmann's face went slack. He answered in a monotone. "The F.B.I."

I froze. "The F.B.I?"

"Why were the F.B.I. here?"

"They were called here," Harmann answered. "They came here yesterday after they visited the Outdoor Education Center."

I exchanged a glance with Sonja; she was just as surprised as I was. Nobody had mentioned that the F.B.I. had been up at the Outdoor Education Center. Debbie didn't mention it, at the very least. If Backman knew, she didn't think it was worthy of mention, either.

Maybe it wasn't that surprising. Maybe Debbie knew a shifter in the F.B.I and called them to help with the search for Leroy, or maybe Backman called someone to ask for backup when the Ancient came through. There were shifters in all levels of government – vampires, too. It wasn't inconceivable that they had friends in the F.B.I. they could call for help.

Except Harmann said that the F.B.I. were here *yesterday*. Before Leroy disappeared. Before the Ancient came through.

It didn't make sense.

Rafael didn't turn; he was focused on keeping Harmann under his spell. "Why were they at the Outdoor Education Center?"

"I don't know."

"Why did they come here?"

"They came to ask about *her*," Harmann spat out the word despite his vacant expression. "They wanted to know everything I knew about her. I told them everything. That she's a dirty criminal. One agent agreed with me, and told me everything she'd done."

Rafael had gone very still. A smarter person would realize how dangerous he was, but Harmann was not a smart man. "And what did that agent tell you?"

"He told me that she was a murderer. He showed me footage from a warehouse in California – she let some pit-fighting dogs out of their cages, and they ripped apart their owners. He showed me a photo of her running away from a burning building on the outskirts of the city, where the mangled corpse of a woman was found shortly afterwards. He showed me footage of her running out of an alleyway, where the bodies of two local men were discovered, both with horrific injuries."

I shrugged. "Welp, color me guilty, I guess."

Rafael's mouth twitched, but he focused on Harmann. "What were the agents planning on doing?"

"They are going to arrest her," he said. "She will rot in jail. They are taking all evidence back to the capitol so they can build a case."

Sonja frowned at me. "You've been burned."

Vampires knew what it was like to get burned, over and over again. A curse of immortality; you needed to come up with a whole new identity every sixty years or so. It was annoying.

I sighed. I'd need new identification. *Again*. Damn it. I'd just gotten used to using the name Imogen. I might have to go back to Imelda. Or Immanuela.

I liked Iman – I used that for a few centuries, except there was a famous model called Iman now, and calling myself that helped people remember me when I really didn't want them to.

Maybe that Iman was dead. It had been a while. I'd have to check.

"I could go back to Im," I said out loud. That was my first name. I always used a variation of it, because it was what my father had called me, and I missed him every second of forever. In my first language, Im had meant star.

Rafael ignored me, and focused on Harmann.

"What else did the agent tell you?"

"He said that she was dangerous, and she'd have to be contained. They said that there was a chance they could use her."

My blood suddenly boiled. *"Use* me?"

"As a weapon," Harmann said dully. "He said she had power, and that they would need a little time to come up with a plan to contain her."

Shit. Now it all made sense.

"They took Leroy," I hissed. "They waited until dark, and they fucking took my kid because they were too scared to come for me." I got up from my seat and started pacing back and forth, too agitated to sit still. "They blew up my house to try and force me out of hiding. Gah!"

Rafael kept his eye contact with Harmann. "Were the F.B.I. driving the black sedan that had been parked out front of this office?"

"Yes."

"Did they identify themselves to you? Do you have their names?" Trust Rafael to ask the right questions. If he left it up to me, Harmann wouldn't have any fingernails left by now.

"Both agents came in, but only one stayed to speak to me. His name was Agent Mullins. The other agent stayed in the car. Where she belonged," he added. "She was unnecessary. Her priorities weren't right."

Rafael let out a slow exhale. "Is there anything else you can think of to tell me?"

"No." Harmann's white jowls wobbled. "Just that she will get what she deserves. Life in a cell, strapped to a table."

Asshole. I picked up the desk and threw it into the wall, where it smashed into splinters. Some of the cinder blocks in the wall came loose. It had only been a couple of months since Rafael had to rebuild it since the last time I'd smashed it. I whirled around, snarling. "Can you let me at him, now?"

Rafael held Harmann in his gaze. "*Mi amore*," he murmured. "Can you not think of a better way to cause him suffering, other than the physical?" He blinked, and turned away from the cop, releasing him from the compulsion.

Harmann immediately shook himself, straightened up, and sneered at me. "You're going away, bitch," he spat out. "You'll get what's coming to you."

Rafael nodded towards him, so I looked at him. *Really* looked. Harmann's mouth twisted scornfully, his flabby cheeks trembling with outrage.

He was *so* consumed with hatred. Every cell in his body vibrated with malice, fully loaded with contempt. Every ounce of energy he had went towards terrible thoughts; a dark loop that went around and around. Now that I was looking at him properly, I could almost see Harmann's soul, and it was filthy and stained with the depth of his loathing for his own existence.

Huh. He was suffering. It really was astonishing. There was nothing worse I could possibly do to him that he wasn't already doing to himself. If I was to rip Harmann's arms off, it might actually relieve his misery for a few moments, in the same way that a depressed teenager slices their thighs to divert attention from their dark thoughts.

I took a deep breath and sighed it all out. "Damn it, Rafael. Could you have waited until I'd punched his teeth out a little before you go all Yoda on me?"

Rafael ran his thumb down my cheek, and I shivered. "He is not worth any of our attention," he murmured. "We have other priorities."

Harmann blustered behind us, spitting out a cacophony of insults and slurs. I tuned him out. "You're right," I said to Rafael, gritting my teeth. "We have to find Leroy."

At least we had a lead now. I guess I could thank Harmann for that.

Sonja had already been busy at Harmann's computer, copying the security footage from outside the station and printing out photos of the agents on the sidewalk, so we'd gotten what we needed. We had no other reason to stay.

Ignoring Harmann completely, we turned around and walked out together, Rafael helping me step over the ruined reinforced door like the gentleman he was. We walked down the steps, and I paused on the sidewalk outside. "Sonja, did you say the vampire who was petitioning for an audience was from Homeland Security? In D.C?"

"Yes."

"Maybe he has insider information on the F.B.I's visit." I furrowed my brow. "See if you can get hold of him."

"Of course." She tapped on her phone.

Wow, Sonja was starting to take orders from me. Maybe the world really was ending.

I squeezed Rafael's hand. "We need to find out more about these F.B.I. agents," I said. "Agent Mullins, and the mystery female agent who stayed in the car. We should find out why they were at the Outdoor Education Center before they came here."

"We will go and speak with Debbie and Cassandra now," Rafael replied.

"Yes." I paused, and winked at him. "But first–"

I let go of his hand and let my power flood through me. Dashing back up the steps, I flew inside the police station, punched Harmann in the mouth, smashing all his teeth, and ran back outside to hold Rafael's hand again before he could even blink.

He frowned down at me.

I smiled and blinked up at him innocently.

Rafael sighed. "Imogen…"

"What? According to your logic, I just did him a favor. Maybe he'll be too busy spitting up his own teeth and he'll forget the depth of his misery for a brief moment in time."

Rafael chuckled and shook his head. "You are incorrigible."

"Welp," I said, pulling him towards the car. "I never said I was an angel."

CHAPTER 6

*W*e piled into the Maserati and drove up the valley in a convoy, heading east, up towards the Outdoor Education Center. My spirits – which had been slightly lifted after getting the tip about Leroy – sank again when I spotted loose rocks on the roads. They were everywhere; most no bigger than an orange, and some little piles of loose gravel slipping down the valley onto the blacktop. I rounded a corner, and cursed.

"Damn it." I slammed on the breaks. A pile of boulders blocked the road in front of me. I got out of the S.U.V. and walked over.

Rafael slipped out of the Maserati behind me and joined me. "A rockfall," he said, dark eyes flashing. "The valley is starting to crumble."

"That asshole is going to bury us." I ground my jaw, stomped over, and kicked a boulder into the trees. It crashed into the trunk of a huge cedar and snapped it in half. With an enormous groan, the giant tree bent over and fell to the forest floor in slow-motion. "Oops."

"I will get a team here to clear the rubble as it comes down," Rafael muttered.

"If the Ancient causes a big enough quake, there won't be time to move the rubble, Raf. The portal will get buried, the telluric field will be interrupted, and ghosts and monsters will flood this world." I ground my teeth. "Then, we'll all be damned."

"I don't think he wants to do that."

I tossed a boulder off the road and turned to face him. He was far more perceptive than me, but I'd gotten that vibe from the Ancient as well. "Yeah, I thought so, too. He had a hint of fear in his eyes when I said he'd destroy the world. He doesn't want to do it. But he will, just to get back at me for some made-up offense I committed." I squeezed my eyes shut and cursed. "I wish I could understand what the hell he is talking about. I don't know any Sariel."

"Let's hope these quakes don't get too bad. He only has three days."

"Does he, though?" A thought had been niggling at me. "He's in a pocket dimension. It's outside of this reality. It has different rules. The laws of physics might force him out of *this* realm and back to his own after three days…"

Rafael stared at me grimly. "You're right. Time works differently in a pocket dimension."

"We have no idea how long he'll stay there for," I said. "He could stay for a month and shake the valley until it's buried."

I tossed another boulder and frowned. "Maybe I should send Brick down to sing Karaoke to him, and he'll get annoyed and leave."

Rafael's eyes flared wide. "No, my love." He shook his head, horrified. "That is a torture that no creature could withstand. If anything, I would imagine the Ancient would rather self-combust. The resulting implosion may cause a black hole which will suck all of our reality into nothingness."

I chuckled sadly. Brick's singing really *was* that bad.

* * *

W<small>E GOT BACK</small> into the cars and drove up the valley towards the Outdoor Education Center, stopping twice more to clear the roads. The gate across the driveway was bolted shut; Rafael and I got out. I took his hand.

"Sonja has gone to try and contact our vampire from Homeland Security," he told me as we walked up the driveway. "We do need to try and chase all the leads."

Cassandra, the camp counselor, met us at the front entrance. "Come on in." She swished her hips as she walked. "We've just gotten back from a hunt. The kids are all napping or taking some down-time in their room. Debbie's running the perimeter, she'll probably scent you and join us." She led us to the rec room.

"No sign of Leroy?" I couldn't keep the hope out of my voice.

She glanced back at me and shook her head. "I'm sorry."

I collapsed into a squashy sofa. Rafael draped himself beside me, the picture of masculine grace. "You had visitors from the F.B.I. yesterday," he said.

Cassandra tilted her head, confused. "No…?"

There was a beat of silence.

I frowned. "No one from the F.B.I. came here yesterday asking about me?"

She shook her head. "No. Of course not. I would have told you if they did."

Hmm. Maybe Harmann lied about that for some reason. I glanced at Rafael. "Why would he lie about that?"

He turned back to Cassandra. "You had no visitors yesterday?"

"Well, just the usual. The grocery delivery came yesterday, and some parents came to visit their kids. The gates have been shut, so the visitors buzz, and I'll send someone out to escort them in."

My brows shot up. "You had *parents* come in?"

She gave me a sad smile. "Well, as you know, most of the kids are here because they've been abjured by their families, or they're in hiding, so there's not many parents coming to visit. Especially not any fathers."

The Alpha movement had torn apart a lot of families. The kids here at the shifter school were mostly victims of domestic violence, smuggled out and hidden by their mothers because their idiot fathers wanted to embody the stereotype of the Alpha Shifter. They demanded total submission, and often beat their wives and children. It was ridiculous, unnecessary, contrary to the whole of shifter history, and it was completely and utterly heartbreaking. The family unit had broken apart because a handful of idiots had read some fiction in the nineties and decided that they needed to be 'alphas'.

That wasn't the only reason for the school. Other kids were here because their parents hated being shifters – they were often religious extremists who thought shifting was unnatural and evil. They wouldn't let their children change into their animals, and would beat them when they did, so they ran away, and Backman took them in.

Things were getting better. There hadn't been any new shifter kids come into the school in the past six months. Slowly, the Alpha movement was being revealed for what it was – straight-up child abuse – and the religious extremists knew better than to go up against Backman.

The kids were safe here. Except, the F.B.I had somehow gotten in…

Cassandra shifted in her seat. "Some of the kids aren't here just because their parents are assholes, you know. Sometimes it's because of their own behavioral issues."

I leaned forward. "Who came to visit yesterday?"

"Darla's parents," Cassandra replied.

"Darla?" I wracked my brain. There was important information here, I could feel it. "Her parents are accountants, aren't they?" I vaguely remember her telling me that the school was more of a Brat Camp for her, rather than a shifter sanctuary.

"That's right. I'd never met Darla's parents, but they swung by for a visit yesterday."

I glanced at Rafael, and back at Cassandra. "You'd never met them?"

She shook her head. A spark of alarm flared in her eyes. "Why? What's going on?"

"We were told that the F.B.I. came up here yesterday, asking questions about me," I ground my teeth. I glared at her. "Darla was busted for hacking, wasn't she?" I leaped to my feet. "*Damn* it!" All the pieces crashed together in my head at the same time.

"What is it?"

"She's done it again, I bet you. She's blown up some coal mines or sunk some sea trawlers, or something, and she's been caught. The F.B.I. threatened her and squeezed her for information, and she rolled over and offered me up instead."

"Offered you up?" Cassandra peered at me through her flinty eyes. "Why? What have *you* done?"

"Oh, tons of bad stuff," I said, waving my hand dismissively. "That's not the point. The point is this: She's called the F.B.I and burned me. They've come here, gathered as much information on me as they could, and grabbed Leroy as a hostage to lure me in."

She gasped. "No. Darla wouldn't do that!"

I chuckled mirthlessly. "It's amazing what people will do when their backs are to the wall."

"But she's been so good lately! She's been accepted for environmental studies at Georgetown. She's studying very hard."

I stared at her. "Always on her computer, huh?"

Cassandra cursed, and rose to her feet. "We better go and talk to her."

We walked through the rec room into the courtyard beyond, and took an outdoor corridor through to the girl's dormitories. Each kid had their own tiny room, it seemed, which was nice for a boarding school.

I glanced into some of the open doors as we passed. Various kids were napping on their beds, sprawled out, some still in animal form. The further down the hallway, the older the kids got. Cassandra shimmied forward down the hallway and knocked on the door right at the end. "Darla?"

"Yeah. Come in."

Darla was sprawled on her bed, tapping away on her laptop, the picture of languid grace. Her animal was a panther, if I remembered correctly, and she seemed to embody the elegance of that particular predator in human form, too. Lithe, long-limbed and exceptionally beautiful, with glowing dark skin and huge, shimmering eyes, she had a way of making it look like she was horribly bored even while an intense battle raged around her.

She gazed up at us coolly, giving no indication she even knew who we were. "Can I help you?"

Her attitude, which I normally admired, pissed me off. I shouldered my way past Cassandra. "What did you tell them?"

She paused for a moment, and blinked her big eyes lazily. She was giving me every impression that she was about to fall asleep out of boredom. "What did I tell... *who*, exactly?"

"What did you tell the F.B.I?"

"I haven't told the F.B.I anything."

I growled. As a powerful immortal creature, it was desperately humiliating to stare into the face of a bored teenager and be intimidated, but here we were. "Bitch," I snarled. "Where is Leroy?"

Some of her attitude wobbled. A flash of concern touched her expression. "I don't know where he is."

"Well, who took him, then? You know that much, don't you?"

She sighed deeply, as if I was a tiny irritating fly, swung her legs underneath her long body and sat upright. "I don't know who took him," she said. "I already told Ms. Backman everything I know. Leroy was with us last night until we got to the lake turn-off, and he rode off."

She stared at me. "I offered to go with him. I've got a little brother his age; I miss him. But my little brother isn't a powerful witch, so I let Leroy go by himself, and I didn't worry about him after that."

Her concern touched me for a second, but I brushed it off. "The F.B.I. came to visit you," I snarled. "What did you tell them?"

She raised one eyebrow and stared at me. "It's finally happened," she drawled. "You've completely lost your mind."

I snarled, and took a step towards her. Cassandra hissed softly behind me; a warning.

I flicked her a glance over my shoulder. She met my eyes. I could almost see the calculations going on in her head as her eyes flickered bright-green. If it came to a fight, it would be her, Debbie the lion shifter, Darla... The older kids could try and fight me...

75

I let the silence hang heavily in the little room for a second. "You have no idea," I said quietly, my voice ice-cold, my eyes fixed on Cassandra's gleaming slit-pupils. "I could destroy this whole school in a heartbeat, you know. I could rip you both apart in an instant and kill everyone in this building." I raised an eyebrow. "You think I'm on the edge of a breakdown? I *am*. And the last time that happened, I burned a whole city to the ground. Don't you dare hiss at me again."

I turned back to face Darla. "I'm going to ask you one more time. What did you tell them?"

Darla swallowed heavily. I'd finally frightened her out of her sullen attitude. "Imogen, I'm sorry, but I don't know what you're talking about."

"Who came to visit you yesterday?"

"Nobody. I didn't have any visitors yesterday."

Cassandra stepped closer. "Your parents were here."

She shook her head. "My parents?" She pointed to a photo on her desk.

Cassandra's mouth fell open. Clearly, it wasn't the same people.

"My parents are still in Detroit." Darla frowned. "Why would you think my parents came here to visit yesterday?"

The snake shifter hissed again, a mad gleam in her eye. "Because two people showed up here yesterday, claiming to be your parents. They signed in, and they were escorted through to the courtyard to meet you."

There was a pause. Darla raised her eyebrows very slightly. "And who was it that escorted them?"

I gritted my teeth. It had never made sense that it was Darla who rolled me. But there was one kid in this place that definitely had it in for me. "I think I can guess."

Cassandra nodded at me. "Sebastian."

CHAPTER 7

*S*ebastian was crying so hard his whole face had gone bright red. Fluro-red, even. Usually pale, supercilious and scornful, Sebastian clung to the tree branch and sobbed so dramatically I thought he was going to pass out.

Cassandra, guessing the reason why Sebastian had betrayed me, made me promise I wouldn't hurt him. She took the news of Sebastian's screw-up as well as can be expected, cussing under her breath the whole way around the center as we walked around looking for him. "I can't believe this happened under my watch. I'm going to have to notify Backman," she hissed. "She's supposed to be taking no-contact leave so she can concentrate on looking after Marigold."

"You don't need to tell her," I said. "It's done, now. Maybe wait until after Marigold stops levitating and throwing fire-balls when someone sneaks up on her."

"She's got almost eight months to go in her pregnancy. I doubt Backman will leave her alone any time soon."

Cassandra sighed out a breath. "Maybe it's a good thing she's stepping back. She has to let go of the school sooner or later."

"Why?"

"The shifter world is leaning on her more and more," Cassandra explained. "Backman doesn't want to be Queen, you know. Before her, we didn't have a ruler. There was no use for one. Shifters were family units, and ruled themselves. But when the Alpha movement came along, she fought for the kids more than anyone else, and people started turning to her for help. Of course, she always wants to help as many shifters as possible, so she started cleaning up other people's messes, then slowly, she started mediating between warring clans. Before she knew it, people were calling her Queen."

I sniggered. "I wish I was there when she found *that* out for the first time."

Cassandra giggled. "Oh, she was mortified." Her laughter faded. "There's no one else, though, so she has to do it. If she publicly abdicates responsibility for the shifter community, it will leave a power vacuum, and I know for a fact there's a lot of people willing to fill it for their own shitty reasons." She glared around the clearing, scanning for Sebastian. There was no sign of him so far. Cassandra sighed. "Even now, every six months or so some wolf or big cat shifter will gather a few followers under their boot and declare himself the Shifter King. Most of the time Backman will ignore them until there's signs of abuse, then of course she'll head in and shut it down."

"Does she get challenged?" I asked. "The shifter books I read always talk about dominance challenges, and how shifters fight to the death for the role of Alpha. They make it sound like the Alpha was always beating off challenges."

"Oh yeah," Cassandra said. "Unfortunately that little aspect of the Alpha movement also carried over from fiction, too. Backman gets challenged all the time." Cassandra giggled. "She just ignores them. They hate it. And every now and then, some asshole will show up here and demand a fight with her." Her smile flattened out. "Backman will rip their head off within thirty seconds, every time. It's not even a competition. No," she sighed. "That poor bear has enough on her plate, with her crown, and her mate pregnant. I think I'll keep Sebastian's fuck-up quiet for now."

We'd found him hiding up in a tree at the agility course. Darla heard him first, because he was crying.

My anger at him almost evaporated. *Almost.*

I gripped the tree trunk between my hands and wobbled it. "Sebastian," I growled. "You know I could rip this tree up by the roots."

"No–hooo–hooo," he sobbed. "Please! Imogen, please. I'm sorry. I'm so, so, so sorry."

"That doesn't make it any better!"

"I just love him so much. I love him soooo much," he howled. "But he loves *youuuuuuu*."

I banged my head against the tree trunk. "Goddamnit, Sebastian." His distress was making it really hard for me to be angry at him.

"I'm sorry. I really am sorry. I'm *so* sorry. I regretted it the second I called them. I don't know what I was thinking."

I let out a rude noise. "You wanted revenge, that's what you were thinking."

"No! Well… sort of, I guess. I just wanted to hurt you in the same way you hurt me. I feel like I'm being stabbed in the chest, over and over and over," he wailed.

"For fucks sake," I muttered. *Teenagers.* This was ridiculous. "Dude," I shouted up at him. "I didn't steal Brandon from you. I don't even want him!"

"That makes it *wooooorrrssseeee.*"

I ground my jaw. "It's not my fault!"

"I know! I– I just got so angry about him being obsessed

with you. It got so intense... I thought I was going to explode!"

"So you called the F.B.I. on me."

"No! I called a police tip line and told them you were stealing boys away. I– I ranted on the phone for a little bit. I just wanted to get it all off my chest. But– but– but some federal agents called me back straight away!" He screwed his face up and howled for a full minute.

I huffed out a breath, crossed my arms, and waited.

He finally calmed down, and carried on. "I was so scared. I tried to backtrack, but they insisted they needed to find you. I've been watching the road for days because I knew they would show up. They did," he squeaked. "Two of them came here and I was such a coward, I snuck out and met them at the gate. The agent was a black woman, so I made them pretend to be Darla's parents so I could cover my tracks!"

I frowned. "That's pretty despicable."

"I know! I'm the worst person in the history of the u–u–u–niverse!" He dissolved into some sort of weird panting sob.

I waited for him to finish hyperventilating. "So, what did you tell them?"

He wiped his nose on his sleeve. "I spoke to the woman, mostly. Agent King, her name was. The male agent hung back, I never got his name."

I nodded, silently gesturing for Sebastian to carry on. We already got his name, anyway. Agent Mullins. Now we knew the names of the people who kidnapped Leroy.

"The male agent was just watching everything around us, like a security guard. I told Agent King all about you and Brandon," Sebastian said. "She didn't really care about him." A touch of outrage crept into his voice. "She asked me some questions about you. Both agents were human, though, so I didn't mention any of the supe stuff."

I cocked my head. "She didn't know you were a supe? Or me, for that matter?"

"Nope," Sebastian said, shaking his head. "I checked her for the Sight, too. She didn't have it."

He would have been able to tell that she was human just by sniffing her, that part was easy. But just because she was human didn't mean she was unaware of the supernatural element in the world. Almost every human who had been exposed to the supernatural had an extra sight, like they could see things on a wider spectrum beyond normal human comprehension. Most supes could tell just by looking into a human's eyes whether they could See or not. There was a clarity there, like a veil had been stripped from their eyes.

"She had no idea about anything to do with the supe world," Sebastian went on. "She was just a normal human woman. She was really nice, actually," he added, sniffing dramatically. "She seemed like she was only here to make sure you weren't stealing children. I told her you weren't – I admitted I'd just gotten carried away because my heart was broken. She asked me a bunch of questions, though. I gave her your address."

My shoulders slumped. "Ugh." Well, they knew all the supe stuff, anyway, since they went to visit Harmann right afterwards. He would have told them everything.

Or maybe he didn't. Harmann might not have mentioned that he'd been turned into a pig by a fae queen. And if he did, then they probably thought he was just crazy.

Maybe the agents been hunting me because of the murders in California, and they'd jumped on Sebastian's tip to track me down. Maybe they thought I was just a human serial killer, like Harmann said.

Except... Agent Mullins told Harmann I was a dangerous

weapon. I took that to mean they definitely knew I was a supe. And they took Leroy to lure me in.

I frowned. Something wasn't adding up. The male F.B.I. agent told Harmann I was a powerful, dangerous animal, and he was going to lock me up and try to use me as a weapon. But the female agent had no idea I was a supe?

Something fishy was going on.

The expression on Rafael's face told me he thought the same. These agents knew exactly who I was. They were hunting me for my powers. Maybe Agent King couldn't See, but Agent Mullins probably could, and that's why he stayed back. At best, they were human government agents, out to capture me and experiment on me. *Again.*

At worst, they were supernatural creatures themselves, some sort of evil monstrosities that could shield themselves, who were hunting me for reasons unknown.

And now, they had Leroy.

I sighed and rubbed my chest. It felt so tight; like I couldn't breathe. "Can you come down, please, Sebastian?"

"Never," he cried. "I'm going to stay up here and starve to death. It's what I deserve." He wrapped his arms and legs around the branch and cried fat teardrops on the dusty ground below.

"You're just going to get dehydrated and pass out, you know," I muttered.

"Then I hope I die in the fall," he howled dramatically.

"You're only a few feet above my head. Rafael could probably pull you down from here."

"*Amore,*" he said. "His heart is broken. Leave him be."

A gust of wind blew through the trees around us, and suddenly, Sonja was beside us. "My King." She bowed deeply. "Consort. I've spoken with your subject from Homeland Security. He has information regarding Leroy's abduction."

I grabbed her by the arms and thrust my face close to hers. "Seriously? He knows where Leroy is?"

Sonja eyed me steadily. "Calm down. He says he has information, but it is difficult for him to relay it to us. His partner is a human, and he does not wish to break his cover. He does not have a secure line out – I've only been able to get fragments of information. We may need to go to him."

I looked at Rafael. "Time for a road trip."

He raised one eyebrow ever so slightly. "Road? No. We're taking the helicopter."

"It's just an expression."

"Imogen," Rafael pulled me in. "It might be best if you stay here."

"What? No. No chance. I have to find my kid." Right on cue, the ground rumbled beneath our feet, and I ground my jaw. "And we've got to find him as soon as possible. It's not just that I'm insanely worried he's being hurt, it's also because we need him to break open the pocket dimension. The Ancient is going to destroy the whole world, Raf."

"Yes, but I am worried about your identity being known to the authorities. You are a target, now."

"I'm used to it." I eyed him steadily. "I've always been a target."

"More now than you were before," he clarified, touching my lips with his thumb. "Now they know your identity, your alias."

"I'll do my hair differently, or something."

I should probably do something about the fact that I was still glowing golden, too. I took a breath, concentrated, and, with a little effort, dialed down the star energy coursing through my body. Immediately my color returned to normal. I looked at the skin on my arm, my usual golden-brown color. As much as I liked my extra power, I preferred my skin to look the way it always did.

I sighed. I'd have to dye and cut my hair shorter, so I wasn't immediately recognizable. "I usually have a few back-up I.D. but they were all cooked when my cabin exploded."

Sonja jabbed at her phone, both thumbs a blur. "I'll have identity documents prepared now, and have the chopper ready."

"Give me a red bob on the I.D, would ya?"

Sonja snorted. "No. You will be caramel blonde. Red would clash with your wedding gown."

My protest died on my lips. The prospect of my wedding to Rafael seemed like a dream, like a fantasy in some far-flung land that I would never get to. A life with a partner and a kid that I adored, free from my enemies relentlessly pursuing us.

God, I wanted that dream. I wanted it so bad I could tear down the barrier between worlds myself.

I clenched my teeth. We needed to find Leroy, squash whatever government agency was gunning for me, open the pocket dimension, find the mysterious Sariel, and smack the Ancient in the mouth before he left our reality…

And I'd finally be happy.

CHAPTER 8

*W*e landed in D.C. outside a private hanger and were escorted to a convoy of armored Range Rovers by Rafael's security. Rafael seemed distracted, on the phone the whole time, issuing orders in twelve different languages. "I apologize, my love," he said to me once. "It seems there is a sudden surge of rogue vampire behavior on this continent. Innocent people have been hurt."

He frowned deeply, watching new messages come through on his phone. "It is unsettling. The usual nest chain of command are having difficulty keeping up with breaches. The Enforcer of D.C. has filed concerns. I will need to meet with him while I am here."

I squinted. "There's an Enforcer in D.C?"

An Enforcer was a human nominated by supe leaders as their proxy if they couldn't immediately take care of a problem themselves. Enforcers had immunity from retaliation, and were provided intelligence and financial support from all the different supernatural factions. Since they were always human, they were supposed to be impartial to the shifter-vamp-witch power struggles that sometimes went on.

Trouble was, not many humans had the balls nor the strength to deal with supes on a daily basis, so not many cities had their own Enforcers. They were rare and formidable characters. I had a boyfriend who was an Enforcer once, a few hundred years ago.

"The capitol needs an Enforcer, so I am glad he is there," Rafael said. "It has been decades since a suitable candidate has been chosen, but this one is more than capable. In fact, he practically appointed himself to the role of Enforcer."

"Hmmm. I'd like to meet him."

Rafael huffed out a chuckle. "Not a chance."

"Why?"

He looked up and met my eye, and grinned. "Conrad Sinclair is possibly the most attractive man I've ever met before in my life. I am not a jealous man, but I am not a stupid one, either."

I let out a rude noise. "Come on. He can't be that good-looking."

Rafael tapped his phone, then flipped it over, showing me a photo of the Enforcer, Conrad Sinclair.

"Oh." I swallowed roughly. "*Wow*. I see what you mean." If explosive masculinity and blistering-hot sensuality was a person, he would look like the man on the screen.

"I am very sure in my sexuality," Rafael said. "But even I struggle not to lick my lips when Sinclair is in the room. I must meet with him today, though." He glanced out the window, brooding. "Something is going on."

"What do you think it is?"

He frowned. "I don't know. There is something dark stirring in this city."

I left him to his brooding. "Where are we headed?" I asked Sonja, as the convoy moved at snail's pace through D.C.'s horrendous traffic.

"The King's hotel," she said. "Our Homeland Security

informant will be able to contact us there." She frowned down at her own phone. "He is being unfathomably reticent with information."

I winked at Rafael. "You have a hotel in D.C?"

"He has five," Sonja said shortly. "The stylist will meet us there."

We reached Dupont Circle and got out of the cars. Rafael's hotel was right in the hustle and bustle of the city, a beautiful old-world French architecture building, with its original facade restored and gleaming with new paint and shining stained-glass feature windows. The lobby was light and airy, with grand high ceilings and a soaring staircase leading up to the second level.

I took a second to admire the beauty of the building. Rafael was distracted; his Washington D.C. head of security walked beside him, reporting on the rogue vampire issue. He gave me a smile in apology and let himself be dragged away by his security team.

A second team escorted me and Sonja in as we walked straight through the lobby, uninterrupted. Four receptionists with model-perfect good looks bowed deeply to us from the reception desk.

"Hello!" I waved cheerfully back at them.

Sonja dragged me by the elbow towards the elevators. "Please have a little decorum," she said out the side of her mouth. "The King's subjects in Emerald Valley might be used to your... little mannerisms. But please keep in mind that these people don't know you. They will be expecting the King's mate to be cool and reserved."

I flattened my mouth in a line. "That sounds like a 'them' problem. I don't really care what they are expecting. They will take me exactly as I am."

Sonja pushed me into the elevator and glared at me for a full minute. Never one to pass up a chance to annoy her, I stared back, unblinking, so she'd know we were in a staring contest.

After a moment, she blinked.

"I win!"

She sighed deeply. "You're right. I don't know why I bother."

I gasped dramatically and put my hand on my chest. "I'm right? Did the great taciturn and stoic Sonja just tell me I was *right?*"

"The old King is dead. The danger has passed. There is no need to keep up appearances," she sighed again. "Maybe it is time to let the world know exactly who our King is marrying," she muttered. "It's going to have to happen sooner or later."

"You don't have to say it like that."

"If I sound disgusted, it's because I am," she curled her lip. "You are wearing *sweatpants.*"

I laughed. "I thought you were still angry because I'm not a vampire."

"Your fashion sense offends me more than your genes."

"Jeans before genes, huh?"

"*Sweatpants,*" she sniffed haughtily. "The King's last girlfriend was wearing a ballgown when she visited this hotel for the first time."

"Well," I muttered. "I suppose you liked her a lot more than you like me?"

"Of course not," Sonja replied, her tone icy. "I have despised every single one of my King's partners." She ran her gaze over me, wrinkling her nose. "You, unfortunately, are the best of them all. If you were only a vampire, then I would go to my final death a happy woman."

I grinned at her. "Aw. I love you too, Sonja."

The elevator dinged and opened directly into an enormous suite. The penthouse was two-storied and furnished in soft pastels, with charming priceless watercolors adorning the walls and soft pink and lavender peonies on delicate side tables. A grand curved staircase soared into the upper level, and I could spot another staircase heading up from that, probably to the rooftop. "Nice digs," I hefted my overnight bag onto a yellow silk chaise lounge.

"That chair belonged to Louis XV," she muttered. She took a deep breath. "Come," she ordered. "Your colorist is waiting for you in the bathroom."

* * *

I EMERGED THREE HOURS LATER, vibrating with impatience, with brand-new caramel hair with honey-blonde highlights cut into a very chic textured bob. I looked great, but I wasn't happy.

It didn't do me any good to sit still. Every second I was stuck here, hiding in the bathroom, Leroy could be getting tortured for information. I was desperate to find him.

Rafael, waiting in the lounge area of the suite, pulled me into his arms and kissed me deeply. It settled my nerves slightly. "You look delectable," he murmured in my ear.

"Good enough to eat, huh?"

"Don't tempt me."

I shivered. "Later," I promised him. "When we've found Leroy, I'll let you eat every single part of me."

Sonja dumped a charcuterie board on the coffee table in between us with a clatter. "Our informant has made contact," she said. "He will be running surveillance with his human partner on a suspected K.G.B. agent in Lincoln Park in one hour. He will attempt to break away from his partner and meet with us."

"It's a little odd that he's so hamstrung by his partner, isn't it?" I frowned. "I would have thought it would be fairly easy to get on a secure line and tell us everything he knew quickly. Or just use a little compulsion on his partner, and meet with us."

"He is in Intelligence." Sonja said, her voice dripping with disdain. "They all behave in an unnecessary clandestine manner. All our operatives prefer to give information in person, so that things cannot be misinterpreted or missed. It is annoying, but meeting with him directly is the fastest way to get the details we need to continue our pursuit."

I nodded. "I don't really care, as long as we get Leroy. He could be here, somewhere in the city. They could be hurting him." I clenched my fists. "I just need to get to him."

"They will not harm him," Sonja placed a cool hand on my arm, obviously trying to soothe me. "We're running under the assumption that it is some black-ops government agency attempting to contain you for research purposes. They will threaten him with injury to lure you in, but they will have no cause to do anything until they've made contact with you."

"That's not particularly comforting, you know," I muttered. I let out a low, frustrated hiss. "Oh, I just want to break something."

"Save that thought." Rafael buttoned his jacket. "We will meet with our informant first. Then you can go and break something."

"Who is this guy, anyway?"

Sonja consulted her tablet. "His name is Squires. Agent Simon Squires: a newly born vampire, only turned fifteen years or so. He lived his human life in Mississippi, and became the plaything of Mary Benedict, one of the nest leaders in the south. Just after he was turned, Mary Benedict apparently went rogue, slaughtered all her female children, butchered a few local human police officers, and was reluctantly extinguished by the male members of the nest."

"Hmm. Nasty."

Sonja frowned deeply. "I always wondered about it. It was a great shame about Mary Benedict; she was a bonne vivante and enjoyed her vampire life very much. It felt strange to me that she would succumb to madness and risk everything."

I shrugged. "Maybe she just went mad like all old vampires eventually do."

"Oh, she wasn't ancient, only a hundred years or so older than me. She was odd, that was certain, but I never thought for a moment that she would start indiscriminately slaughtering her female children for no good reason."

"Well, it's a good thing she was put down before she could do too much damage," I said absently.

"Indeed. In any case, Squires went into law enforcement himself and became an intelligence operative on our orders. It pays to have people everywhere."

"If he can get us information about Leroy, it will be worth it." Hope stung my chest, along with the echo of bitter disappointment. God, I missed him. I ran my fingers through my hair, pulling up short. "Oh. I forgot about the hair. I must look quite different."

"Different enough," Rafael ran his fingers through it. "Although it might be good to get you out in the open, so that whoever has kidnapped Leroy can try and make contact." He pulled me close. "My love, I am sorry I will not be with you, but I have to meet with the Enforcer."

I nodded, and winked at him. "Keep your hands off him, okay?"

He smiled back and kissed my nose. "I'll do my best."

* * *

SONJA SENT a security team ahead to Lincoln Park to sweep for danger. They were under strict orders to stay unnoticed, and they were doing an excellent job, because even I couldn't tell who they were in the throng of tourists wandering through the park.

Sonja and I walked alone, strolling slowly down the paths and idly inspecting statues. I let myself be seen. Hopefully, whatever rogue government agency that took Leroy would make contact with me and issue some demands. It was hard to pretend to be so nonchalant when all I wanted to do was smash open every building in the city and search for my kid.

I also made sure Sonja issued an order to her security team to let me be taken if anyone tried to abduct me. I wouldn't try and fight my way out; not when Leroy's life was on the line. At this stage, I'd let myself be experimented on for years if it meant getting Leroy back.

No one was trying to touch me, though. Nobody approached me. Morosely, I bought myself an ice cream and forced a berry sorbet cone on Sonja, and we walked in circles around a fountain in the center of the park.

"Agent Squires is not going to show," I muttered, trying to lick ice cream off my chin.

She frowned. "He will. He must. He would not defy the King's orders." Her eyes narrowed. "Although, I must say, he is overwhelmingly annoying, and I haven't even met him yet. He has made contact at least four times already, and each time he hasn't told me anything useful. He demands to speak with the King, and tells me nothing. He is filled with riddles and abrupt hang-ups."

I huffed out a breath. "Well, he better show up." I squinted at her. "We could go and get him. You keep tabs on all the vampires, don't you? You know where he lives?"

"Yes. I've already had security check it out. His official address is just a front. The apartment he leased in his name has not had any vampire inside of it for more than a week."

"That's not a red flag?"

"He will be keeping his resting place secret. It is not unheard of. Vampires are vulnerable when they rest, especially the new ones like Squires. Since he is in Intelligence, he will be more paranoid than most."

"Right," I muttered. "So we can't just go and find him."

"If he does not show up, then we will attempt to locate him." She frowned. "If we burn him, we burn him."

We made another circle around the fountain. I finished my ice cream and wiped my sticky hands on a paper napkin.

"That is no good," Sonja said. She pulled a wet wipe out of her purse. "Here."

"Thanks." We sat down on a park bench by the fountain so I could clean the ice cream off my hands. Balling up the wet wipe, I launched it into the trash next to the park bench, and hugged myself. It was a cold winter day, I was aware of the temperature, but I really couldn't feel it. I'd dialed down my star energy so I would fit in amongst the humans, but my extra powers were still coursing through my body.

I'd always been strong and fast, and, annoyingly, unkillable, but that's as far as my half-human-half-star powers ever went. Now, my senses were all super-charged. Like my hearing, which had been depressingly human before, was sharp to the point of distraction. I could hear conversations going on across the park if I concentrated hard enough. My sense of smell, too, had improved beyond comprehension.

So far, that wasn't a good thing. The smell of the trash can next to me made me feel sick to my stomach. A young mother walked by with her toddler, apparently completely unaware he had a giant stinky turd in his diaper. I had the pleasure of having them wander slowly past us, watching – and smelling – the kid mash his own poop between his legs as he walked. Even Sonja wrinkled her nose in disgust. I was so glad I'd gotten Leroy after he'd been toilet trained.

I groaned. "Am I ever going to get him back?"

"We will. We will leave no stone unturned."

My attention pulled towards a man in a long, black woolen overcoat with the collar turned up. He wore mirrored sunglasses and a flat cap pulled low over his face, and he walked with the air of a man with absolutely no goal at all other than to enjoy the day. He wandered by and sat behind us, facing the open fields next to the fountains. I stiffened, immediately smelling the overpowering scent of sunscreen.

It was a cold winter day. Who wears a thick layer of sunscreen on a day like today? Unused to deciphering new scents, I tasted the air with my tongue. I couldn't tell.

Sonja was more skilled than me. "Squires?"

"Don't turn around," he said under his breath. "Keep facing forward. Don't look at me."

I let out a breath. Thank God. He was here.

"Where is Leroy?" I whispered.

There was a long moment of silence. Agent Simon Squires reached into the pocket of his coat. I waited, almost vibrating out of my skin with impatience. Slowly, very slowly, he pulled out a small, bulging paper bag. Carefully, he unfolded the top of the bag, rolling it back down onto itself, exposing the contents.

I waited, my breath in my throat.

He dipped two fingers inside the bag and took a pinch of whatever was inside. Moving slower than a sloth, he brought his fingers out and stretched his hand, sprinkling the pinch of what smelled like dried seeds on the ground at his feet.

Immediately, a flock of pigeons swarmed the seeds, flapping their wings and pecking the ground frantically.

I pursed my lips. "Seriously?" I muttered, looking away. "You're feeding the birds?"

Sonja cursed in German under her breath. I didn't catch what she said, but Germans always seem to have the appropriate expression for any niche situation, so whatever she said probably meant something like 'at a time when we are meeting with a secret agent, I cannot believe he is behaving exactly like a secret agent.'

Squires scooped up another small handful of seeds and dropped them on the ground, and spoke so quietly I barely heard him even with my own new enhanced hearing. "I was expecting our liege to be here. Where is he?"

I spat out quietly through clenched teeth. "Where is Leroy?" I asked again. "Where are Agent King and Agent Mullins?"

"I do not know who either of you are. I will only discuss these matters with the King."

Sonja tilted her head, still looking away from him. "You know who I am. I am the King's Valet. Tell us what we need to know."

"It is sensitive information," Squires murmured. "I do not know you. You are a mere woman, and as far as I know, you do not have clearance. I will speak with the King, and the King only."

Sonja bristled. I doubt I'd seen her so offended. If Squires wasn't such an asshole, I'd be in awe of how much he riled her up. "I am the King's right-hand vampire," she snarled softly. "Everyone in the Kingdom is aware of who I am. I have his proxy in all things. This is his fiancé, his *mate*. You do us a great insult, Squires."

I casually looked sideways, glancing at him in my peripheral vision. He was a handsome vampire, with chin-length black hair swept back off his face by the flat cap, skimming his collar, a straight, proud nose and thick black brows above the mirrored sunglasses. A slight smirk touched his thin lips.

He was enjoying holding this information over us, I could tell. What I couldn't understand was why he would do it. Sonja was much older than him and could crush him into dust in a heartbeat. I, myself, could rip him apart with my bare hands. He must know how old and dangerous we were.

He just didn't care. That was strange.

Taking his time, he scooped up another handful of seeds and scattered them at his feet. Pigeons frantically flapped and pecked again. Some of it bounced beneath the bench, and the little flying rats scuttered underneath the chair. I lifted my feet up and shivered involuntarily.

"I will only speak with the King," Agent Squires said, his mouth not moving as he spoke. "This information is too sensitive, and I don't think either of you rank highly enough to have the clearance for it."

Sonja growled. "This is his *mate*."

"Even so, I very much doubt he will allow her to have the information before he gets it himself. Perhaps you are operating without permission. It would be irresponsible of me to allow you to have such sensitive information."

I took a breath to try and calm myself down. Agent Squires was getting to me, too. I was acutely aware that some of the older vampire relationships were stuck firmly in the dark ages. Some arranged pairings were more slave-and-owner than a marriage on equal footing. Rafael's father, General Lucius, had bought his mother and treated her like a possession for her whole long life. Maybe Squires was operating under the assumption that Rafael was just like his father, and would be angry if he gave us anything.

I turned my head away, and spoke out of the corner of my mouth. "Listen here, Maxwell Smart, you absolute buffoon. I'm Rafael's intended bride. I'm his Queen. But that's neither here nor there." I lowered my voice, my tone ice-cold. "If you don't tell me what you know about Leroy's kidnapping, I'm going to rip your head off right here in this park and finger-paint anarchist symbols on the fountain in your blood, just for kicks."

His own tone didn't waver. "Then you will never see your child, Leroy, again," he murmured. He curled his lip. "I would never let a woman talk me into breaching important security protocols."

There was an odd groan, the sound of metal being bent out of shape. I looked down. I'd twisted the wrought iron armrest on the park bench out of shape.

My heart was thudding uncontrollably, I could hear it in my ears, but it was the background to every single noise in this park. Sound assailed me, high pitched children's screams, low mutters, gravel crunching beneath tired feet. I could smell the dusty cold-cream vampire smell underneath Squire's thick layer of sunscreen and the rank, musky dirt odor of the pigeons at my feet, and further out, the obvious sting of chlorine in the fountain water. I pinched my eyes shut. The man on the other side of the fountain was wearing a cologne I vaguely recognized. The woman next to him was on her period. I could smell that, too.

It was too much; too overwhelming. My anger was spiraling out of control. I felt close to exploding.

Sonja reached over and took my hand, and squeezed it.

I looked down. My skin was glowing gold. With enormous effort, I swallowed down my fury, and dialed down my star powers.

Agent Squires chuckled once, his voice harsh, and balled up his paper bag, tossing it carelessly into the trash can. He stood up. "There's a diner on eighteenth near the Library of Congress. If your King really does need this information, he will meet me there in an hour. Otherwise, I don't know when I will be able to get away again." He paused, and frowned. "Maybe it won't be in time to save Leroy."

He turned, and walked away, while I festered and burned on the park bench.

CHAPTER 9

Sonja was almost as angry as me. She was just better at controlling herself. We stalked out of the park, power-walking with her leading me by the hand so I didn't break anything else.

"I promise you, Consort," she growled. "Once he gives us the information we need on Leroy's location, I will personally gut that puffed-up little cockroach myself."

"No, don't do that."

Her steps faltered. She glanced at me.

I looked her in the eyes. "Don't deny me the pleasure, Sonja. I'll make it a slow gutting."

She snorted. "As you wish, Consort. Bah," she waved her hand as we strode through the park. "I cannot believe the nerve of that man. He knows who I am. He is entirely aware that I outrank any of the King's security. His *generals* report to me, for St Peter's sake." Her mouth twisted. "For him to withhold information like this…" She kicked a stone in her path. "I do not know what his game is."

"Oh," I said bitterly. "I can guess what his game is."

Sonja raised her brows.

"He made several references to the fact that both you and I were mere women."

Realization dawned and her brows fell. "Is that it?"

I nodded. "He's just a simple misogynist," I said. "He hates women. He probably hates having to answer to you, or me, for that matter. I've known men like that throughout history. They despise women who won't defer to them."

"Homeland Security must be a tough place for him, then," Sonja picked up her long-legged stride. "More than half of the senior agents are women now."

"It wouldn't matter. He'd do the same thing to his female superiors that he's doing to us right now. He'd make up excuses to withhold information, go over their heads, deliberately provoke them into a reaction... and I bet you anything he'd just get transferred somewhere where his boss isn't a female. Men don't get fired for being assholes to their female bosses. It's usually the female bosses that are reprimanded for not being able to handle their underlings."

Sonja scowled. "You are probably right." Suddenly, she brightened. "Well, it won't matter soon. I will pull him from duty myself, and have him stretched out on the rack and ready for you to eviscerate as soon as we have Leroy back in your custody."

"Sonja, babe." I wrapped my arm around her waist and hugged her. "You do say the nicest things."

Her phone buzzed; she glanced down. "The King will meet us at the diner. His meeting was abruptly cut short too."

That was a shame. I was hoping we could somehow crash his meeting with the Enforcer. Another day, maybe.

* * *

THE DINER AGENT Squires mentioned wasn't far away, so I insisted we walk there. I felt like I needed to keep moving, to keep a forward momentum, otherwise I'd explode. The energy buzzing around my body needed an outlet. Sonja busied herself on her phone, barking orders in German. By the time we'd reached the diner, the hour was almost up.

"The King is inside," Sonja told me, quite unnecessarily, since I'd already spotted one of his security team lounging next to the door of the diner, casually smoking a cigarette. She pulled open the door, and we went in.

The diner was a classic American layout, with a long counter running the length of the room, and booths arranged along the wall with shiny red upholstery and faux-marble Formica tables. A few patrons sat on high stools at the counter sipping coffee and eating pie. A couple of the booths were occupied by what looked like a mixture of foreign tourists, examining everything with fascinated concentration, and businessmen swigging black coffee and barking at each other about podcasts. Sonja slipped into a booth, issuing orders in twelve different languages into her phone. Two other vampires joined her, studying the menu and talking quietly amongst themselves.

Rafael sat at the counter, sipping an espresso. I slid up onto the seat beside him and immediately felt the tension in my muscles release just a fraction. "How was your meeting, honey?"

He turned and smiled at me. "No better than yours, from the sounds of it."

I ground my jaw. "Agent Squires is an asshole."

Rafael took another leisurely sip from his tiny cup. "He may just be diligent. My father was a tyrant, as you know. Squires might be overly cautious."

"Or he might just be an asshole who hates women."

"For his sake, I hope he is just being diligent."

The waitress sashayed over, put a cup down in front of me and poured coffee. "Pie, honey?"

"That sounds amazing." I took a sip and put my cup down. The coffee tasted like dishwater. "So, what happened with the Enforcer?" I waggled my eyebrows.

Rafael smirked back at me. "He was called away on a matter of urgency."

"Is it to do with the rogue vampire situation?"

"Yes. Although, as it turns out, the drainings that have occurred in this city are not the work of rogue vampires."

"Well… who did it then? Non-rogue vampires? Blood witches?"

Rafael's face darkened. "Both."

"Both?" My mouth dropped open. "You mean both, as in, together? Vampires and blood witches acting together?"

"And shifters, it appears."

"No. That can't be possible. Vampires and shifters and witches all hate each other."

"Not necessarily. They'll work together if they find some common ground. Remember that group of Alphas who attacked the Outdoor Education Center? They were united by the fact they thought themselves disenfranchised."

I pursed my lips. "Good point."

"This might be the same sort of thing. There is a figure-head in this city who calls himself Lord Seth. Nobody knows what kind of supernatural creature he is, but Sinclair has heard whispers that he is a demon of some sort. He has been gathering followers to himself, acolytes who believe that Lord Seth will help them shake off their shackles so they can embrace their power over humans."

"Urgh. Is this like a Lord Voldemort thing?"

Rafael looked at me blankly. "What?"

"Sorry. He Who Must Not Be Named."

"You are the strangest woman I have ever met in my life."

"You need to get out more. Anyway, did Sinclair cut the

meeting off because he had to run off to catch this Lord Seth?"

"No." Rafael didn't laugh, but his eyes twinkled. "He has deputized a powerful psychic to help him in his investigations, a lovely young woman, apparently. From the sounds of it, this business relationship has morphed into something extremely personal. And she has a knack for getting into trouble." He took another sip of his espresso.

"Aww. Good for him." I wrinkled my nose. Rafael's coffee smelled delicious. I eyed his tiny cup enviously. The waitress had given me the old coffee from a percolator. "Where did you get your espresso from?"

The door jingled. I glanced over and sighed in relief. "Finally."

Agent Squires swaggered in, not removing his cap or mirrored sunglasses. He made a beeline for the seat next to Rafael, and swung himself onto it, facing away from him.

Rafael ignored him, and took another tiny sip of his espresso. I glared at his little cup, looked up, and glared pointedly at the waitress. She stared blithely back, the ghost of a smile on her lips.

It took me half a second to realize that she was a vampire, too.

I inhaled, tasting the air around me. Hmm. This whole diner was filled with vampires. No wonder Rafael got the good coffee.

"My King," Agent Squires murmured to the empty spot beside him, still in deep-cover mode. "Thank you for meeting with me."

Rafael sighed, and turned to face him. "Squires. Listen to me."

Alarm flared in Agent Squire's face. He froze for a second. "Sire. I am undercover. There are civilians here."

Suddenly, Sonja was sitting next to Agent Squires. One

minute she was in her booth, the next, she was right next to him, staring into his eyes like a cobra.

She'd ripped the mirrored sunglasses off his face, too. I'd never seen her move so fast.

Rafael put his cup down. "Agent Squires, Sonja is my right arm. Do not insult her ever again. Do you understand?"

There was a beat of silence, and Squires nodded once. I could see confusion and defiance warring on his face. The fact that Sonja had just displayed her insane vampiric powers – in public and in full view of the King of the North – had finally thrown him off his game.

"Sonja is my right arm, and Imogen is my heart. Insult them, and you insult me. Do you understand?"

He nodded again. The muscle in his jaw twitched.

I tugged on Rafael's sleeve. "Switch seats with me, babe. I want to talk to the secret agent man."

He obliged, picking up his coffee and moving to my other side.

"My King," Squires stammered. "We are in public…"

Sonja leaned forward until her face was one inch from his. "You think we are in public?"

His eyes hardened. "I am underco–"

"Are there innocent civilians here?"

"This is a public diner," he growled back. "My partner thinks I am picking up cake for our stakeout."

Sonja raised her voice so it almost echoed around the room. "Any unsuspecting humans in here?"

The diner went dead silent for a fraction of a second, then, every single patron recited back to her. "Kein, Kommandant!"

"Is this building secure?"

"Ja, Kommandant!"

"Who owns this building?"

"Sie, Kommandant!"

The room fell silent. Sonja stared at Squires.

The skin around his eyes tightened. He was furious.

Every single person in the diner was part of her security team. She'd managed to buy the whole building and stock it with her vampires in less than an hour. I was impressed. "Now you may speak freely, with no reason to hold anything back." Sonja stared at him, unblinking. "Imogen, ask your questions."

Squires gritted his teeth.

I leaned forward eagerly. "Tell me what you know."

He paused for a long second, and swallowed, bitterness written all over his face. "A week ago," he began, speaking as though the words were being dragged out of him by force, "We received an anonymous call alleging you'd been involved in human trafficking. Because of your involvement with the King, my instructions from my nest master was to flag anything involving you and bury it straight away. I'd already taken steps to bury the tip. I called the tipster back and had him admit it was a hoax. But while I was trying to suppress it, someone from Langley picked up the investigation."

"Someone from the F.B.I? Who? And why?"

"I don't know. Your name has been flagged, I guess. They've been looking for you." The tightness disappeared from his eyes; a tiny smirk lifted the side of his mouth. He was enjoying my predicament, I could tell. "An agent from California came out here to ask a few questions about the tip, so I got myself involved."

"Mullins?"

The smirk twitched. He didn't like that I knew the names of the agents that took Leroy. He enjoyed holding information to himself. "No, Agent King. She and Mullins drove out to Emerald Valley to get you."

They wouldn't get me. It would take an army to bring me down. So, they got Leroy instead.

I glared at Squires. "You're not telling me anything I didn't already know."

He eyed me back steadily. "I know where Agent King is."

"Does she still have Leroy?"

"Maybe. I don't think so, though. From what I understand, he's not in D.C anymore. But she knows where he is."

I leaned forward, baring my teeth. "Where is she?"

Squires hesitated, drawing out the moment, a tiny smirk on his face. He clearly got a kick out of holding this tiny bit of power over me. "Hotel Engany in Crystal City, not far from the Pentagon," he said, scribbling an address down on a napkin. "She is staying there."

He slid the napkin over and glared at me. "You will have to be discreet," he said, curling his lip. His arrogance had come flooding back. He gestured to all the vampires in the diner. "This little game won't fly anywhere near the Pentagon. There are agents everywhere."

I snatched up the napkin. Squires got up abruptly. "I must go. My partner does not know I am a vampire, and I'll get burned if I get caught giving information to civilians." He made an awkward bow towards Rafael, avoided Sonja completely, turned, and scurried out.

CHAPTER 10

J watched the diner door slam behind him, and wrinkled my nose. "Well. He was entirely unpleasant."

"Indeed." Rafael wrapped an arm around me. "At least we have a lead on the woman who took Leroy."

I nodded. "Yeah." Glancing down on the paper, I read the address of the hotel room again. "It's strange, though. No mention of Agent Mullins. Only Agent King."

"That thought did occur to me, too. Although Sebastian did say that King was more interested in Leroy, and Mullins was interested in you."

I pulled my bottom lip through my teeth thoughtfully. "Maybe King has got Leroy in a safe zone for witch kids, and Mullins is with some black-ops military organization and they're trying to come up with something to contain me."

Sonja looked down at her phone and sighed. "Maybe."

I glanced at her. "What's wrong?"

"Brick has another concussion."

"Oh no! What happened?"

She looked up at me and frowned. "He is helping the crew

clear the valley as the rockslides occur." Her frown deepened. "Apparently he was doing an impersonation of Sisyphus and he got hit by another large boulder."

"The valley is still shaking, huh?" I'd almost forgotten about the Ancient in the pocket dimension, shaking the town to rubble. It almost didn't matter to me that we needed Leroy to help open the dimension and save the world.

I just needed him with me. It hurt that I didn't know where he was, or what they were doing to him. The world would fall to ruin if we didn't find him soon, but I didn't care about that.

I just wanted my kid back.

Rafael, reading my mind, drew me closer in. "It's not self-ish," he murmured, kissing my temple. "It proves the depth of your love for him. You want him home safely. That's your only priority."

"I guess there's no home if we don't find him, though, right? The valley crumbles, the portal gets buried, the telluric field gets disrupted, and the ghost of your mean Aunt Hilda comes blazing back out of the lower Astral plane to fuck up your whole duplex."

He nodded, his jaw tight. "The crews are working over-time to clear the rubble. I've brought in engineers to help stabilize the ridges, but so far they have not had much luck."

I let out a long, slow breath. "Can we go? Can we go and beat up this Agent King woman now?" I clawed my hands, cracking my knuckles. "I need to punch someone. I can't believe I've gone this long with my star powers and I haven't beaten anyone up yet. It's unimaginable."

"You punched Harmann in the mouth," Sonja mumbled, not taking her eyes from her phone.

"It was only a tiny punch."

"You knocked all his teeth out."

"I held back! For some insane reason, I didn't want to kill him. So, I held back, and it was *intensely* frustrating."

Rafael pulled me off my seat. "We will go to Crystal City to find Agent King now. If anyone knows where Leroy is, it will be her."

"Hold that thought." Sonja stood up. Her jaw was set, her blue eyes blazing. "I've found Agent King. She's not at that address."

I squinted. "Where is she?"

"At the airport. We must hurry."

CHAPTER 11

e drove in convoy towards Reagan National, with Boris driving us in the lead Range Rover.

"I cannot begin to express how much that cretin Squires irritated me," Sonja explained, still gritting her teeth. "He strung us along with promises of information but gave us practically nothing. We have been wasting time," she growled. "As soon as I realized this, I put out an alert on Agent Mullins and Agent King, based on their names and the surveillance footage we obtained from the police station in Emerald Valley. I sent it to our people in all major transport hubs as a matter of priority. We got a hit." She held up her tablet. A grainy still of a tall, middle-aged woman striding down an airport corridor flashed on the screen. "No sign of Leroy or Mullins, but Agent King is booked on a flight to San Francisco, leaving in one hour."

I leaned forward. It was exactly the same woman who had been at Emerald Valley police station.

I replayed that footage in my head. The camera from the police station had been facing the sidewalk directly outside. Mullins and King had gotten out of the black sedan and walked inside the station. After only a few minutes, King walked back outside and got into her car, and occupied her time making notes on her laptop until Mullins joined her around ten minutes later, and they drove away.

They'd driven away to wait until Leroy was alone, then they'd snatched him off the road in the dead of night. And they blew up my house, too. Maybe Mullins did that, while King snatched Leroy.

Yeah, that made sense. Mullins crept around my cabin, torching it somehow, while King talked Leroy into getting in the car, where he was then magically disabled. It was Agent King's scent on the handlebars of his bike, so she must have tossed it into the forest as soon as Leroy was subdued. Then, she drove up to pick up Mullins, and they left Emerald Valley.

"Drive faster," I snapped to Boris.

"There's no need," Sonja said, pinching the bridge of her nose. "I have an engineer on the ground at Reagan National. He is stalling the flight to San Francisco for us." She rubbed her forehead, and sighed.

She looked more annoyed than usual. I eyed her carefully. "Are you okay?"

She met my gaze, and frowned. "I am worried about Brick."

"I don't blame you. I've known him for little over a year, and he's had, what, maybe four concussions in that time?"

"Six," she said shortly. "Bah. He is lucky he is a vampire, or he'd be a vegetable by now." She stared down at her phone again. "He is so brave and so stupid. He will get crushed by a boulder if someone is not watching him."

Rafael tapped her knee. "As soon as we get to the airport, take a chopper back to the Valley, Sonja. Guard your mate."

Her shoulder sagged, and her eyes blazed with relief. "Thank you, my King."

Boris steered the Range Rover right to the departure gate and we got out. I gave Sonja the most awkward hug I could possibly manage and walked briskly away, hand in hand with Rafael. Our security team fanned out, blending into the crowd around us.

According to Sonja, Agent King was at the departure lounge, killing time inside a cafe. We followed her directions, and it took us around thirty seconds to find her.

She sat in a booth with both hands wrapped around a steaming mug of tea. A blueberry muffin lay on a plate next to the teapot, untouched. She stared at it morosely.

She wasn't what I expected. Agent Squires had behaved like a Bond movie spy, all clandestine flickering glances and calculated movements. This middle aged motherly-looking woman stared at her blueberry muffin like she had the weight of the world on her shoulders.

I watched her for a minute. She barely moved. Rafael nodded at me.

"Go ahead," he said. "Question her. If you need to knock her out and take her elsewhere to torture her for information, do it. Boris has his EMT equipment ready to go, he can transport her to the private hanger and we can take her back to Emerald Valley with us."

"I like the way you think," I muttered, watching Agent King stare unblinkingly at her muffin. I took a deep breath, walked forward, and slipped into the booth opposite her.

She glanced up. Her expression barely changed.

We stared at each other for a long moment.

Finally, she signed, and sat back. "I wondered if you would catch up with me."

I lifted my chin. This woman had abducted Leroy. "You wondered correctly," I growled.

I waited for some flicker of fear to pass over her expression, but none came. She seemed resigned. It was a little strange. She looked into my face without a hint of worry.

"Do you know who I am?" I asked, blisteringly aware of how arrogant I sounded.

"I do," she replied. "Of course I do." She huffed out a harsh chuckle. "Mullins kept a lot of things to himself, but he did warn me, and I'm not stupid. In this line of work you come across things that don't add up sometimes," she said quietly. "People doing strange things, behaving in strange ways. I've known for some time that there's more to this world than the ordinary, but I've never had anything too bizarre shoved in my face. Until now."

"I don't want to shove anything in your face," I said coldly. "I just want my kid back."

Her lips curled up into a tiny smile. "I thought that local cop was insane, you know. Officer Harmann, was that his name? He ranted about you like you were some kind of demon."

I stared at her. "Maybe I am."

She chuckled bitterly. "Maybe you are. I don't think so, though." Her laughter died in her mouth. She stared at me for a good minute, then shrugged. "You know, I love my job. I get orders, and I follow them, and for the most part, I like to think I'm doing some good in the world. Protecting people, y'know? But there are certain aspects of my job that I find hard to stomach sometimes." She eyed me steadily. "Taking Leroy was one of them. I've regretted that since the second we picked him up."

Oh, she was feeling *guilty* for her part in taking Leroy.

Maybe she had a kid his age, and she knew someone was going to hurt him to get to me, and her conscience was killing her.

But she wasn't scared of *me*. She must have known I could torture her into insanity. Maybe she'd been so worried I'd catch up with her and kill her, and it was a relief now that I was here.

This whole thing was so weird. I glared at her. "Why hasn't anyone come for me yet?"

"I don't know. I'm not privy to any other orders coming out of Langley. My job was to get Leroy, that's it. Nothing to do with you at all. Mullins did say that they had plans for you, though. I'm sorry."

She sounded sorry.

Sebastian did say that she was nice – a normal human woman. At the time, I assumed she was just a really good FBI agent, playing a role. Seems Sebastian was right. Maybe she was just a federal agent who was given a job to do that she really hated.

She sighed. "I suppose you want to know where he is."

"You suppose correctly."

Agent King stared at me in silence for a whole minute, then pulled the napkin from underneath her muffin and jotted down an address. "I'll get fired for this, you know." she scribbled. "If anyone knew, I could get thrown in jail."

I bared my teeth. "That's the least of your worries." There wasn't too much bite to my snarl, though. Agent King and her weird remorse had thrown me off my game.

She handed me the napkin. "He's not at this address yet, but he will be. He's due to arrive there on Friday. He's with another agency, and he's still in transit, from what I understand. He's being transported by road. Why, I couldn't tell you."

Probably because he was a powerful witch who might blow up a plane. Whoever had him now clearly wasn't taking any chances. I looked at the napkin. An address in Los Angeles, in Central City East. Literally in Skid Row. You couldn't get a worse area in the whole of the United States.

Agent King pointed at the paper. "There's still some issues to sort out, but he'll be there by Friday."

They were probably fortifying some black-ops safehouse for him, something witch-proof. I swallowed roughly. "Is he being hurt?"

"Not that I know of." Her voice dropped to a whisper. "Not yet, anyway. Just go and get him." She looked me in the eye. "Please."

"I will." I stared back at her, a million questions on my lips, but none I could think of clearly enough to voice. I glanced back down at the address again. "So should I worry about Mullins coming for me? Is he getting a team ready?"

"I don't know what he's doing," she replied, huffing out a sigh. "He has different orders from me. He wasn't the nicest person to have to work with, you know. He was a pain in the ass in Emerald Valley. I don't know about him assembling a team to take you down, but last I heard, he was back with his partner. Both of them were supposed to escort me to Emerald Valley, but only one of them did. Squires stayed here, for some reason."

Based on what Harmann had told me about Agent Mullins, it definitely sounded like they were coming for me. I suppose it was only a matter of time before–

Wait.

I paused, and furrowed my brow. "Did you say... Squires?"

"Yeah," she said, she took a sip of her tea. "Mullin's partner. He was the one that took the tip and relayed it to us. He was supposed to escort me to Emerald Valley, but he stayed here, and sent Mullins with me instead."

My mouth dropped open. "Agent Squires is Mullin's partner?"

She cocked her head. "Yeah?"

"Pale guy, chin length black hair, thin lips? Always wearing mirrored sunglasses and a hat?"

She nodded. "That's him." She let out a derisive snort. "Asshole."

"Oh," I growled, "he's a lot more than just an asshole." I stood up. "And I'm going to rip him a new one."

"Go on, girl," she replied. "You have my blessing."

I looked down at Agent King. Damn her to hell, I was actually looking forward to beating someone up, and she had to go ahead and be the nicest F.B.I. agent in the whole country. Something definitely wasn't adding up.

Instincts were a new thing for me, and I was beginning to trust them. Agent King was a good person, and good people don't go around stealing kids from the side of the road.

She clearly regretted it. Maybe she was being blackmailed herself, or maybe they lied to her and she thought she was helping. Maybe, because King was so lovely, they recruited her to charm Leroy into getting into the car that night to reduce any magical fallout.

I didn't know, and neither did she. But I had to punish her for her role in this somehow.

I glared down at her, and swiped her muffin off the table and brandished it at her. "I'm taking this with me."

CHAPTER 12

We power-walked back to the Range Rovers, the rest of the security team blending into the crowd behind us. Luckily, Rafael had been lingering close to where me and Agent King had been sitting in the cafe and had heard our entire conversation, so I didn't need to fill him in.

"I have ordered Squire's nest master to bring him to me immediately," he told me quietly as we walked. "He is unaware of his location at this stage, but the net will tighten on him." The muscle in his jaw clenched; he was furious. "He lied to his King."

"What do you think this means?" I muttered to him, forcing myself not to run. "Why would he lie like that?"

"I would assume the worst," Rafael said darkly, his eyes flashing. "We already knew Squires was the one who picked up the tip from Sebastian, but instead of burying it like he said he tried to, he notified other government agencies instead. He is working with Mullins to capture you. He is a traitor." The words ripped like a low snarl from his throat.

"The address he gave us for Agent King," I said. "What do you think it really is? A trap, of some sort?"

"Without a doubt. I assume it is whatever they have put in place to contain you. It is in Pentagon City, after all."

"So Squires thought he could bait us, then have us walk into a hotel room, where I'd get, what? Hit with a tranquilizer dart and shoved into a cage?"

Rafael pinched the bridge of his nose. "I'll have a team head out there now."

"No," I put my hand on his arm. "Let's go there. Let's go there ourselves. Squires will be there, I bet you anything, Mullins, too. Let's pretend to walk into their trap and then we can beat the living shit out of them." We stopped at the curb outside Departures. Immediately, Boris whipped the Range Rover beside us, leapt out, and held the door open. I got in the back and bounced around on the soft leather seats, too agitated to sit still.

"Please, Rafael," I begged. "I need to punch someone."

He stared back at me. "It may be too dangerous."

"*Please*. We've got some time to kill before Leroy gets to whatever holding cell they've got for him in Skid Row," I said bitterly. "Squires and Mullins, and whoever they work for need to go down."

Rafael frowned. The muscle in his jaw clenched again, and I smoothed it with my fingers. "Fine," he sighed. He nodded to Boris. "Crystal City," he ordered. He glanced back at me. "I'm having both teams follow us in, just in case."

"Great," I said, cracking my knuckles. "We're not going to need anyone else though. If it's the same agency that captured and tortured me back in the fifties, they're only aware that I'm strong and fast and immortal. No one knows about my star powers," I smiled widely, showing my teeth. "They're about to get a nice surprise."

"I thought you destroyed that whole facility."

"I did. I killed everyone associated with it, too. That doesn't mean that someone in Intelligence hasn't picked up a file somewhere and made a note to try and capture me again."

Crystal City was only five minutes' drive away, but the traffic was insane. I itched to get out, to run, so I could rip off someone's arms. Within ten minutes, we were at the hotel address that Agent Squires had given us.

Boris walked ahead, compelling the reception staff to ignore Rafael and I, and the twelve other vampires behind us. We packed into the elevator and rode up several floors. It took a few minutes to find the right room.

I knocked on the door. "Just a second!"

I glanced at Rafael and frowned. The voice from inside the room was middle-aged, and female. It sounded exactly like Agent King. But I'd left her in the cafe no more than fifteen minutes ago. There was no chance it was her.

Rafael took my hand and squeezed it.

The door cracked open. "Can I help you?"

It was Agent King.

I glanced at Rafael. "Uh..."

He looked back at me, a crease between his eyebrows. He had no idea what was going on, either.

I looked back at Agent King, or, rather, the sliver of her face I could see in the crack of the door. "Uh... Housekeeping?"

"Oh, no problem," she said, smiling at me, then up at Rafael, standing close behind me. She shut the door again, and slid the chain off, and opened the door wide. Immediately, she turned her back and walked away, with not a trace of fear or suspicion to her movements. "You can get started," she called out. "I've just packed anyway, I'm ready to go. Just let me get my stuff from the bathroom."

There were no tense movements. No hesitation. She didn't recognize me.

I glanced behind me, where a handful of vampires lined the corridors, waiting to swarm the hotel room. Raising my eyebrows at Rafael, I shrugged. We had enough firepower with us to rip apart a whole team of F.B.I. agents, and enough resources to clean up any trace that we'd even been in this hotel in the first place. I inclined my head at Rafael, and we stepped inside the room.

I looked around. It was a plain, ordinary, no-frills hotel room. She'd stripped the bed and piled the sheets in the middle of it. The remote control for the T.V. was lined up next to it. Nothing seemed suspicious at all. Was this Agent King a fake, or was the one in the airport departure lounge a fake?

Most likely, the one at the airport was the fake. She'd been too nice; too quick to give me Leroy's address.

Although we found her through our own efforts, so that didn't seem likely either.

This whole thing was driving me crazy. I looked at Rafael and mouthed at him: *What the fuck is going on?*

His eyes were narrowed in suspicion. He scanned the room, and breathed in through his nose. "Something smells strange," he murmured to me softly. "There is old blood here; very old blood. Ancient."

"It's a hotel room. There's probably bodily fluids splattered everywhere," I whispered back.

"There's something else…" He shook his head, perplexed. "It is an odor I have not smelled before. I cannot place it."

That was odd, for a vampire. Their sense of smell is second only to a werewolf. Rafael has had many lifetimes to catalog every smell on the planet, so for him to be stumped by an odor was definitely a red flag.

I sniffed. He was right. My sense of smell was only

recently developed, but there was a cold, tangy-metallic odor in the room that I'd never smelled before.

"I'm afraid I might have stained the carpet," Agent King's voice called from the bathroom. "I dropped a piece of pizza on the floor last night." She walked out of the bathroom and smiled at us.

There was a beat of awkward silence. "Oh. Uh, really?"

"Yeah. Just here," she said, maneuvering around the bed. She pointed at the floor.

Rafael and I walked over and looked down. There was indeed a stain on the carpet. It was more than a stain – it was a burn mark, etched so deeply into the carpet I could see the gray concrete underneath. It swooped around, almost in a circle, with the edges disappearing under the bed.

Hang on. Maybe it *was* a circle. I blinked, and looked up. My heart stopped.

Everything happened all at once.

Rafael shouted an order; a call to the security. Immediately, the door exploded inwards, and vampires swarmed in.

Agent King smiled triumphantly, clapped her hands and shouted a Word. Her face blurred.

Boris, the vampire closest to me, ran forward, fangs bared and hands clawed, but he hit an invisible wall and bounced back, smashing into the T.V. opposite me.

Blazing black light filled my vision completely, and the world tilted upside down. I moved forwards, trying to grab onto something, trying to clutch at Rafael but my hands felt like rocks.

Then, a chime split my head in two, and I fell into nothingness.

CHAPTER 13

I blinked frantically, trying to clear my vision. My eyes were open, but the blazing black light had blinded me completely. My ears rang. I felt like I'd gone both deaf and blind in an instant. It was terrifying.

I took a panicked breath in. "Rafael? *Rafael?!*" I could barely hear my own cries, but they were there, echoing to my ears from what sounded like very far away. My hands reached out, fluttering helplessly, patting the black space in front of me.

I found him. He pulled me close, cocooning me in his arms. "... here, my love... I'm here."

Thank *God*. I could hear him. I pinched my eyes shut again, and breathed. *Focus, Imogen.* Mentally, I calmed and centered myself, pulling at my star power so my senses would heal as quickly as possible.

Something had just happened to us; something terrible, and I felt like we'd been completely disabled.

No sight, no sound. No vampire guards. Nothing.

I had never felt so vulnerable in my whole life.

Next time I blinked my eyes open, gray shapes appeared

in front of me. Slowly, my vision sharpened, and color melted in. The endless loud chime in my ears began to fade.

"You're okay. You're okay," Rafael said, his voice strained. "I'm here."

I pulled at him desperately as his face came into focus. My relief turned to chilly fear as his eyes gazed down on me sightlessly. "Rafael. What happened? What the *hell* just happened?"

He blinked. His pupils were fully dilated. "I cannot hear you well, my love," he muttered, running his fingers over my bare skin. "I cannot see. Give me a moment. It's coming back."

I caressed his face with my palm gently and forced down my rising panic. He could feel me. I held on to that fact with desperate hope. He wasn't healing as fast as me, though. Slowly, the darkness in his pupils receded; the beautiful deep brown color edged slowly back. My own vision sharpened quickly, and I reached out with the rest of my senses.

What the hell just happened? An explosion of some sort?

The first thing I saw was the bed beside me, or part of it, in any case. It had been cut in a perfect arc as if a giant laser had punched out a circle on the hotel floor. I looked past the dissected bed, and saw a brick wall. I shook my head, trying to clear the last of the ringing from my ears.

We weren't in the hotel room anymore.

My pulse roared in my ears. Rafael rubbed his eyes. "It's coming back," he whispered. "What happened?"

"The circle," I muttered. "The goddamn circle."

"Was it a worm gate?"

"It was a worm gate," I confirmed.

It was the deepest and darkest of blood magics. No wonder Rafael could smell old blood in the hotel – the spell to open a worm gate took buckets of blood from innocent sacrifices to key. It was dangerous too; the witch who performed it essentially opened a wormhole between two locations, and had to be present for the trip. The pressure it put on a mortal body was enormous; you could lose all your senses, and end up at the other end of the gate, unable to see, hear, touch or taste anything. You were locked in darkness, in silence, forever. Barely any witches would ever dare look up the ritual required for this, let alone perform it.

They must have wanted me so badly. I huffed out a bitter chuckle. Well, they got me.

I reached out with my hand, trying to push past the point where the bed had cut off. I wasn't surprised when my hand hit hard air. I pushed, flexing, seeing if the ward would give at all, but it didn't.

That was surprising. They must know about my star heritage to key a ward to keep me in place, although I had no idea how they managed it.

Frustrated, my fear mounting, I punched at the hard air. My knuckles scraped against the nothingness in front of me. It didn't even tremble.

"That's not going to work." Agent King's voice sounded smug, and nothing at all like in the airport cafe. "You're not getting out."

I blinked, trying to focus, and turned towards the sound of her voice. She stood over by a metal bench on the other side of the room. The surface of the bench was littered with vicious-looking metal tools, bundles of twigs, piles of tiny bones, and opaque bottles filled with magical ingredients.

Agent King crossed her arms over her chest, grinning at me. "Punch all you like. It won't give. Not for anything."

"How did you get out, then?"

She chuckled. "I have more power than you, that's why." Her face blurred again, dark skin fading briefly to dull beige.

A tiny bit of relief pierced my despair. This was not Agent King. The real one had been the one in the cafe, which meant the address she gave me in Skid Row was genuine. I could still find Leroy.

If I could ever get out of this circle, that is.

Watching the woman carefully, I took a stab in the dark, lowered my voice and snarled at her. "Mullins."

"You're not as dumb as I thought," she laughed. "I'm surprised." Slowly her face melted, turning paler and more ruddy in the cheeks. Her scraped-back black hair morphed into a military-style brown fade. The statuesque female body bulged and rolled in a manner that made my stomach churn until eventually, Agent Mullins stood in front of me.

He smirked at me, clearly proud of his power.

"You're a blood witch," I said. "Is that why you took Leroy? You want to lure him to the dark side?"

He laughed. "I didn't even take Leroy. I don't care about him."

I mashed my mouth into a harsh line. He wanted *me*.

I glanced around the room. It was a fairly large space enclosed on all sides in brick – not pretty red-brick of a feature wall, but more functional, and sturdier, like what you would get in an old industrial building. There were no windows at all, which violated a lot of building codes, but then again the worm gate violated laws of physics, so whoever built this room clearly wasn't fussed about keeping to code. Apart from the long metal benchtop littered with creepy magical ingredients, sinister-looking tools, and a couple of metal fold-out chairs leaning against the wall, there was nothing else in the room. The only exit was one heavy-looking gray metal door. It gave the impression we were in a giant vault, a locked workshop of some sort. "Where are we?"

"We're not in Crystal City anymore, Toto," Mullins chuckled.

"Ha ha ha," I chuckled back mockingly. "I figured that out already, *Dorothy*."

His eyes narrowed. I'd hit a nerve. "Don't call me that," he snapped.

Hmmm. He didn't want me to call him a woman's name? I'd definitely hit a nerve, so it was time to hammer on that nerve until he snapped. "You just quoted her, you moron. You were literally pretending to be Dorothy. What do you want me to call you?" I laughed. "You want me to call you *Cheryl?*" That was Agent King's first name. Thanks, Sonja, for the thorough information.

"Shut up, bitch," Mullins snarled.

"Calm down, Cheryl." I widened my eyes, and raised my hands in a placating manner. "Don't get your knickers in a twist."

Mullins glared at me and clenched his fists so hard his knuckles whitened.

"Come on," I giggled. "Why are you so offended? You were Cheryl only a couple of minutes ago."

"The means to an end," he spat. "Bait for the trap."

"You must have enjoyed it, though. You wouldn't have done it otherwise. Pretending to be Cheryl was probably a lot of fun for you, that's why you decided to do it. I'm sure there was probably another way to trap me, let's be honest, here." I grinned widely. "You could have just hit me with a knock-out spell in Lincoln Park. You could have had Squires drop a roofie in my coffee at the diner. There were probably a million ways to lure me away."

"This is not about you," he spat out.

"So it's about you, and you wanting to dress up like a powerful woman? Oh, I get it. That makes sense," I nodded seriously.

He let out a snarl and stomped forward.

The door clanged.

"Ignore her," Agent Squires said from the doorway. He walked in slowly. "She's baiting you, trying to get you to lose control. Relax, brother. We have them right where we need them to be." A smirk pulled up the edges of his mouth.

"To be fair, it's weird that he's so offended by the idea of pretending to be a woman, when he was just *pretending to be a woman.*"

Mullins' face twitched. He stepped forward again, but Squires put an arm on his shoulder and he paused, his mouth trembling in anger. He clearly had rage control issues. And some homicidal tendencies. And some seriously bad trans-phobia, from the looks of it.

"It's okay," Squires told him. "All we have to do is wait."

"Wait for what?"

Neither of them replied. The anger on Mullin's face melted into scorn, and he moved back and started tinkering with the tools on the metal benchtop.

I stared at Squires, the dirty traitor. "I see you got some new sunglasses," I said. "They don't suit you. I liked the other ones better, but I'm guessing Sonja smashed them when she ripped them off your face in the diner."

Squires tilted his head, watching me coldly. "She'll suffer in the end, too. I have every confidence that she'll try and come to rescue her king, and I'll teach her a lesson as well."

Rafael slumped slightly in my arms. I tensed. I thought he was healing, but I could feel his strength waning.

I had to get him out of here. I needed more information. "What lesson would that be? How to commit treason and defy your king? How to betray your people for personal gain? How to do the worst Loki cosplay ever?"

Squires chuckled darkly. "You have no idea, do you? You have no idea what's going on?"

"I know you're in deep shit." I growled back.

Suddenly, I made the connection in my head. A vampire and a blood witch banding together... "You guys are part of that Lord Seth bullshit, aren't you? You've got a brand-new asshole to worship, and he's sucked you into his little cult, right?"

"Oh, it's not a cult," Mullins growled from beside the metal table. "The Wraith has shown us the depth of true power. It's like nothing you could ever dream of. Lord Seth brings us the truth, when we've been lost and sunken in lies."

I widened my eyes. "Oooh. Charismatic leader? Mystical doctrine? A monopoly on the 'truth'? Promises of salvation?" I huffed out a chuckle. "Sounds like a cult to me."

"Our coven leaders and kings have been lying to us for our entire existence," Mullins said softly. "True power is ours to take, and there's no reason at all why we shouldn't take it. We were born for power," he said in a low tone. "Born to rule over those weaker than us."

"Who? *Humans?*" I sneered at him. "Get a new narrative. Harry Potter already did that one."

"No," Squires said simply, a cold smile on his face. "Women."

There was a beat of silence.

"You're kidding." I cocked my head. "You're kidding, right?"

"They are the weaker sex," Squires said with a gleam in his eyes. "We were born to lead. All of us powerful creatures have that in common; we are stronger than our female coun-terparts. It's time we took our rightful place at the head of the table, and put them back underneath us where they belong. Human women should be at the bottom of the ladder. They are like cattle," he said, screwing his nose up in distaste. "Breeding stock, and food."

I let out an exasperated breath. "Oh my God. You're not kidding, are you? Sweetheart, let me out of here, and I'll show you who is more powerful out of the two of us."

Rafael sagged behind me. Despite my bravado, my anxiety was spiking. Something was going on in this circle, and I had no idea what it was. Rafael was crumbling, and I could feel my powers rapidly draining, too.

Squires laughed out loud, and Mullins echoed him stupidly. "You're not powerful. That's the whole point. I don't have to do anything to you." He took off his mirrored sunglasses, leaned closer and stared at me. "I just have to wait."

A cold chill tingled through my spine. My palms went clammy. "What is this place?" I whispered.

"A chapterhouse for the Blood Kings," Mullins replied, flipping a wrench in his hand. "Our brotherhood. This is where we perform our magic, and build our strength and resources."

I made a rude noise, but I couldn't force any scorn back into my voice. My head was almost spinning, and I was feeling weaker by the second. I was properly scared. "How did you key this ward for me?"

"It's not a ward." Squires leaned over and snagged a fold-out metal chair from beside the bench, and dragged it over slowly. It made a grating, high-pitched screech on the floor that almost burnt the back of my throat. I forced myself not to flinch. Swinging the chair around backwards, Squires straddled it, and rested his head on the back of the chair. "It's something else." He grinned. "The key to our new power."

"Really?" A sweat broke out on my forehead. Behind me, Rafael dropped to one knee. His strength was rapidly draining.

"Uh-huh." Squires smiled broadly. "It's called a Spirit Circle."

"Sounds cheerleader-y." I started to pant softly. My breath wasn't filling my lungs anymore.

"A gift from Lord Seth. The magic in this circle will sever your spirit from your body."

That sounded pointless. There were faster ways to kill someone. I pursed my lips. "That doesn't sound very useful."

Mullins let out a dirty chuckle. He held up a lumpy leather pouch and waved it at me. "It is if you can siphon that spirit into a fetish and use it in your own spells," he told me, tapping his nose.

I stared back at him. "That can't be done. You can't drain a spirit from the body. If you do that, the body dies, and the spirit disappears immediately into the ether."

It wouldn't work on me in any case. I'd tried variations of this sort of thing before in my mission to end my immortality, and it never worked. Once, I had a sorcerer try to pull my spirit out of my body and then stab me in the heart, but my spirit snapped straight back like a twanged bra strap, just in time for me to feel all the horrendous pain of healing. Fun times.

Mullins smiled like a snake. "But what if you tether the soul to the body and keep it alive..."

I gazed at him, horrified, and he laughed again to see my expression. "Then, you can use the severed spirit for whatever you like. That's what the circle does, you know. It tethers the soul to the body permanently and lets you drain the person's spirit. And spirit, taken by force, is more powerful than the freshest blood." He paused, and ran his tongue over his lips. "The tortured screams of the most innocent child pales in comparison to the raw power of a severed spirit."

Fuck.

I forced my brain to think, but it was getting harder. He could be right. Body, soul and spirit. Your body was physical and temporary, your spirit was your personality in its current manifestation. Your soul was eternal, not part of our reality but connected to it. If your body died, your spirit was released into the ether where it rejoined your soul, and melded with all the other manifestations of who you had been in other lives.

If your spirit was ripped out, your body would die immediately. You can't drive a car without a driver.

But if you forced your soul to hang on to your body somehow...

Oh, shit. Theoretically, it was possible. It was both spirit and soul that gave the body life. The body would still live, but you couldn't use it because your spirit wasn't in it. No, your spirit was being tortured by an asshole blood witch. I couldn't imagine the suffering.

Maybe they were full of shit.

I squinted at him, sweat beading on my head. "How do you know this works?"

"We've already done it many times," Mullins chuckled. "What do you think this room is for? How do you think we've amassed so much power? Why do you think our movement is growing so much? We get results, that's why."

It still didn't make any sense. "But what's the point of doing it to *me?*" I gritted my teeth. Now that they'd explained it, I could feel what was happening. There was a sick, sucking feeling deep in every single cell of my body. It was made even more sickening by the fact that I knew it wasn't going to work, anyway. I'd long suspected that my soul and spirit were too tightly bound to my body, and since my body could heal instantly, the connection between the three wouldn't sever. "You won't be able to cut my spirit from my body. This circle is just going to make me feel uncomfortable," I spat out.

Mullins and Squires both laughed, like I was missing something very important. The sick feeling in my stomach morphed to a desperate, panicked anger. "What's the *point*," I seethed. "Just to keep me here and make me feel sick? Seriously? You can't let me out; I'll destroy you. You can't use my spirit. It won't sever from my body. I've tried before. It doesn't work."

Squires grinned widely. "You really think this is all about you, don't you?"

My breath hitched in my throat. "What?"

"You think we set this all up for you?" He shook his head slowly, a smug smile on his lips. "You're nobody. Why would we do this for you?"

Oh.

I glanced behind me. Rafael was on one knee, his head in his hand. Desperately holding on. Fuck.

Squires laughed. "You should see the look on your face. You really thought this was all about you, didn't you?"

It took me a whole minute. My brain wasn't working properly. The constant pressure; the stomach-churning sucking sensation pulling at me made it hard to think. I squeezed Rafael's hand, and finally, I realized.

"The King," I panted. "You wanted him the whole time. You want him… gone."

"Of course," Squires said. "The Blood Kings have been working on plans to assassinate the so-called Vampire King for months now. When the tip came in about you, it was the perfect opportunity to lure him here." He grinned down at Rafael, slumped on one knee in the circle. "There's no room in our new world order for him, so he must go. He doesn't see the world the way we do, and he has no vision for how things could be for us."

Squires let out a huff of scorn. "He's a traitor to his gender. He defers to that German bitch Sonja – he even takes orders from *you*. He already proved to the world that he's a female sympathizer when he let that idiot Samara take the throne of the East. General Lucius would *never* have let that happen."

"Yeah, but General Lucius isn't here anymore, is he?"

"It's a shame. He would believe in our cause," Squires said, tilting his head. "He knew the natural order of things. Strength and might at the top of the pyramid. Everyone else underneath."

I squeezed Rafael in my hands. "So that's it, is it? You're going to keep us here, drain my boyfriend's spirit and kill him. Then what?" I asked. My voice dropped to a whisper. The sickening sensation was starting to overwhelm me. It wasn't getting any worse, it was just... constant. Constant, stomach-churning pain. "What are you going to do with me?"

"Why, leave you in there, of course," He grinned. "Forever, if need be."

Oh, no. No no no. Stuck in a circle made of negative space, with Rafael's comatose body. With this constant vacuum sensation fixed directly on my spirit, never severing it, and never stopping, either.

Eternity in torment. No.

I lashed out, punching at the edges of the circle, smashing my fists into unyielding empty space over and over again. My knuckles split; blood splattered onto the cut-away bed and dribbled onto the floor. I kept going, hammering against the circle until I felt the sobs catch in my throat. "No. No, no no. *No!* Let us out! Let. Us. Fucking. *Out!*"

"Imogen..." Rafael's voice sounded like it was coming from very far away.

I dropped my fists, and wrapped my arms around him. "Raf...?"

He said something; I didn't catch it. "What? Babe..." I sandwiched my hands over his face; the blood from my knuckles painted his cheeks. "What did you say? Rafael. Speak to me... please..."

He let out a croak. "Fiancé."

"What?"

"Fiancé. You keep calling me… your boyfriend. I'm your… Fiancé."

I cried out once, and thrust my lips on his, kissing him desperately, hungrily, hoping for one last piece of him, of his beautiful spirit, his indomitable personality before it was sucked away from him forever. I blocked out the smug laughter of Squires, standing at the edge of the circle watching us, and I ignored Mullins' low chanting as he performed the ritual to transfer Rafael's spirit into the fetish. I ignored my bleeding knuckles and the sickening sensation of my own spirit constantly being sucked from my body. I blocked it all out, and I kissed my lover, until he sagged in my arms.

"… Love you… forever…"

I closed my eyes, and cried out, and held on to him as tight as I could.

Mullins's chants rose in volume. In the back of my consciousness, I heard a faint crash outside, beyond the brick prison.

I glanced up. Squire's head cocked, he frowned, and moved towards the door to investigate.

Suddenly, the metal door exploded inwards, hitting the vampire with a sickening thud. He flew back, hit the brick wall and crumpled on the ground in a heap, stunned.

I looked towards the door, shocked out of my misery.

A huge figure stood there in the doorway, a terrifying creature made up of red smoke, whirling black hair and a billowing black gown, with gleaming red eyes, sharp claws and a deathly white face.

I froze. Was it a demon?

Slowly, with menacing, terrifying grace, the creature stalked into the room, snarling with an intense, over-whelming rage. Fierce emotions streamed through the room, anger and retribution rolled over me like waves, shocking me out of my despair. What the hell?

Whatever this thing was, my torturers clearly weren't expecting it. Mullins scrambled to his feet, his chants cut off abruptly. His eyes flew wide. "What the fu–"

In an instant the demon was on him, its black-clawed hand around his throat, squeezing. Mullins choked, his face turning purple immediately. He scrabbled with the creature's billowing black gown, his eyes wide and panicked. The demon was too strong; he made no dent in the face of its towering rage.

The creature pushed its face close to his, its flashing ruby pupils glaring straight into his wide, terrified eyes. Its other clawed hand swooped down in an arc, stabbing straight into his stomach. Still holding eye contact, the demon pulled those razor-sharp claws upwards forcefully, gutting Mullins, splitting him from groin to chest. With another low, furious growl, it pulled its bloody hand out, drawing out a big hunk of purple flesh.

His liver.

I watched, shocked into stillness, as the demon – still holding eye contact with Mullins – thrust his liver into its mouth and chewed on it with obvious relish, gulping it down like a shark eating a baby seal. Mullin's mouth moved helplessly, but the words died on his lips. His face turned gray as the demon thrust a hand into his chest cavity again, this time pulling out his still-beating heart. Moaning in pleasure now, it worried the muscle between its teeth, tearing out a chunk and swallowing it. Blood spurted, coating the walls.

Whoa.

Rafael twitched and moved in my arms. The drain on his spirit had stopped. Mullins' spell had been interrupted. Rafael was recovering, but we were still stuck inside the circle. And now there was a bloodthirsty demon raging around us. "Imogen?"

"Shush," I said. "It's okay." I ran a thumb over his lips and glanced up again at the terrifying demon chewing on Mullin's heart, only a few feet from where I knelt. "We'll be okay," I mumbled.

Maybe it will fill itself up on bad guys and leave us alone. I swallowed down my new fear and watched the demon moan in satisfaction as it took another big bite.

Wait. Not it. *She*. The demon was a female, judging by the billowing black gown and wild hair, and the distinctly feminine way she ran her tongue over her black lips, savoring the heart's blood.

Squires, stunned when the door hit him, leapt to his feet and immediately charged at the demon with a wild cry. She unceremoniously dumped the rest of Mullin's heart on the ground and dropped his body, whirling to face the vampire. He reared back, dodging her swiping claws, ducking under her reach and tried to scuttle around and attack her from the side.

He wasn't as fast as her. Letting out a scream of rage that rattled the bricks around us, the demon swooped downwards. Thrusting her arm out, she caught Squires by the ankle and yanked him off his feet. He flailed in the air, helpless, shouting in anger.

With an air of graceful, predatory contempt that I might have admired if I wasn't so scared, the demon caught his other leg in her hand and yanked.

His leg tore off. The sound it made when his bones disconnected and broke made me retch, but I didn't look away. Squires, upside down and scrambling at the floor with his fingertips, screamed in mortal agony. Unmercifully, the demon yanked again, severing the leg completely, and tossed it at the wall. It hit the brick, leaving a flower-shaped splatter, and landed with a wet thump on the floor.

I swallowed my bile. I'd seen some shit in my time, but this was truly something. Rafael's eyes had blinked open; he watched too, focused intently on the demon as it caught hold of Squire's arm, and tore that off for good measure. She tossed it carelessly on the ground and swung him like a pendulum, still clutching him by one leg. On one upswing, she pushed her claws into his body and ripped out a rubbery strand of intestines.

Sheesh.

Rafael, rapidly gaining his strength back, got to his knees and wrapped his arms around me. I helped him to his feet, and we stood at the edge of the circle, frozen, holding each other, watching the demon pull Squire's intestines out of his gut like a magician pulls at a length of scarf tucked up his sleeve. It just kept coming.

Suddenly, the demon seemed to become aware of us.

Her movements slowed. Her head twitched towards us. Squire's bowels flopped to the floor, his tortured screams dying off to pitiful moans. The demon's terrible, white face turned slowly to face us.

I swallowed.

Those burning ruby eyes focused on me, and I flinched.

And waited.

There was a beat of silence. Then, inexplicably, her eyes widened. I sensed… recognition.

Recognition… and a little embarrassment.

Red smoke suddenly whirled through the room. The demon shifted on her feet, her towering height shrinking rapidly until she was no taller than me. The wild black hair shortened, too, becoming paler and softer until it was a pretty gold shade. Her white face flooded with color, her cheeks grew pink, and her eyes blinked from ruby red to a deep blue.

Finally, instead of a huge, terrifying demon, Sandy Becker stood there in front of us, the tops of her ears and the apples of her cheeks flushed red with embarrassment.

"Imogen!" She chuckled awkwardly, and waved at me with her free hand. "*Hiiiiii.*"

I swallowed, and cleared my throat. "Hi, Sandy. How are you?"

She gave me a perky smile. "Oh, great, I'm great. How are you?"

"Just dandy." I grinned at her. "It's great to see you. I heard you moved to D.C."

"Oh, I did. Finally took your advice," she nodded sheepishly. "I left Terry. Things have been pretty crazy, but I'm so much happier now."

"Well," I said, chuckling. "You *look* great." Deliberately, I tilted my head and nodded towards her right arm, where she still held the bloody, disemboweled Agent Squires by the foot.

Sandy followed my gaze and flinched. She gave a little squeak and dropped Squire's foot, and his body slumped to the ground. She visibly shuddered, dusted off her hands and turned to face us. "Oh, good grief. Sorry about that."

"Oh, don't mention it."

Rafael coughed. "My love," he said, his voice tense with strain. "Won't you introduce us?"

"Oh, of course!" I said. "I forgot you two don't know each other. Sandy, this is my boy– my *fiancé*, Rafael. Rafael, this is Sandy."

"Nice to meet you!" She smiled at him widely.

Rafael inclined his head in a bow. "The pleasure is all mine." He glanced at me with a loaded expression, which I happily ignored.

I'd forgotten to tell him about Sandy, but we'd been rescued in the nick of time. There was no chance he could be mad at me about it. All's well that ends well, and all that.

"What are you guys doing here, anyway?" Sandy asked me.

"Those two," I said, nodding towards the various pieces of Squires and Mullins that littered the ground in bloody lumps. "Kingnapped us. They wanted Rafael out of the way."

Sandy paused, and cocked her head. She looked at Rafael. "Oh! *You're* the Vampire King?" She blushed again and dropped a quick curtsy. "Imogen, you didn't tell me that your boyfriend was the Vampire King."

"Fiancé," he growled in my ear.

"Oh yeah," I told her, ignoring him. "That's my man, right there."

"I saw you both at Benson's funeral," she said, her smile fading. Suddenly her eyes filled with tears. "I drove down for a couple of hours, but I stayed in the back, out of sight, because I was afraid my mom would see me." She frowned. "I'm still avoiding her."

"You were at the funeral? I didn't see you!"

"It was so sad. I'm sorry I didn't come over and say hi, but I couldn't stay for the wake. I had Dexter with me, too. He was a bit of a handful." She frowned deeply for a second. "He found a stray cat in the woods behind the church, and insisted on taking it home with us. It's... a bit weird. Mavka tells me there's a demon stuck inside it. Dexter is obsessed with the cat, though, so I can't get rid of it."

I nudged Rafael. "Sandy here has a cute little three-year-old kid. He's an adorable hellraiser."

He stared back at me. "*That's* the part you think needs a little more explanation?"

I sighed. "Rafael, honestly. You can't expect me to remember to tell you every little thing that happens to me." I nodded at Sandy. "So I guess you didn't come here to rescue us. Are you cleaning up the whole magical woman-hating cult they've got going on here?"

She groaned theatrically. "Oh, God yes. I'm trying to. I know all about it. There's some hideous magical monster they call Lord Seth here in D.C. – he's started up some blood cult for misogynists. They call themselves the Blood Kings. It's actually pretty bad," she said, frowning. "I've been working with some people here to try and find out who this guy is, and take down his gross little network."

Rafael blinked at her. "Are you… are you the Enforcer's psychic? You're Alessandra Montefiore?"

"Ah-hem. Um." She bit her lip and looked away. "Yeah."

I leaned forward eagerly. "Ooh! The Enforcer? The hot guy?"

Sandy grinned at me. "The hottest."

"Good for you!" I grinned back.

Rafael cleared his throat. "Miss Montefiore… You're a little more than just a psychic."

"Yeaaaaah." She shifted on her feet uncomfortably. "I don't suppose you could keep this to yourself, could you? Sinclair doesn't exactly know about Mavka. I'm worried he won't take it very well. I mean," she added, chuckling awkwardly. "There's no good way of telling someone you've got a vengeance demon sharing your body who eats the internal organs of evil men. Sinclair is the Enforcer, after all. I'm not sure where Mavka sits on his morality scale." She gave Rafael puppy-dog eyes. "Could you maybe not mention this to him? *Please?*"

"She's been through a lot," I added, squeezing his hand.

Rafael's head whipped from Sandy, to me, and then back again. Finally, he locked eyes with me, and gave me a meaningful stare. "You knew about this? The demon?"

"Technically, she's not a demon. She's a pontianak. And

it… uh… It kinda might be… my fault." I trailed off in a little voice.

Rafael rolled his eyes. "Of course," he muttered. "Of *course* it was." He shook his head, looking at me in wonder.

I gazed back at him. "You love me because I'm full of surprises, right?"

"Right," he sighed. He tilted his head, holding my gaze. "She only eats the evildoers?"

I grinned at him. "Oh, of course." I lied happily. "Only the worst of the worst."

Sandy shuffled her feet awkwardly, but kept her mouth shut.

Rafael took a very deep breath. Finally, he turned to Sandy. "Miss Montefiore," he said, his voice low, rolling the words sensually. "Of course, I will keep your dual nature to myself, if you so desire it. You have done us a great service by destroying these men, so I thank you for that," he said, bowing his head graciously. "I don't suppose you can free us from this prison, can you?"

"Oh!" She shuffled forward, nimbly hopping over the disemboweled corpse of Squires. "Yes, I think I can. This circle looks a little different from the other one I smashed, but I think I can do it."

"It's the end of a worm gate," I explained. "That might be the difference."

She wrinkled her nose. "What the hell is a worm gate?"

"A portal between two locations. We were in Crystal City twenty minutes ago. Where are we now, anyway? Are we still in D.C?"

She nodded, examining the circle. "Yeah, in Georgetown. This is one of the Blood King's properties. I was just doing a little clean-up from our last mission. Sinclair and I have been trying to weed out this Lord Seth character." Her expression grew thunderous. "One of my client's sister's boyfriend's sister was found unresponsive at a frat house not far from here, and we found the reason why. These damned circles."

She walked over to the metal bench, rummaged around, and picked up a little heavy-stitched pouch. "This should be it." She tossed the pouch towards us. There was a flash of black light, and an electric pulse shot through me.

Tentatively, I stepped forward, pushing my hand out of the circle. "*Yessss.* Oh my God, thanks, Sandy! You're a lifesaver!"

"You're welcome!" She stepped forward and hugged me. "It's good to see you, Imogen. Your hair looks amazing, by the way. Let me do your regrowth when you're next in town, okay?"

I grinned. "Sandy's a hairdresser," I told Rafael.

He smiled back. "Well. That seems like important information to share," he muttered sarcastically under his breath.

Sandy held on to my hands and smiled at me fondly. "Are you guys in D.C. to help with the Lord Seth situation?"

"Ah. No," I shook my head. "Unfortunately, we've got bigger fish to fry. I'm looking for my kid."

Sandy gasped. "Leroy? Leroy is missing?"

"Mullins took him," I said. "He gave him to some other agency. I'm assuming he's safe for now, and I've got a lead on where to find him. But I kinda need to find him soon, or else a powerful ancient creature might shake the town to rubble and bury the portal, triggering the apocalypse," I finished lamely.

She nodded at me knowingly. "It's a Tuesday in Emerald Valley."

"Yeah," I said, laughing. "*Exactly.*"

CHAPTER 14

The second Sandy deactivated the spirit circle, my phone started spitting out missed call and text notifications. Rafael growled into his own phone once, and within two minutes, Boris and a fleet of armored cars were outside the little warehouse in Georgetown.

I had a million missed calls from Backman. Nervously, I called her back.

"Little drill bug," she answered the phone. "You found him yet?"

"No. But I've got a lead on him. Apparently, he's still being moved, but I've got the address of where he will end up. He'll be there by Friday, so I've been told."

She let out a little grunt. "Well, you might have to come back home in the meantime."

"Why?"

"The ridges of the valley are starting to destabilize rapidly," she growled. "That little monster of yours stuck in the pocket dimension is going to bury us all."

Rafael, still on the phone, shot me a glance and nodded. He was getting the same reports as me. The Ancient was upping the earthquakes, trying to force my hand. He wouldn't care that I couldn't do anything without Leroy.

"You might think about coming home, see if you can talk some sense into him, stop him from shaking the town apart," Backman said. Her voice sounded strained. "Marigold is trying to magically stabilize the valley, but it's taking a lot out of her."

"I got it," I muttered. "Keep her hydrated and her feet on the ground."

"I'm doing my best." She hung up.

I threw my phone on the seat opposite me. "God *damn* it."

Rafael took my hand and squeezed it. "I'm sending scouts to see if we can find Leroy en-route to the address in Skid Row," he told me. "And I'll send a team to monitor the whole neighborhood."

"I want to go *now*," I snarled, tears of frustration leaking out of my eyes. "But they might change the location of his prison if they know we're coming. We need to do this by surprise, or else we might never find him again."

"Yes," Rafael agreed. "We must wait until Leroy is there."

Hopefully they're not hurting him. Yet, Agent King had said. He's not being hurt yet.

I let out a groan. "It's so ironic," I said quietly. "I've never been more powerful than I am right now. And it's making exactly zero difference to all this heartache. We still got caught in Mullin's trap, Leroy still got taken, and I still can't go and get him."

"Not just yet," Rafael reassured me. "We will, though. We will. We know exactly where he will be the day after tomorrow," he murmured, kissing my knuckles. "And we will get him, I promise you that. For now, let's go home."

CHAPTER 15

The air in Emerald Valley felt more charged than usual; like all the atmosphere was loaded with tension and electricity. The clouds hung low, their thick white bottoms drifting on the edges of the crumbling ridges of the valley. I could almost feel the invisible web of the Earth's telluric field trembling in fear as it watched the boulders tumbling down; I could almost sense the portal shiver in expectation.

Rafael and I swooped into the valley through the thick clouds by helicopter. Sonja and Brick, sporting heavy bandages around his head, met us on the helipad and walked us to the main building.

Usually, we would have spotted a country club member and their entourage by now, hanging by the pool or chipping away at a golf ball on the golf course, but there was no one around at all. The place was deserted. It felt eerie.

"Nice turban," I nodded at Brick. "It suits you."

"I lost half my scalp," he admitted sheepishly. "When your friend decides to shake the valley, those boulders really start to move."

Sonja looked more worried than usual. "The quakes are getting worse. We have evacuated the valley," she reported. "The E.P.A. are not taking any chances, so they didn't take much convincing. We've planted some scientific reports that there is a blind fault underneath the lake which is causing the current stress."

Rafael nodded. "Good. It's best if the innocent are kept far away from this place."

"I need to go and talk to the Ancient." I gritted my teeth. "He needs to stop this now."

"The engineers need to speak with me," He leaned down and kissed my lips. "I want to survey the valley, see how bad it's gotten. I need to know how long we'll have to evacuate if the Ancient starts to bring down the ridges."

I held him so tight he winced. "I'll join you in the square as soon as I'm done," he promised. He kissed my nose, and let me go.

I zoomed down the valley in Rafael's Maserati. I fishtailed down every corner and floored it whenever I saw a boulder, hoping I would lose control and smash into a wall. My new powers were absolutely good for nothing so far, so the least they could do was heal me after I had worked out my frustrations on the car.

I reached the town square within minutes, mounted the curb, pulled the handbrake, drifted the Maserati on the grass into a perfect circle and got out.

Huh. Brandon was still there, sitting on the grass underneath the portal. He looked like he'd never left. He lounged easily on the grass, a cigarette hung on his lips. Claude, the gargoyle, sat frozen solid next to him. "Hey, buddy," I greeted Brandon. "What are you still doing here?"

He shrugged. "Waiting for you, I guess." He inhaled deeply and passed the cigarette to the gargoyle beside him. "This seems like the place I'm supposed to be."

"It is the end of the world," Claude intoned, taking a drag on the cigarette and exhaling. "The end of all things. All we can do is watch and wait."

I sighed. "You're such a downer, Claude." I was so tired. Idly, I wondered when I'd last slept. Did I need to sleep now? Despite all my useless powers, I was still half human, so I probably did. The last night's sleep I'd had was the night before Benson's funeral. That had been on Sunday. Leroy had been taken Sunday night. Today was Wednesday. Had it been that long?

I yawned, and waved at Marigold who walked briskly over the grass towards me, with Backman shadowing her. It was after five now, the light was starting to fade.

Marigold looked stressed and as tired as I felt. I nodded at her. "You okay?"

She shook her head. "A long way from it, unfortunately. Stabilizing the valley isn't working, so I've been trying to find a way of pushing the creature back through the portal by force." She looked at me frankly. "He's not moving, Imogen. He won't go back. He's going to destroy the world."

I frowned. "I really don't think he wants to do that. He just wants me. Ripped into little pieces."

"Or Sariel," Backman chipped in. "He said he wanted Sariel back."

I clenched my teeth, suddenly overwhelmed with tiredness and frustration. "Goddamnit, I don't know who Sariel *is*," I hissed. "I don't know what this asshole wants from me." The grass suddenly glowed golden under my feet. It was coming from me; I was showing my star nature again.

Marigold took a step back. "Please try and talk to him again," she said, her expression pleading. "We have to do *something*."

I took a deep, deep breath, and sighed it all out. "I don't know if it's going to do any good," I muttered. "But I'll try."

Marigold nodded, and walked up to the blank space under the portal, chanting under her breath. Immediately, the air in front of her shivered with lavender light, then faded, leaving the window hanging in midair

I stepped forward, and looked inside.

The Ancient stood there in the window, looking back at me, with no expression on his face at all.

The sight of him suddenly filled me with an intense rage. "Do you know what you're doing?" I hissed at him. "Did you know that you're shaking the town to pieces? You know that it's going to destroy the entire Earth?"

He tilted his head back and glared at me. "I have no desire to destroy this creation, but it is not me that is tearing it to shreds. It is you." He narrowed those glowing eyes. "It is you who are destroying the Earth, because you will not give me back Sariel."

"I don't know who Sariel is!" I screamed back at him. "Take some goddamned responsibility for this, you asshole!"

In the background, I could hear Backman's voice, gruffly telling me to cool it. I ignored her, and smacked a fist on the glimmer window. "It's *you* that's causing the earthquakes. It's *you* shaking the town to pieces. It's *you* who won't fucking leave this dimension."

His eyes glowed white. "Why should I leave? You trapped me here. You tortured me with your presence and trapped me. I will not leave until you face the consequences, or give me Sariel back."

"I don't know who Sariel is!" I screamed, smacking the window again. "I haven't done anything to you!"

The Ancient shot forward and put his furious, terrible face right up against the window. "You ruined my eternity," he screamed. "You stole from me, and you torture me, over and over again, you flaunt my loss in my face!"

"You. Are. Fucking. Insane!" I screamed back. "Whoever

the fuck you are! You know what, go ahead! Shake the town to rubble, I don't care!"

A hand clutched at my arm, tugging. Someone was pulling at me, but I wouldn't budge. I thrust my face closer to the portal and screamed at the Ancient. "Do it. Destroy the Earth, I dare you!" I punched at the window. "I. Fucking. Dare. You!"

He snarled back at me. The earth began to shake underneath my feet. I lifted my chin, defiant. A hand roughly pulled at me again.

Backman growled at me. "Imogen. Stop it."

I whirled around and faced her. "Back off," I spat at her. "This has nothing to do with you."

"You're going to destroy the valley." Her eyes blazed yellow, she stared me down. "I can't let you do that."

Frustration boiled over; I couldn't contain it. I clawed my hands and screamed. "What do you want from me! You want me to talk to him? I'm talking. He can't be reasoned with. I can't find Leroy. What are you doing about it! What the actual fuck are you doing, Backman? Nothing!"

The earth rumbled.

Her eyes narrowed. "You need to calm down, little drill bug. Right now."

"I will not fucking calm down! The asshole in that dimension has been ripping me apart for millennia, and now he wants me to magically find some mysterious person that I have no fucking idea about, or else he's going to destroy the world. It's not me, Backman! I'm not doing it. I'm not doing anything! Everyone is always trying to kill me, trying to destroy me, over and over again and it never works!"

The ground shook again. My heart pounded in time with it. I clenched my fists to try and stop them from shaking, too. I was so mad, I thought my skin would rip open and I'd erupt like a volcano.

"Stop it," Backman growled, lowering her head.

"Or what?" I let out a harsh bark of laughter. "What are you going to do about it?"

Marigold shifted on her feet behind her wife. "Imogen..."

I threw my hands up, a red-gold light streamed from my pores. My powers blazed through my skin and wafted around me, I was literally vibrating with strength and might...

But I was essentially, wholly useless right now. That thought made me grind my teeth in frustration. Marigold peered around Backman, looking at me, hesitant.

"Why are you all acting like this?" I screamed. "It's not me who is going to destroy the world. It's not me!"

The ground shook. Marigold and Backman exchanged a glance. Marigold took a step back, behind her wife.

"Oh," I laughed harshly again. "You're scared of me, aren't you? You're scared of *me*."

"I don't think it's that creature shaking the ground right now, Imogen," she said. The fear sparked in her eyes. She backed away.

It hurt. God, it hurt.

Backman's huge, muscular body shivered. "Back off, drill bug," she rumbled. "Now."

A snarl ripped from my throat. "Make me."

She lumbered forward, exploding into a huge mass of fur, and as a giant prehistoric bear, she roared.

I roared back, and tackled her.

Her teeth snapped at me, grazing my skin, cutting deep furrows where her fangs found purchase in my flesh. I screamed in her ear, deafening her, and pushed back, grappling with her mighty paws. We rolled on the ground in a tumble, me tearing at her fur, her snapping at my neck. I punched her in the gut, she let out an agonized groan and batted me off her with an enormous paw. I flew back and landed on the tips of my toes, glared, and ran forward again, tackling her.

"Stop it!" Marigold screamed in the background. "Imogen, stop! Don't hurt her."

"Don't hurt *her?* She started it!" My frustration bloomed out of control; it was unfair, it was so unfair, I was being blamed for everything and it wasn't my fault. I pounded into Backman's fat hide with my fists, venting all my frustration. She whirled and pinned me with her arms, mashing my face into the ground, roaring. She sat on my back, pulled my head up, and slammed my head into the ground again.

I bucked, sending her over my head, she rolled and lumbered to her feet instantly, padding forward on giant paws, lips pulled back from her muzzle in a horrifying grimace.

I punched her in the mouth. She spat out a gob of blood, her black eyes flashing, she raised herself on her back feet and lashed out, smashing her paw into my shoulder, ripping open the flesh. I screamed back, moved into a crouch, and tackled her.

There was an enormous crack. Backman went limp in my arms.

CHAPTER 16

*A*n icy cold chill washed over me; a shock so horrible it chased away everything else in my head. My arms were still full of Backman, still clutching her enormous hide. She'd gone deathly still. The whole valley was silent.

"Barbara?" Marigold's voice shook. "Barbara?!"

My breath hitched in my throat. Desperately, I slid my fingers through her fur, trying to feel for a pulse, but I couldn't feel a damned thing. I turned her head. Her eyes were closed. "Backman?" I whispered. "Backman…" Something had broken; I heard it quite clearly. The snap was loud and absolutely sickening. Please, God, don't let her be dead…

I let out a terrified sob. "Backman… please…"

Marigold flew forward, her tiny white hands fluttering over her wife's body, patting her frantically. "Oh, no no no no no…"

I pinched Backman's eyelids; her pupils weren't dilated. "She's alive," I said, relieved. Suddenly, her eyes moved. "Oh, thank God."

Marigold slumped on her wife, sobbing. "Barbara. Barbara, are you okay? Please talk to me," she cried. "Please."

She didn't move. Her eyes fluttered from side to side, her mouth slack. She couldn't move.

I ran my eyes over her body, thinking about the way I'd tackled her. "I think I might have broken her spine. Marigold, I'm sorry," I whimpered. "Oh God. I'm so sorry." I sat back, running my eyes over Backman's huge body, looking for any other clues.

The bear let out a low groan. Marigold leaned down, dropping a kiss on her furry muzzle. "It's okay, babe. It's going to be okay. We'll get you fixed."

She groaned again but didn't move. Her eyes whirled around in their sockets. It was the only part of her that she seemed to be able to control.

She was paralyzed.

I blinked back tears. Could she be fixed? I didn't know. Shifters could recover from most injuries, but some things couldn't be knitted together. I'd heard of shifters that had their spinal columns severed, and they were paralyzed forever. Most of them ended up asking someone to kill them, and they went to their graves, broken. Brandon's leg wouldn't have grown back if it wasn't for some crazy experimental magic that Leroy dreamed up.

I let out another whimper of fear. Leroy wasn't here either.

I needed to get some help. I jumped to my feet. "Stay here," I said to Marigold, slumped, sobbing over Backman's huge body.

There was only one place I needed to go. The only person I could think of that could help. I zoomed down Main Street, praying that he hadn't evacuated yet, and burst through the door of the vet's office.

Jamieson was sitting at his reception desk, tapping away at his computer. He looked up at me, his gentle smile wobbled when he spotted my face. "Imogen?" He leapt to his feet, so nimble for a man in his early seventies. Even in my desperate, panicked state, I noticed he was wearing his red scrubs that, along with his neatly-trimmed white beard, made him look like Santa in the off-season. "Are you okay? What's wrong? What happened?"

Swallowing heavily, frozen in the doorway, I hesitated. I didn't want to say the words out loud; not to Jamieson. I didn't want him to be mad at me. Everyone else could be mad at me, but Jamieson had never judged me, and he'd never been frightened of me.

I just didn't want to disappoint him. But I needed his help. I needed to admit that I'd done something unfathomably, criminally stupid.

"I hurt Backman," I finally mumbled, avoiding Jamieson's clear blue eyes. I'd never felt more ashamed of myself in my life.

I had *wanted* to hurt her. I needed to take my frustrations out on someone, and she'd been the best candidate. All that power coursing through me; I had to get it out somehow, and I'd taken it out on my friend. We'd sparred so many times before, I knew her body, and I knew exactly what I was capable of. "It's my fault." My voice wobbled, and I started to cry. "I hurt her. We were fighting, and I tackled her. I took it too far."

"Where is she?" Jamieson moved around the counter and picked up a bag, in business mode. "What is her condition?"

"She's in the town square. She's paralyzed," I said, my voice shaking.

He glanced up. "Totally?"

"I think so. I think... oh Doc..." I squeezed my eyes shut. "I think I might have broken her spine." I said, hugging myself. The tears started welling up in my eyes, overflowing. I sniffed. "I broke her spine."

His brows pinched together; he came up to me and

tugged lightly at my arm, unfolding my hands from my waist. His palm felt dry and warm, and far stronger than it looked. "Come on," he said patiently, taking my hand. "Let's go and see. It will be alright, Imogen." He looked into my eyes, and nodded. "Everything always works out in the end, exactly how it's supposed to."

* * *

THE ENORMOUS BEAR lay deathly still on the reinforced table in Jamieson's surgery. Somehow, he'd managed to get a neck brace on her. It looked ridiculous, but she couldn't do anything about it. Her eyes flashed at me. She was absolutely furious.

"I'm sorry," I said pathetically, for the billionth time. "Backman, I'm so, so sorry."

Marigold slumped at her side, still sobbing, and running her fingers through her wife's fur. "You'll be okay, babe. You will be. You have to be." She swore under her breath, the sound of it hurt my chest. I didn't think I'd ever heard Marigold swear before.

"Well, you're right," Jamieson said, checking the x-ray image on the computer. "It looks like a C2 C3 spinal injury." He shot me a stern look. "Her muzzle is cracked, too."

I cringed pathetically under his gaze. "I'm sorry."

"Really, Imogen," he frowned. "You need to be more careful. You clearly don't know your own strength. No more roughhousing," he said, wagging a finger at me.

"Never again," I said vehemently. "I promise."

"Good. Now, the question is, what do we do? I must confess, if she were only a bear, I'd have euthanized her by now."

Marigold glanced up, her eyes flashed ruby red.

"Whoa, there, girl," I put my hand on her arm. "Let the good doctor finish."

Jamieson bustled around the table. "But she's not only a bear, she's also a woman. Again, if she were a woman with this injury, the prognosis is not particularly good, either." He popped the earpieces of his stethoscope in his ear and listened to Backman's heart for a minute. "You'd be looking at complete quadriplegia, for life, unfortunately."

A low snarl built up in Marigold's throat.

Jamieson, completely unfazed, pricked Backman's paws with a pin, and checked her reaction. The man had absolutely no fear at all. "But based on the knowledge that you lot have forced on me, I understand that shifters do heal remarkably well, so I'm not sure what to say to you. She might get better on her own. She might not."

The light in Marigold's eyes flickered, and then she slumped again.

"Let me do another x-ray in an hour's time," he said. "I'll be able to check to see the rate of healing, see how she's coming along. But in the meantime," he put a gentle hand on Marigold's arm. "Why don't you do some of your fabulous whiz-bang witchcraft to hurry things up?"

She looked up at him, confused. "I wouldn't know what to do," she whispered.

"Oh, come now," he scoffed. "I know what you're capable of. You're pregnant, by magical means. You grew back young Brandon's leg. That would have been impossible, but I saw him no less than an hour ago, doing yoga on the lawn with what looked like a little gray dragon," Jamieson trailed off, frowning. "The dragon was moving. I thought I might have dropped some ketamine in my coffee by accident again."

"Ha ha," I chuckled mirthlessly. "Nope, that's a gargoyle. He's a right little asshole, too."

Jamieson made a face.

"That wasn't me that came up with that spell," Marigold said. "That was Leroy."

I shook my head. "He came up with the idea," I said. "I hate to point this out, Marigold, but you've been holding yourself back your whole life. You've been too scared to embrace your magic because you're worried about corruption." I squeezed her hand. "You *know* this."

She hesitated, and glanced down at her paralyzed wife. "I know," she whispered.

I waited for a long moment, then nudged her. "So, what are you going to do? You're going to come up with something to knit up Backman's spinal cord, that's what you're going to do."

Her eyes flared wide for a second. "Actually, that's a good idea. Knit." Her brow furrowed. "I know a spell I can modify to help a broken thing knit together..." She trailed off, gazing into space. "I'll need some lovage and tulsi, and some gold leaf." She glanced up at Jamieson. "Can you draw some of her blood for me? I'll need that to mix the spell."

"Good girl," I said to her encouragingly. "That's the spirit."

She glared at me. "I'll need some of your blood, too."

"Why me?"

"Because you did this to her." Marigold thrust out her chin. "I need the blood of the remorseful. The life essence of the one who broke her in the first place."

"Well, you're lucky that I'm extremely remorseful," I chuckled, meeting Backman's furious gaze. I was almost glad it had been such a bad injury, so Backman couldn't retaliate right now.

Jamieson pulled a little vial out of his drawer, along with a syringe in a plastic packet. "I'll wait until after you've done the spell, then do the x-ray, so we can see if it's working," he said, breaking open the packet.

I watched them bustle about, drawing blood, drawing

runes, marking up ingredients, checking vital signs, painfully aware that I was useless when it came to fixing things. I'd broken Backman, possibly permanently, and I couldn't put her back together again. I sent up a fervent prayer to whatever gods were listening that Backman would get better.

* * *

MARIGOLD MIXED up the spell right there in Jamieson's surgery; the smell of magic made me sneeze. For a whole hour, she'd been frantically sourcing ingredients, poring over her books, weighing out herbs, writing the spell, and swearing non-stop under her breath. Finally, with her blonde hair sweaty and her cheeks blushed pink with effort, she held up a tiny amber vial filled with a thick silver liquid. "Here it is," she said. She paused, and frowned. "This needs to get to the exact site of the injury, though. Doc, do you think you could do the honors?"

"I'd be glad to help," he said, taking the vial from her. "Let's just say I'm glad Backman can't feel anything, because this would hurt like a bitch." He nodded to me. "Can you help me roll her over?"

At least there was one thing I could help with. I gently tipped the giant bear on her side. Feeling through Backman's rough fur, Jamieson expertly found the right spots, and without hesitation, drove the needle into her thick flesh and pushed the plunger. Backman let out a pathetic gargle. Even more gently, I placed her back down on the table.

"Now all we can do is wait," I said, sitting down on a swivel chair. Jamieson settled himself into his squashy armchair in the corner of the surgery and pulled out a book about Antarctica, clearly intending on waiting with us. I smiled at him fondly, watching him get comfortable in his chair like a cat settling down for a nap.

Marigold sat opposite me, on the other side of the bear. She picked up Backman's huge paw in her hand and patted it.

I took the other paw. Marigold smiled when she saw me. "Thanks for the pep talk before," she said. "You're right. I'm capable of so much more. I haven't done enough."

She looked away; her face darkened. "I've been trying, though. I've been trying to stabilize the valley so it doesn't crumble, but nothing is working so far."

Right on cue, the ground shook beneath our feet. In the distance I heard a faint crash. Another huge boulder had come down. I cringed, hoping that Brick was nowhere near it.

Silence fell around us, and I yawned. God, I was tired. My eyes blinked shut for a moment.

Another loud rumble made me jump – it was coming right from this very room. My head whipped towards the sound. Jamieson had fallen asleep in his armchair, and was snoring so loud it sounded like thunder. I got up and removed the book from his arms, covered him with a blanket, and took my seat next to Backman again, and waited.

Rafael called, checking in. He had a whole team trying to move the biggest boulders out of the valley, and a fleet of engineers trying to come up with ideas to help stop the earthquakes. Sonja had dropped in some gold for Marigold's spell and gave Backman her best wishes. She looked exhausted. We were all spread too thin. The apocalypse was fucking us all over.

The three-day time limit had come and gone, and the Ancient was still in the pocket dimension. My fears had come true; I had no idea how long he could stay in there for.

Marigold looked at me, her face pale. "This might be all for nothing."

My face crumbled. "I'm sorry." A tear overflowed and ran down my cheek. "I just don't know what else to do, either.

The Ancient won't leave until I'm ripped to shreds. I would have done it a million times by now, but I can't find Leroy. I can't find this mystery Sariel person, either."

Marigold frowned. "I would do a location spell to find him, but I don't know what to fix the intention on. A name is not enough," she said. "We need to know who it is."

I pinched my eyes closed. "And the Ancient won't tell us. It's hopeless."

Marigold reached out and took my other hand. "Never. Not while we're all still breathing. There's still hope."

CHAPTER 17

I swallowed. My mouth was dry, and tasted like dirt. I smacked my lips together a couple of times and swallowed again, awareness sinking into my sluggish brain. I was lying on thick, musky-smelling fur. I'd been asleep.

Abruptly, I sat up. Whoops, I'd fallen asleep with my head on Backman's belly, and I'd drooled all over her. Quickly, I checked her face. Her eyes were closed, her breath steady. She looked like she was asleep. Thank God for that; I'd never hear the end of it if she caught me napping on her belly and drooling on her.

Marigold was fast asleep on the other side of me, curled into Backman's side in a much more elegant position. I yawned and stretched, feeling my bones shift and tendons pop. The sky was light outside, a watery brightness that told me it was very early.

"Good morning," Jamieson strolled in, wearing clean baby-blue scrubs that matched his eyes. "Did you sleep well?"

"I'm not sure if you could call what I was doing sleep," I told him. "That felt more like a coma than anything else."

"Well, you probably needed it." He handed me a coffee cup.

I sipped gratefully. "You're a lifesaver," I said, checking my phone. There was a message from Rafael that simply said: *Sleep tight, I love you.*

"He called in," Jamieson said. "Twice. He insisted you be left alone. You looked very comfortable, snuggled in next to the bear," he chuckled.

I flicked a glance towards Backman. "How is she doing?"

"I don't know. She's still alive, that's the main thing. When she wakes up I'll do another x-ray to see if Marigold's magic spell worked." He nodded towards the back of his surgery, gesturing for me to follow him. "For now, it's best we let them both sleep as much as possible."

"Yeah." I nodded, and followed him to the rear of the vet surgery. Flicking a button on the wall, he lifted the garage door at the back open, and we ducked outside.

Beautiful morning sunshine flooded the alleyway behind his clinic. Directly opposite the back door, on the wall of the store across from his clinic, he'd planted a vertical garden of lush ferns and trailing vines. "That's nice." I pointed to it. "Really makes a difference to an ugly functional alleyway, doesn't it?"

He'd even done a little mural on the walls on either side of the roller door at the back, an abstract of bright golds and silvers and greens that looked like thousands of little feathers. It made the alleyway look so cool.

"It doesn't take much effort to make something beautiful," Jamieson replied. He took a couple of folding seats from beside the door, popped them out, and gestured for me to sit in one of them. "This alleyway was a gray concrete energy-sucker a couple of years ago," he added. "And all it took was a couple of plants and a splash of paint, and now it's a pleasure to sit out here. It's such a tiny thing, but the reward is never ending."

I nodded, and sat back, nursing my coffee, letting the early morning light warm my face. It was a tiny moment of simple bliss, and I savored it like a mouthful of priceless whiskey.

Jamieson leaned back in his chair and sighed in satisfaction. "I love sitting out here with my coffee. The morning light is such a wonderful reminder that you have another brand-new day in front of you. It's like the first crisp blank page in a journal."

I took a sip of coffee and grinned at him. "You're such an optimist. How are you so perky after so few hours of sleep?"

"I've traveled a lot. I think once you spend enough time napping on packed trains in India and jumping multiple time zones within a week, you get pretty good at getting quality sleep while you can." He suddenly frowned, and peered at me closely. "Speaking of quality sleep... you were dead to the world before. How long has it been since you've slept?"

"Days," I muttered, taking a sip of coffee. "You may not have noticed, but I'm caught up in a pretty serious world-ending drama."

He snorted. "Again?"

"Yup."

"What is it this time?"

I sighed deeply. "Are you sure you want to know?"

"If you'd asked me a year ago, I would have said no." He chuckled once, his expression resigned. "I was always quite adamant that I didn't want to know anything about the supernatural element that sits alongside the world that I adore. I always felt that my ordinary world was enough for me." He smiled, and tilted his head. "Do you know what I mean?"

"I do. You're very good at finding the extraordinary in the ordinary."

"Exactly." He took a sip of coffee. "When I was mayor, and I became aware that your lovely fiancé was a vampire, I was quite frightened. I feared for the ordinary world that I inhabited. Turns out, I had nothing to worry about."

"Not from Rafael," I said. "Other things, absolutely."

"And you, yourself, are from that supernatural world. You're a wonderful young woman."

I huffed out a bitter chuckle, although not with my usual sullenness. "We're not all sunshine and roses, you know. I've behaved quite badly in the past. And there's always some supernatural jerk wanting to destroy the world." I smiled back at Jamieson. It wasn't easy to be depressed right now – not with the morning sunshine warming my face, a mug of coffee in my hands, and Jamieson calling me a 'wonderful young woman'. I found myself preening like a little girl with a new headband.

"Well, you fight against those things that threaten the world that I love, so you're all sunshine and roses in my book," he chuckled. "You're brave and strong. I guess I can be, too." He straightened up in his seat. "Do you want to tell me about it? About what's going on?"

I sighed. He had such kind, twinkling light-blue eyes. He looked adorable in his matching scrubs. "We're in a bit of a pickle, Doc," I began. "There's lots of backstory to cover. Hmm, where to start." I tapped my chin. "I should probably start with me. I'm... I'm kind of unique, you see."

"Yes, of course you are," he nodded.

I blushed slightly. "Yeah, but not in the way where you think I'm a lovely young woman. I'm immortal, Doc. I can't die."

"I did notice that. I watched you grow back the lower half of your body in the space of a couple of weeks. I was lucky enough to pull a unicorn horn out of your spleen, remember?"

I grinned. "Well, one thing I haven't told you is that I'm very *very* old. I've been around for a couple of hundred-thousand years."

There was a beat of silence. Jamieson's mouth dropped open. "No."

"Yes."

"You're not older than me."

"I am."

He shook his head. "No chance."

"Sorry, but it's true. I seem to have frozen at maturity, a few hundred-thousand years ago." I held up a finger so he wouldn't interrupt. "Before you ask why I'm not really really wise or insanely rich, you should know my brain is *very* human and I forget stuff all the time. Most of my memories feel like dreams I had a long time ago. I'm not super-intelligent, because I wasn't super-intelligent when I was born. I've just been around for a very, very, very long time. I don't know what I am." I shrugged.

His furrowed eyebrows smoothed out. "You don't know what you are? You don't know where you came from?"

"No," I shrugged. "I was born to a human woman, and I grew up, but then... I never got any older. And I never died. I *can't* die," I said, frowning. "It used to be my only goal. My greatest wish." I glanced inside to where Backman and Marigold lay cuddled on the giant table, and my voice grew softer. "Things have changed a little in the last year or so."

"I understand," Jamieson said, nodding. "Wow. Okay... so what is the world-ending danger we're in right now about?"

"See, there's this... creature, I suppose that's what I could call him because I don't know what he is. He's been hunting me for my whole life. He's from somewhere else, another dimension." I peered at him. "Whenever I try to use all my abilities, the superhuman ones, he storms into our dimension to hunt me. You following me?"

He nodded. "I'm following."

"When he finds me, he rips me apart. Into tiny, tiny bits."

"Ouch." Jamieson winced. "And you heal."

"And I heal. It *hurts*." I paused, and pouted. "I don't know why he does it. I have no idea why he hates me so much."

"That is despicable."

The outrage in Jamieson's voice made me laugh. "Maybe you can have a chat with him and tell him that."

"Oh, I would." He clenched his fists. "I would give him a piece of my mind." He looked so angry. It was sweet.

"Anyway, recently, Marigold and Leroy put up a pocket dimension around the portal in the town square, to stop other things falling through accidentally. A little side-effect of this is when the Ancient came hunting me when I used my extra powers, like he always does, he got stuck in the pocket dimension."

Jamieson tilted his head. "He's here? Stuck in the portal?"

"He's in the pocket dimension that covers the portal. He's not stuck; he can go back to wherever he came from at any time. But he won't." I sighed. "He's responsible for all the earthquakes in the valley. He's shaking the town to pieces."

Jamieson paled slightly. "Oh."

"I spoke to him for the first time ever, only a couple of days ago, and he said he wouldn't leave until either he ripped me to shreds, or I gave him back some dude that I supposedly stole from him that I've never even heard of."

He shook his head. "Back up a little. Is that the reason why he's hunting you? He thinks you stole from him?"

I nodded. "He says I stole a person called Sariel. I don't even know if it's a man or a woman. I've never heard of someone by that name."

"Is it possible he's confused you with someone else?"

I chuckled bitterly. "There's no one else on this Earth like me, so I don't see how that is possible. But he's demanding this Sariel back, and I can't give him something I don't have. And the alternative is letting him out of the pocket dimension so he can rip me to shreds again. He *hates* me."

Inexplicably, my eyes welled up with tears. Somehow, telling Jamieson this story made me feel very, very sorry for myself. I'd resigned myself to the Ancient hating me for my whole existence. Right now, the injustice of it all felt like a weight in my chest. It was so unfair.

"You can't do that," Jamieson sounded horrified. "You can't let him hurt you."

"I can't do it even if I wanted to." I sniffed. "As a side-note, I have a mysterious government agency hunting me, probably trying to get me so they can experiment on me and try to take my powers. They took Leroy as a bargaining chip, and he's the only one who can take down the pocket dimension."

Jamieson's mouth dropped open. "Leroy's been kidnapped?"

I nodded, my chin trembling.

"I see," he nodded. "Quite the pickle."

I laughed and wiped away a tear. "It is, indeed, a pickle, Doc. I know where Leroy will be very soon, so we're going to get him tomorrow." My fist clenched; my coffee cup exploded in my hands. "Oh, shit. Sorry," I said, gathering up the dusty remains of china.

"Don't worry about it," he said. He took the broken pieces out of my hands and dumped them in a trash can just inside the clinic door, and handed me his own coffee cup. "So, this creature is going to keep shaking the town until it collapses?"

I nodded. "The portal isn't just a hole between dimensions, it's the beginning and the end of an energy field. Because Emerald Valley is below sea level, it's currently sitting very low on the surface of the Earth. If it gets buried, the field will be interrupted. It's a protective layer," I explained. "It keeps our dimension separate from all the others. If the field fails, then all sorts of monsters could pop through on our plane of existence."

Jamieson rubbed his chin thoughtfully. "I see." He looked at me. "And this Ancient creature can't be reasoned with at all?"

"He's stubborn. He won't leave until he gets this mysterious Sariel, or he gets me. If he can wait a couple of days, he can have me," I muttered.

"No," Jamieson said, frowning deeply. "That's not acceptable. This creature cannot just come to this world and torture you." He shook his head. "I won't have it."

"You can go tell him, then."

"Maybe I will." He squared his shoulders. "I'll go and give him a piece of my mind."

"Jamieson," I said, wiping another tear off my cheek. "He's an ancient, powerful supernatural creature."

"So are you," he said.

"I'm not as powerful as him."

He squinted at me. "Is he… is he the same as you? You said you don't know what you are. Maybe *you* are Sariel. Maybe this is all a giant misunderstanding."

"The thought had occurred to me," I admitted. "We seem to share a similar vibe, if you know what I mean. I'm half-human, though, so I'm nowhere near his strength. I'm not Sariel either. I've never gone by that name before."

Jamieson leaned back in his chair, thinking. "You said that you and this creature share a similar vibe. Do you think he is related to you somehow?"

"It's likely. My father was a powerful supernatural creature of unknown origins, a star, apparently. It's possible that this Ancient creature is a star, too."

"Well, could this creature you have trapped actually be your father? *You* could be Sariel, and he could be your father, and just not know it. Or he might know, and he's trying to kill you anyway, because of some mysterious force pressuring him to do it." He shrugged. "This could be Star Wars all over again. You're all stars, so it would make sense."

I laughed. "No. My father was a star, but he died a human. He *became* human, right in front of our eyes. And he's been reincarnated as a human, thousands of times over the course of human history."

Jamieson went very still.

I took a big sip of his coffee, and went on with my story. "I've been looking for him my whole life. Sometimes I find him, but our time together is always too short, and always interrupted." I took another gulp of coffee, and sighed out a breath. "It's why I came here, actually. He's supposed to be in Emerald Valley somewhere. I was looking for him again, hoping he could finally tell me how to become human, too, so I could die."

There was a long moment of silence.

Jamieson looked at me.

I looked at him.

He blinked, turned away, and looked at me again.

I stared back at him.

He raised an eyebrow, and *looked* at me.

I laughed out loud. "You were literally the first person I thought of, Doc. My first suspect," I chuckled. "It's not you, though. My informant told me that my father's spirit resided in Emerald Valley, but wouldn't be here when I arrived. You've been here the whole time."

There was another long pause.

Finally, Jamieson cocked his head. "I was backpacking in Tibet when you came to Emerald Valley," he said, his voice barely above a whisper. "I'd just unpacked my bags when Rafael brought you to me, with half your body missing."

His words hung heavily in the air. I froze. The air in the alleyway charged; goosebumps rose on my skin. I didn't dare move. I didn't dare breathe.

I'd never let myself hope it was him.

Jamieson leaned towards me. "I remember it so clearly, Rafael walking into this surgery with you in his arms. I saw your face. You were unconscious, of course, but I couldn't stop staring at you. And I remember my heart squeezing in a way I'd never felt before."

I opened my mouth to speak, but no words came out.

"In all my years as a vet, and before that, as a medic in the army, I've never prayed so hard that someone would live. I've never worked harder on anyone in my whole life," he added, chuckling. "When it became clear that you were healing, I was hellbent on making sure you were as comfortable as possible. And when you woke up, my heart sang with joy. I didn't even know you; I'd never seen you before in my whole life, but I *knew* that I knew you."

I bit my lip. Tears slid out down my cheeks. "It's *you*," I whispered.

"It's me." He laughed once, and waved me forward. "Come here, you silly sausage."

I barreled into his arms, and he hugged me. I cried louder, sobbing with relief and grief and a million different other emotions I couldn't explain. I howled like a dog into his scrubs, saturating his shirt with my tears, while he gently patted my back and made soothing noises.

My father. My dad. *Finally*.

After a long, long time, I got a hold of myself, and eased myself off him. "I can't believe it," I whispered, and cringed. "I'm such an idiot. You were literally the only person in town who felt like my dad, but I discounted it because of the witch's criteria. She was very clear on the fact that my dad had been here, and would return soon." I groaned. "Now I remember when I first heard of you. Benson had made me go and get a mohan out of Tim's pool pump shed, and he mentioned that you probably hadn't unpacked yet."

Jamieson laughed. "I wish you'd told me this sooner. I've been very confused, feeling this way about a stranger. If I was a younger man, I would have assumed that I got a girlfriend pregnant and she kept it secret. You felt so much like a daughter to me that I've been wondering if someone, somehow, froze my sperm."

"Gross," I chuckled. Shaking my head, I wiped my nose on my sleeve. "Honestly, I think I didn't even dare dream it might be you. I've refused to even let myself *hope* that it was you, even though you were the perfect candidate. My father always loved people, loved to travel, loved having fun and loved beautiful things, and you're exactly the same. It made perfect sense this whole time, but because of my terrible luck I always imagined it would turn out to be someone awkward, like Brick. Or Rafael," I shuddered.

"That would, indeed, be awkward," he laughed.

I cuddled into him, and sighed in satisfaction, savoring the moment. For a brief period in time, everything was perfect. I'd found my dad.

Finally, he stirred. "I'm not sure this helps you at all, though," Jamieson said. "I don't know anything about my former life as your father. I don't know what you are, so I can't tell you that. I don't know what *I* was," he said, shaking his head. "I've only ever been human, as far as I know."

"Yeah." I sighed out a breath. "You say that every time. In the past, I've been frantic to find out how you managed to become human, so I can become human too, and die." I gave him a tiny smile. "Honestly, this time, I'm just glad you're here."

He hugged me again. "And I'm glad to hear you've dialed back your suicidal tendencies," he said heartily. He pulled back, and looked me in the eye. "I must be able to help in some way, though. If you think this ancient creature you've got trapped in that pocket dimension has, like you said, the same kind of 'vibe' as you do, maybe he is a star as well." Jamieson shrugged. "Maybe I know him. If I could remember, maybe I could say something to him that will stop him from wanting to hurt you all the time. I could get him to go home."

"I don't want you anywhere near him," I said savagely. "He's a monster. He'd tear you to pieces. He hates me so much, there's nothing *anyone* could say to get him to stop hating me."

"I would like to try, in any case," he said. "I'd like to be able to help you. A little more information never hurt anyone."

I huffed out a breath. "Well... okay. There's a ritual we can do, I've tried to do it before, but it's never really worked," I told him. "We need a lightworker to help you connect to your higher self – your soul. You might be able to access all the information you've accumulated in the past few hundred thousand years." I paused, and frowned. "It's... it's a lot. It's hard to filter all that information into human words. You'll be able to remember your origins, at least, so hopefully you'll be able to put that into words. I haven't managed to get much information out of you in the past, but it's worth a try."

He nodded. "Okay. Sounds good."

A rattling noise from the door drew my attention. Marigold walked over to the open door and planted herself in the sunshine, stretching her arms overhead and groaning. "Morning," she muttered.

"Marigold," I said, grinning. I waved my hand at Jamieson grandly. "Say hi to my dad."

She looked down at me and frowned. Her gaze swung towards Jamieson, grinning next to me. She rolled her eyes. "Well, duh." She put her hands on her hips and stretched backwards. "I've been trying to tell you for a whole year now."

"No you haven't!"

She snorted. "Yes, I have. We all have. You just didn't let yourself believe it because you didn't want to be *insanely* disappointed if it turned out to not be true."

"No!"

"Uh, yes. We all had a good talk about it when you first told us you were looking for your dad. Barbara even tried to set up a betting pool, but Jamieson was odds-on favorite from the start, and no one bet on anyone else. Leroy even tried to tell you last week, remember? When you were wondering who would walk you down the aisle?"

I spluttered. "No!"

"And then when we were setting up that location spell, you know, the time where I accidently called the demon instead? Barbara phoned Jamieson just beforehand to make sure he wasn't doing a complicated surgery or something, because he was about to be interrupted."

I scowled. "I thought you were all being silly."

"Clearly," she chuckled. "Sonja even had a father-of-the-bride suit custom-made."

Jamieson shook his head. "I was wondering why she kept dropping by the clinic to take my measurements."

"All of us knew," Marigold said, shrugging. "You just have to look at the two of you together, and you can tell you're related."

"Gah!" I buried my face in my hands. I took a few long, slow deep breaths. "Okay, fine. I'm the idiot that just didn't want to be disappointed."

"Disappointment is a part of life," Jamieson patted my

shoulder. "I guess you're a bit disappointed that your dear old dad turned out to be someone so ordinary as me. No special powers," he grinned. "No magic."

I smiled up at him. "Are you kidding? You're the most extraordinary person I know. Even not knowing you were my dad, you're the first person I ran to when I needed help."

"Well, you do tend to need a lot of medical assistance."

"You even popped up when that cop was harassing me," I scowled again, remembering it. "It's so ironic. Again, I'm probably the most powerful person in the whole world right now, and it means exactly nothing. I can't find Leroy. I can't do anything about the Ancient. But you," I blinked at Jamieson, tears coming to my eyes. "My dear old ordinary dad, you're here, making me feel better about everything. Helping me. Cleaning up my mistakes." I glanced inside the clinic. "Speaking of that, can you x-ray Backman again? I'm desperate to know if she'll be okay." The tears were welling up properly in my eyes now. I felt so awful having hurt her. Not only were my extra powers useless, it seemed they were only good for hurting people I loved.

"Of course." Jamieson got to his feet and stretched. "And after that, we'll do this higher-self connection, if you like. It's time for you to finally get some answers."

"It's working," Jamieson grinned, looking at the x-rays of Backman's spine on the screen, side-by-side. "The cord is knitting together." He glanced down at the bear's face and waggled his finger. "Don't get excited just yet, young lady. It's still happening quite slowly as it's a very complicated process. I don't think it's a good idea if we move you just yet. You'll have to stay here for the time being."

Backman opened her muzzle and let out a huff.

"She's okay with that," Marigold said. "Shifters always heal faster in their animal form."

The bear let out another huffy groan.

"I'm not going anywhere," Marigold told her. "We'll all stay here for the time being."

I gestured at her. "Can you understand what she's saying?"

"Sort of. I've gotten used to reading the vibe of her language in bear form. She's pretty good at communicating."

"I'm glad she's still a bear," I muttered. "I doubt she's ever going to forgive me for this."

"She will." Marigold squeezed my hand. "Of course she will. She's already forgiven you."

I looked down at Backman, who focused on me. Moving deliberately, she pulled her muzzle back from her razor-sharp teeth, narrowed her black eyes, and very clearly mouthed *fuck you.*

I chuckled awkwardly. "You might want to work on the bear comprehension skills."

Marigold patted her wife's huge paw absently. "I've got the circle ready," she told me. "Do you want to do the higher-self connection ritual now?"

I nodded. "Yo, Dad. Papa. Father. Are you ready?"

Jamieson chuckled. "Yes, darling daughter, I am."

Marigold led him to the back garage door, still wide open, letting in the sunshine. She had set up a big circle ringed with salt and quartz crystals, with two cushions in the middle. "Come, sit," she said, settling herself on the cushion. She let out a little burp. "Sorry about that."

"Uh, oh," I said, leaning against the wall, out of the way. "I'm having déjà vu."

Marigold brushed my concern away. "This is a relatively simple spell, so there's nothing to worry about. I'm not calling any foreign entities, I'm not doing anything that dances around the edges of blood magic." She shifted on her seat again. "This pregnancy is giving me the worst gas."

"That's because you're pregnant with Backman's kids," I told her. "She's full of piss and wind."

The bear growled on the table behind me.

"Hush," Marigold said reprovingly. She leaned forward and took Jamieson's hands. "Now, Doc. All I need for you to do is clear your mind. I'm going to ask your higher self to connect to your body and spirit in this plane of existence, and speak to me through you."

"Sounds fabulous," Jamieson said, wiggling on his cushion in excitement. "If you can, please ask my higher self where I put my passport. I'm booked to go to the Balkans in three weeks' time, and I can't find it."

I chuckled, in spite of myself. The elation I'd felt in finding my dad was slowly giving way to a creeping, soul-chilling dread.

We were still in so much trouble. At any second, the Ancient could shake the town enough for the ridges of the valley to collapse, and bury not just us, but the portal.

The world would get eaten by monsters.

I was acutely aware, too, that every other time I'd found my dad, my time with him was always short. Something always happened to tear him away, or he'd die unexpectedly. Fate always seemed to rub my immortality in my face. I chewed restlessly at the side of my nail, trying to squash down my fear, as Marigold closed her eyes and began to chant.

A soft, white light bloomed out of the circle, so slowly it was almost imperceptible. The light sharpened, hovering in a column over my dad. There was a long minute of chanting, and finally, Marigold blew out a breath.

"Jamieson," she said quietly. "Repeat after me. I call on my higher self to speak through me."

"I call on my higher self to speak through me."

The column of light immediately pulsed, and grew brighter. My dad was bathed in stunning white rays streaming down from the sky. I was absolutely dumbstruck by the beauty of it.

Marigold blinked. "Wow. That was really quick. His connection is incredible." She sighed. "Okay." She raised her voice. "Combined spirits of the one we call Jamieson, please speak to us."

Jamieson's eyes blinked open. They shone like stars in his face. "Holy shit," I breathed out.

The ground trembled beneath my feet sharply. Damn it, that one felt bad. In the distance, far away, I heard a rumbling noise, the sound of boulders crashing through the forest. Marigold peeked up at me, her face apprehensive. "Keep going," I urged her. There was no point stopping now. We couldn't do anything about the Ancient. He was either going to bury us, or he wasn't.

Marigold took a deep breath, and swallowed. She blinked at the blazing light from Jamieson's eyes. "Higher spirit," she began. "Can you tell us who you are?"

"I am many." The voice out of Jamieson's mouth was deep, resonant, and made me want to cry. It was the combination of all his manifestations, every single reincarnation of who he'd ever been in almost three-hundred thousand years. "I am many, but there is still much to learn."

Marigold's brow fell slightly. "Okay... can you tell us who you *were?*"

"In the beginning..." Jamieson blinked. His flashlight-eyes strobed. My heart skipped a beat. "I was nothing. No one. A watcher."

"What did you watch?"

"Earth," he said, his voice echoing through the clinic, feeling like pure energy pulsing through me. I shot a glance at Backman. Her fur was standing on end. "I watched the Earth. It was all we were supposed to do." Jamieson's eyes shone brighter. "The Earth was the most beautiful thing I'd ever seen in all my existence. The plants, the trees, the wind and rain. The *mushrooms*. The bounty that sprang from the soil was magnificent to behold, I could barely stand the beauty of creation. And then..." his voice trailed off.

Marigold glanced up at me, and cocked her eyebrow. "Then what?"

"The *animals*. The fish, the birds, the huge scaled beasts with sharp claws and fangs." His bright eyes grew wider. "Such a sight to behold. I could barely stand it. My heart sang. My essence rejoiced."

I almost laughed. Higher-self Jamieson was just like ordinary Jamieson. Loving life. Loving animals. "Then... then..." his voice wavered, the resonance dipping in and out. "I had to come closer. I came closer. I wasn't supposed to."

"You came to Earth?" Marigold shot me a look. It sounded like Jamieson was looking through a portal, and he'd decided against all reason to jump through.

He nodded. "I came to Earth. Bewitched by the beauty of creation. I told myself I would go back..." He trailed off. "I missed the others."

"Who? What others?"

"My family. My kin."

Marigold ran her bottom lip through her teeth. "Okay. Then what?"

"Then... I found..." His voice softened, deepened, tempered with holy awe. "*Her*."

I let out a tiny sob. He didn't have to explain that one. I knew who he was talking about. My mother.

"She was divinity. She was grace, embodied. Even though my kin screamed at me to come home, I could not leave her."

"Go on," Marigold whispered.

"We coupled. I thought my soul would explode with the joy of it, then, inexplicably, there was more joy, when life sparked within her." His blazing white eyes turned on me, and the pure light pulsed, sending my heart crashing against my ribs. "Every single day I thought I'd reached the zenith of love, the pinnacle of happiness. Every single day, my love grew. Life, in this realm, was so perfect. Chaotic, painful, joyful, serene. It was all these things, a vast spectrum, each one unique. Creation was dazzling and perfect, and I had created. *You.*"

I gazed back at him, tears streaming down my cheeks.

"You had a daughter," Marigold said.

Jamieson nodded. "Im. The brightest star in the sky."

"Then what happened?" She blinked up at me, asking the question she knew had always been in my heart. "How did you become human?"

He smiled serenely. "I lived as a human. I lived. I let go of that which didn't serve me – my old self, so I could learn what it meant to be truly part of this creation. I suffered. I loved. Even not understanding what was happening, I became human."

"You died," I croaked.

He smiled sadly at me. "I died." He cocked his head and grinned at me. "I came back, though."

"Why do you keep coming back?"

"There is still so much to learn," he breathed out. "This world teaches you so much.

Another rumble shook the clinic. "Do you know who Sariel is?" I asked him urgently.

"I do," he answered.

"Who?"

The clinic jerked sideways roughly, the biggest earth-quake yet. I was thrown off my feet. A huge crash sounded outside. Marigold shrieked, jostled sideways. Jamieson's eyes blinked; the light in them extinguished, he pulled Marigold in and covered her. Quick as anything, I slid a bench overtop of them to cover them and flew towards Backman, still lying in bear form on the table.

She couldn't afford to get jostled too much. In an instant, I'd climbed on top of her, sandwiching her body between my legs, and holding her head still. I rode out the earthquake, keeping her steady, until the last of the tremors died away.

CHAPTER 18

I made sure the others were okay, and rushed outside. Rafael met me outside the clinic, in the middle of Main Street, and held me tightly. "The valley cannot withstand another tremor like that," he mumbled into my hair. "The engineers are advising a full evacuation." He placed his palms over my cheeks and squeezed. "We might need to consider notifying world leaders that the veil may soon come down." His dark eyes bored into mine. "The world may soon be at war with monsters."

"No," I cried. "Rafael, no. This can't happen. The world can't end because of *me*. This is bullshit!" I screamed.

He bared his fangs. "It's not because of you," he snarled. "It is because of that creature in the pocket dimension. He is ruining everything."

I sobbed into his chest for a minute, letting myself feel the despair, the desperation of everything, letting it overwhelm me because if I didn't get it out I might explode. Rafael hugged me tight, and let me cry. "I'm not leaving you alone again," he muttered into my neck, sending tingles down my skin. "When we face the end of the world, we'll face it together."

I nodded, and pressed my forehead to his fiercely. "There's something I have to tell you." Quickly, I tugged him into the clinic, and down the little hallway to the surgery.

The place was a mess. Bottles and boxes had fallen off the shelves and littered the floor. Marigold sat next to Backman, dusting plaster out of her fur. "Is she okay?"

Marigold nodded.

Jamieson stood beside her, checking her vitals. "It's still working," he said. "She's healing. It's a good thing you kept her steady."

"Raf," I pulled him over, smiling shyly. "Meet my dad."

Rafael looked at Jamieson, then looked back at me. "My love. Seriously?'

"What?"

"We've been telling you this for months."

"Goddamn it." I kicked a stray bottle on the floor.

"It was obvious," Rafael said, shrugging. "Everyone knew. I think this comes as a surprise to exactly no one."

I ran my hands through my hair. "God, I feel like an idiot."

"You didn't want to be disappointed," he said, rubbing my lower back. "You loved him from the second you saw him. Imagine how hurt you would be if it turned out to be someone else?"

I bit my lip. "For a long time, I wondered if the Ancient was actually my father. If he was the ultimate manifestation of him, or something like that, and he hated me because he created me, and that's why he keeps hunting me and trying to rip me to shreds whenever I use my powers."

Jamieson shook his head sadly. "Sweetheart. That's a terrifying idea. No parent hates their child."

"Sorry, Pollyanna, but that's not true," I replied. "I've known lots of parents that hate their children. I've known mothers that resent their kids because they're a horrible burden. And don't get me started on dads. If they don't like their kids, they just walk out. Mothers rarely do that, but I've seen some unspeakable cruelties inflicted on kids, because their parents weren't ready to be parents, or if their kids don't behave in the way they expect them to. It happens all the time." I hitched my shoulders in a shrug. "I was always worried that the Ancient might be my dad, and he hated me because of what he created." Jamieson looked horrified, so I gave him a reassuring smile. "I've never seen the Ancient and a manifestation of you at the same time, and he felt a little like me, so it made sense."

"Darling. I would *never* do something so terrible to you."

"I know. It's such a relief." I sighed out a breath. "I guess I never realized how scared I was until now. Now, I don't have to worry. All we have to worry about is him destroying the world," I chuckled, slightly hysterically.

A gust of wind blew through the clinic, and suddenly, Sonja was standing there with us. "Sire." She looked flustered.

"Is everything okay, Sonja? Is Brick okay?"

She nodded. "We are fine. The club has sustained minor structural damage. One of the cliffs on the east ridge collapsed, but the engineers managed to direct the rubble to fall outwards. That's not why I'm here."

Rafael cocked his head. "What is it?"

"Our team in Los Angeles has reported a sighting of Leroy, outside the address in Skid Row." She glanced at me. "He's there already."

CHAPTER 19

*R*afael and I ran with Sonja towards the helipad at the country club. "Are they sure it was him?" I shouted to her as we ran.

"They are certain," she replied. "He was walking into a building, escorted by two officials – one male, one female. We were unable to identify the escorts," she added darkly. "There are no matches on any of the military databases we can access. We've even cross referenced all the black-ops information we can get our hands on, and there's no match."

"They must be mercs," I shouted back. "Some megalomaniac's private army. Some rich billionaire has heard of me, and he wants to live forever."

"Leroy was not restrained," Sonja went on. "Although he appeared slightly distressed, he was walking without assistance."

"They were in public, so it makes sense that they wouldn't want to make a scene." I ground my jaw. "They must be threatening him, somehow."

"Make sure our team stays back," Rafael told her. "We

cannot afford to spook them and have them move him again." Sonja barked into her headset as we ran.

We climbed into the helicopter and took off. I glanced down at the valley, my heart squeezing in my chest. "Oh, God, it feels wrong to run away right now," I snarled. "That asshole could shake the town to pieces any second."

"We have no choice, my love," Rafael stared at me, his eyes swimming with fear and anger. "The only hope we have now is to get Leroy, open the pocket dimension, and fight the Ancient. We must stop all this."

I stared back at him. "Fight the Ancient?"

"Of course. What do you think we'd do?"

I mouthed helplessly for a minute. "You can't... you won't... he's too..."

Rafael pulled me in close, and squeezed me. "My love. Do you think we'd let the Ancient anywhere near you? If he wants you, he'll have to go through me, and Marigold, and Backman, and whoever else would stand with you."

"No," I said savagely. "That's not happening. Rafael, I can heal. I *will* heal. In a few years, I'd be back to normal. Yes, as soon as we get Leroy, we'll open the dimension, and I'll do my best to fight the Ancient. But you're not going anywhere near him." I yanked on his hand. "Promise me."

"No," he said, clenching his jaw.

"I won't die," I clutched his shirt. "*You* will. Marigold will, and Backman will. Promise me."

He gazed down at me, his dark eyes boring into mine, blazing with an intense, desperate love. "I will not let him kill you. That is the only promise I will make."

I sighed out in relief. "That's all I want. He can't kill me, so that's all fine."

Within twenty minutes, we were at the airport. Sonja already had the private jet taxiing down the runway, so the second we touched down, Rafael and I hit the pavement and ran towards it. We jumped in, the doors shut, and the pilot lifted the jet into the sky.

CHAPTER 20

*T*he traffic at LAX was horrific, far worse than in D.C. We tumbled out of the jet and straight into Rafael's waiting convoy of Maserati SUVs and crawled, at snail's pace, towards downtown Los Angeles. I chewed my nails down to the quick, and watched them regrow, just so I could chew them off again.

My anxiety spiked. Rafael, sensing my distress, nudged me. "What is it?"

"What if they've broken him?" I whispered, my voice shaking. "What if they've tortured him and it's finally tipped him over the edge? What if he's moving around under his own steam, unrestricted, because they've hurt him so much he's gone to the dark side?"

"My love," Rafael said, trying to hold me together. "Leroy would sooner die than become corrupted. You know this."

I bit off a little chunk of nail. "Yeah. I just– it's been one of my biggest fears since I took him in, you know. He's so powerful, and so damaged."

"So are you."

"Not like him, though. He's such a pure soul. It kills me to think that someone would hurt him badly enough to change him into a monster."

"My love. You are the same, you know. You've been through horrific torture, and you are a pure soul."

I blew out a raspberry. "Rafael, be serious. I'm a monster. I've done some awful, horrible, terrible things in my time."

"Ah, but are you like that now?"

"No," I shook my head vehemently. "I will never be like that again. I'd rather face a lifetime of agonizing torment than hurt an innocent person like Leroy."

He stroked my cheek. "You need to forgive yourself, Imogen," he said quietly. "You need to let go of that guilt."

"No. No, you're wrong. I don't need to let go of it. It's mine. I deserve it."

He smirked at me. "You've atoned for your sins, many times over. When will it be enough?"

There was a long moment of silence, while I tried to let his words sink in. "Never?"

I couldn't let go. I hated myself for the things I'd done in the past. In the grip of my madness, I'd crushed thousands of innocent people while having a stupid tantrum. I'd accidently burned hundreds of people to death while crashing around, having a mad fit about something or other. I'd crushed skulls in my bare hands. Granted, any time I *deliberately* killed anyone they definitely deserved it, but all the deaths I'd caused because of my stupid actions...

"I can't just let go, Raf," I muttered.

"Everyone else gets to let go of their past when they die." He passed the ball of his thumb over my lips gently. "Everyone gets a fresh start. You haven't been allowed to do that, and that's not fair. You need to cut yourself a break, because no one else is going to do it for you." He leaned in and pressed a kiss to my lips. "Forgive yourself," he said. "You're not the same person you used to be."

I exhaled heavily. "You make it sound like it's easy. I'm carrying the burden of thousands of years of selfishness, you know."

"Not anymore. You're different now, aren't you?"

I nodded helplessly. I seemed to be. I felt different. I was still scared, though.

"Then let go of all the guilt and pain from your past, and go forward. Be scared," he smiled, reading my mind. "Life is scary. It's fine to be scared, and hurt, and angry, you know. It's part of being human."

"I'm not human," I muttered, looking out the window at the cityscape before me.

The buildings seemed to have closed in on us; I couldn't see much of a skyline anymore. The streets started to show me the alternative realities of the people who lived in the city; a ramshackle building with boarded-up windows, its sidewalk lined with dirty tents, then, on the next street, a pretty bistro and art gallery with beautiful people standing outside flashing big watches and expensive purses. I saw piles of trash on a corner outside a liquor store and ragged-looking people lining up beside a truck, then on the next corner, a group of beautiful teenagers dancing in front of a gorgeous mural on the side of a brick building.

Rafael straightened up in his seat. "We're here." He gestured to Boris. "Park around the corner." He looked at me. "I've had a couple of my Bravo team go into the build-ing, but I daren't try to have them gain access to the room where Leroy's being held, in case they move him. We're going in blind." The muscle in his jaw tensed. "This is the same as back in Crystal City, Imogen, but there is nothing we can do. We cannot risk letting them know we're coming."

"That's fine with me. I'll just be careful where I put my feet this time," I muttered. "No way I'm going to be accidentally trampling in a circle. We'll stay in the hallway if we have to."

"We will assume the worst. I have a tracker on me, so my team will be able to locate us if we are magically transported again. I have people spread out over the whole city."

I nodded, clenching my fists. Deep inside, I could feel my star power roaring away at my core, almost screaming at me in frustration. So far, my powers helped me with exactly nothing. Maybe now was my chance. I could pull out my full powers and go ballistic on whoever was holding Leroy, and at least, my star nature would be good for *something*. "Have they scouted the rest of the building?" I asked Rafael.

"Yes. It appears to be a normal apartment building. There are residents; my security team has spoken to a few, but were unable to ascertain if they are deep cover agents or just regular citizens. It *is* a government building," he scowled. "I had Sonja check it out."

"So it is the government after all." I ran my teeth over my bottom lip, worrying at the skin. This felt so wrong, in every single way, but we had to go and get Leroy. We had to save him. "Let's go."

Rafael took hold of my hand outside the car. I sensed, rather than saw, his security team fan out, all wearing civilian clothes. They ducked into alleyways and lolled in doorways, melting into the street with the rest of the residents. "Something about this does not feel quite right," he muttered.

"Yeah." My nerves were on edge. "Maybe because last time we walked into a situation like this, you almost had your spirit sucked out of your body?"

"Maybe." He pulled me forward, and we walked around a group of big, ugly concrete buildings, headed towards the address that Agent King had given us.

The building was a wreck, crumbling in places, with graffiti covering the sides. Most of the windows were blacked out; whoever was inside had no desire to see the outside world. My heart thumped in my chest.

The entrance door was unlocked. Rafael, seeing that whatever mechanism that kept it locked had broken a long time ago, pushed it open easily and pulled me inside.

The floor of the entrance was dirty. A garbage bag lay propped up by the door, its side split, an empty frozen meal packet and a diaper bag tumbled out the side. A concrete staircase led up to the higher levels, some of the walls were daubed with more graffiti. At the rear of the lobby, an elevator stood with the doors half-open, the light inside blinking and making an ominous *zzzz* noise.

"I guess we're taking the stairs," I whispered.

Rafael nodded.

We climbed up, two of his security following us discreetly, until we got to the third level. At Rafael's nod, they fell back. "The address Agent King gave us is down there," he murmured to me, pointing.

The hallway carpet was threadbare and heavily stained. The reek of tobacco and incense filled the air, as well as an underlying tang of blood and bodily fluids, smelling to my nose exactly like magic but without the magic afterpunch. My skin crawled, and my instincts screamed at me: *Here lies heartbreak.*

I felt like I was walking into my own destruction.

The door had lost its numbers, only a faded etch told me we were at the right one. I raised my hand, and hesitated.

"Go on," Rafael said. He squeezed my other hand.

I took a deep breath, and knocked.

For a long, long minute, nothing happened. I glanced at Rafael and knocked again.

"Just a minute!" The voice sounded female. I furrowed my

brow. A rustling noise came from behind the door, then a clicking noise, as many locks were turned.

The door cracked. A woman peered at me through the gap, the chain on the door hanging in front of her face. A white woman, quite young, it seemed, maybe in her early thirties, but her expression was much, much older than that. Her face was very thin, bony, even, lined and scarred with pockmarks. She looked like she'd been very sick at some point recently. I stared at her, confused. Who the hell was this?

Fear and suspicion lit up her jaundice-yellow eyes. She peered through the gap in the door, and frowned at me. "What do you want?"

"Uh." I swallowed. "I– I–" My brain wasn't working. I stared at the woman, trying to put the pieces together.

I knew her. I *knew* those eyes.

My heart thudded, and stopped.

Another voice called from beyond the door. "Mom? Who is it?"

There was another rustle of movement, and I saw him, framed by the crack in the door.

Leroy.

CHAPTER 21

*T*he woman's eyes suddenly narrowed, she jerked her whole body like a snake. "Is this *her*, Leroy? Is this the woman who *stole* you?" She reared back from the door, her face screwed up in outrage, and slammed the door in my face.

I tried to shout, but nothing came out of my mouth. I felt like my lungs had turned to stone. Rafael grabbed me and held me tight. "Wait," he whispered in my ear.

I bucked against him. The world had tipped sideways. Leroy was here, just beyond the door. He was okay.

"No. No, Mom." I heard his voice quite clearly through the door. "That's not her. And I told you, she wasn't a bad person."

"Well, you didn't tell me much of anything. Didn't tell the cops much, either." The woman's voice cracked, sounding high-pitched, pleading.

Oh, God. It was his *mother*, the boogeyman herself, the one we'd been talking about in therapy for over a year now. What was her name? I couldn't remember, the shock had blasted away every detail.

192

Glenda. That was it. Leroy's mom. "I've been looking for you for over a year, Leroy. A whole year. I've been worried sick. I got clean so I could find you," she whined. "It's so hard, but I did it. I did it for you. Every day is *so* hard."

"I know."

"I've been so worried…"

"I told you." Leroy sounded patient and firm. "I was fine."

"Well, the cops didn't seem to think you were," Glenda snapped back. "They said a murderer had gotten you. They'd got footage of her running off with you. The murderer, the one who killed that woman, the counselor," she said suddenly sounding frantic. "She told me she was going to look after you, remember? That was the last time I saw you." Her voice took on an even whinier pitch. "I didn't know she was going to hurt you. She lied to me. That's not my fault."

"Yes, Mom. I know that, of course."

My breath caught in my chest.

"That counselor was just going to look after you," the woman said sulkily. "That's what she told me. She was going to help me."

"I know, Mom."

Leroy's mom *sold* him to that blood witch. She knew that Leroy was going to be tortured. He'd told me that the last time he'd seen his mom, she was desperately counting the cash the blood witch thrust at her, nodding carelessly as the witch warned her that she wouldn't be getting him back in one piece. His mom replied that she didn't care what she did to him. She barely noticed the witch dragging him off to his doom.

Leroy had nightmares about it almost every night.

I could hear his mom pacing back and forward on the hard concrete floor inside. "Is she here to steal you away again? Is she coming to take you from me?"

"Mom, no. You're being crazy."

"No, baby. No. I'm sober now. I'm not crazy." Glenda paused. "You're different though, you know that? You're not the same. She took you, that murderer," she spat out bitterly. "She changed you. You're not my sweet boy anymore."

"I grew up." He sounded firm. Thank God, he wasn't hurt. Not yet, anyway. I rested my forehead against the door and listened. "I don't know that woman," Leroy went on, and my heart cracked in two. "You just slammed the door in a stranger's face."

"Well, too bad. I don't know them, either. They can fuck off."

"Whatever they want, they'll just go to the neighbors," Leroy raised his voice. "Or they can find what they need at the shelter across the road."

Rafael tugged me. "Come on."

"No." My feet refused to move. I wanted to bust down the door, I wanted to kill the woman inside and bundle Leroy up in my arms and run away.

But Rafael tugged me from the door, and pulled me away.

* * *

WE RAN DOWNSTAIRS. "He's trying to protect you," Rafael said to me.

I cried as if my heart would break, tears blinding me as we ran down the steps. My soul was leaking; I could feel it, my whole soul, dribbling out of me. I couldn't imagine that anything would hurt as much as this. Seeing Leroy behind that door, with the monster he called Mom. Pretending he didn't know me.

The pain hit me like a truck. I'd been expecting soldiers, mad scientists, evil witches, perhaps, and a bloody fight to the death. I'd imagined Leroy strapped to a table, stuck in a tiny cage, forced to do magic tricks as they shocked him with a cattle prod. I'd expected to fight my way through a whole team of mercs, crushing skulls, snapping necks, until I could find my beautiful kid, and bring him home.

The truth was so much worse. The shock of it was almost unfathomable. Leroy hadn't been taken by an evil dictator or a black-ops military agency. He'd been taken by social services, and given back to his mother, because that's where he *belonged*.

I sobbed out loud. Rafael led me gently down the stairs, wrapped in his arms. "I've lost him," I cried. "I've lost him, Rafael." I was losing something else, too, but I couldn't figure out what it was. It seemed like more of me was breaking off and drifting up into the aether. I reached out, trying to understand what it was, but all I felt was pain.

My poor, beautiful kid. My talented, perfect boy. My heart bled, pouring out a torrent of misery.

"We need to go to the shelter across the road," Rafael muttered. "He will meet us there, you heard him."

My kid. My poor kid.

My head was spinning. Rafael dragged me across the road towards a building with its doors wide open. The light inside was bright. A plump, smiling lady handed out packages across a counter, while a few older people stood in circles, chatting, sipping tea out of steaming Styrofoam cups.

I barely noticed anything. I felt like I was dying and being reborn at the same time.

Rafael led me to the corner, and pushed me down into a chair. "He will come," he said, gazing across the street. "He said so. He is smart…" He glanced down at me. "Imogen." his voice suddenly sounded urgent. "What is happening to you?"

Something was wrong. I felt like I was being both torn in two and put together at the same time. Like two opposing forces were battling for control within me. I had no words for this feeling, this emotion overwhelming me.

It didn't matter, though. It didn't really care if my head had been cut off. "My heart," I sobbed. "My heart is breaking."

Rafael's beautiful dark eyes fixed on me. "I would say you are being overly dramatic, but..." His eyes roamed over my face. "Something is happening to you."

There was a bang across the street, his eyes flashed away, sparking with relief. "He's coming,"

I took a breath; my lungs rejoiced. Even my breath was feeling different, more urgent, more overwhelmingly satisfying. I *needed* to breathe. I blinked the tears out of my eyes; fresh ones came, blinding me again. Through the haze I spotted Leroy running across the road towards me.

He ran so fast. He barreled into the shelter, and straight into my arms. "Immy!"

"Buddy." My breath came in sobs. I rubbed his back and gently tugged his hair at the back of his neck. "Oh, my little guy. Thank God you're okay!"

We held each other and cried for a moment. Finally, he pulled back. "I can't stay for long," he said, wiping his cheeks. "She'll get suspicious." He looked at me; his eyes roamed around my face, alarm flared in his expression. "Imogen... what's happening to you?"

"I don't know," I sobbed. "I'm just so goddamn sad. And happy that you're okay. Leroy, what happened to you? We thought you'd been abducted by some sort of rogue military agency, a black-ops thing, and they were holding you hostage. Or using you for your powers, or something."

"Nothing that dramatic." His lip wobbled. "I'm so sorry, Immy. I've been trying to get a phone to call you, but none of the child services people would leave me alone for a second. I didn't want you to get into trouble." He blushed. "And I don't remember your phone number."

I laughed in spite of my tears. "You dickhead. What happened, Leroy?"

"I was cycling home from Benson's funeral," he said. "And a couple of F.B.I. agents stopped me on the road. One of them, I could tell, was a good person."

"Agent King," I said, nodding.

"Yeah." He paused, and took a sharp breath in. "You didn't kill her, did you?"

"Ha. No. She was the one who gave me your address."

"Okay, good." He let out a relieved breath. "Well, the other one was a blood witch. He stank of dark magic." Leroy furrowed his nose. "I played along when they stopped me. Agent King said they'd been looking for me for ages, and that my mom had reported me missing so they'd dug into mountains of video footage to try to find me. Finally, they got a tip, and Agent King flew all the way across the country to come and get me. She said that someone had reported you for being a human trafficker, so the F.B.I got involved. I didn't know what to do, or how to play it," he muttered, looking at his shoes. "I didn't want to hurt Agent King – she only had good intentions. I also got a feeling that the other one, the blood witch – Agent Mullins – might hurt Agent King if I didn't come quietly. He wasn't in Emerald Valley for me. He was there for you."

"I know." I smoothed his hair back. "I know, buddy."

"I got in the car with them and told her I'd been on my own for a long time. Said I didn't know anything about you. I played dumb," he said, grinning. "But they already had your address, and they were driving up to the cabin to see if you were there. Agent Mullins was determined to get some evidence that you'd stolen me, so I triggered the clean-up charm."

I paused, and blinked the tears out of my eyes. "Clean-up charm?"

He blushed. "I blew up the cabin before we arrived."

I cocked my head. "*You* did that?"

"I didn't want them to find any evidence of you!"

Another piece of the puzzle slid into place. "You said you'd been alone the whole time?"

"Agent Mullins asked me a billion questions about you. I told him I didn't know anything. They had videos of us running away from that wellness center after we torched the therapist's room. They also had a still from when you saved me from those two human traffickers. Agent Mullins said you were a murderer and he was going to find you, so I played dumb, and said I didn't know what happened to you. He was so angry, but Agent King calmed him down. We drove back to D.C. and Agent King placed me with a social services agency, who arranged to have me driven back to L.A, because I said I was worried about flying." He looked at me, and gave me a wry smile. "I'm so glad you didn't kill her. She was really nice, Immy. I ended up telling her that you'd saved my life, and you were the best person I'd ever known."

He looked down at his feet. "She believed me. She had already interviewed my mom." His voice dropped to a whisper. "I don't think she has much faith in my mom's new sobriety. She told me she was sorry that she tracked me down."

"She told me that, too," I muttered, hugging him close.

"My mom's clean," he said, desperation flaring in his eyes. "But she's paranoid. She'll call the cops if she thinks you're back to steal me away again. She's so on edge... And I'm worried they're watching you, Immy," he said, shaking his head. "Something bad is going to happen, I can tell." He worried the bottom of his lip between his teeth. "I'm stuck with my mom for now, but it won't be for long."

"She might hurt you, buddy," I whispered. Another violent emotion rocked through me, shaking me to the core. I took a shuddering breath in and felt parts of myself click together again. I couldn't fall apart now. Not right now.

"She can't hurt me now," he mumbled. "I'm not a little kid anymore."

I stared at him. She might not be able to hurt him physically, but she definitely would hurt him emotionally. He was distraught, I could tell. The way she was rewriting history to make herself look like the victim, trying to gaslight him into thinking she'd never done anything wrong... She was still hurting him. God*damn* it.

"What do you mean, it won't be for long?" I asked him, feeling another piece of me fade away. A tear ran down my cheek. "Will you run away?"

"Agent King already lodged papers to get me emancipated," he said, a sad smile on his lips. "I have a court date next week. I'm fourteen now, I just have to prove I can live by myself. She's going to testify that I'd lived in Emerald Valley by myself, so it should be easy."

"Next week?" It would be too late. The world would have ended. "Buddy, I hate to rush you, but we kind of need you back in Emerald Valley now."

He glanced at me. "Why?"

I opened my mouth, but closed it again.

It wasn't fair. None of this was fair on him. *Nothing* was fair on him. I swallowed, and gave him a tiny smile. "Never mind."

Rafael read my mind. He bent down so he was eye level with us, his phone already to his ear. "I'll get the court date moved to tomorrow," he said. He frowned, and muttered under his breath. "What good am I as a billionaire vampire king if I can't get a court date moved up?"

Leroy glanced back at me and smiled. "I have to go," he said, patting my cheek. "I love you, Immy. I'll see you tomorrow."

"See you tomorrow, buddy." My voice broke. I had to let him go.

He turned, and ran back into the dirty apartment building. He didn't look back. Maybe he was worried he'd turn into stone if he did.

I let out a low, agonized, pitiful cry.

Rafael gathered me up in his arms, holding me tight. They were right, something *was* happening to me, I was fading away. Parts of me were morphing, pulsing, fading and drifting off into the aether. I screamed and sobbed, crying as if I'd lost my heart but gained a new one at the same time. I was pulled apart and put back together, I lost myself, and found myself again.

Another pair of arms wrapped around me, along with the scent of sugar cookies and hand soap – it was the plump lady from the counter. A total stranger, comforting me, rubbing my arms, making soothing noises. Another hand clutched mine, squeezing, the hand dry and papery; an elderly man, someone I'd never seen before, holding me together. Suddenly, strangers surrounded me, solid, earthy humans, commiserating, giving me succor. They enclosed me completely, a thick wall of empathy, with me huddled inside, like a caterpillar in a cocoon, patting, soothing, comforting me in my greatest hour of need.

Finally, the tempest subsided. The wall of people let go, and broke apart, and I emerged from my cocoon.

As a human.

CHAPTER 22

*R*afael carried me in his arms back to the car, never taking his eyes off my face. "You are so beautiful," he whispered to me. He dropped a kiss on my lips. "The most beautiful thing I've ever seen in my life."

"I'm human," I croaked. My voice sounded strange to my ears. My senses didn't feel dull, they just felt… different. I didn't feel weak, but I obviously lost my enormous strength. I felt… normal. It was as if I'd lived my whole life blue, but suddenly, I was green, and I felt like I'd always been green. It was completely bizarre, but entirely natural at the same time. "Why? How did this happen?"

"It's been happening for days. Months, perhaps. This was the final thing your system needed to make the transition complete. You didn't run away from your pain, my love. You chose to feel it all, just like Jamieson said. You embraced humanity," he said, kissing my lips again. "You let yourself be loved. You're human," he said, grinning down at me.

"Well, it wasn't as if my star powers were doing me any favors," I muttered. "How come you're so happy about this?"

He licked his lips, staring at me. "I've always *loved* human women."

I smiled in spite of myself, as he gently placed me in the car, not ever letting me go, never taking his eyes off my face. It was true; before I met him he'd had a never-ending string of girlfriends, and every single one was a human. I'd assumed they were just arm candy, but he seemed to always treat them with respect and dignity. "Human women are perfection," he murmured into the nape of my neck, his lips brushing my skin. I inhaled sharply, and looked at him.

The expression on his face took my breath away.

It was another thing I'd dare not hope for; the idea that Rafael would love me even when I was a weak mortal. From the look in his eyes, it seemed like the reverse was true. He loved me *more* as a human woman. Seeing my incredulous face, he smiled down at me. "You have no idea how beautiful you are now. Your skin. Your hair. Your breath," he leaned down, brushing his lips on mine, and inhaling deeply, he made a low, male noise in his throat. "Your *scent*."

I laughed, feeling the delicious way my chest expanded with extra intake of oxygen. It felt so real, so normal. So *good*. I'd assumed the loss of my star nature would mean dullness and weakness, but this felt almost like I'd been wearing goggles and gloves my whole life and now they'd been taken off.

I was feeling things properly now. *Seeing* them properly. Rafael's love for me was hitting me, filterless, and it was glorious.

Within a few minutes we'd pulled up at a hotel, and, never taking his eyes or his hands off me, Rafael escorted me inside. His security fanned out, dealing with all the mundane things while we were swept inside and into an elevator, and rode to the top of the building. I didn't notice anything except glinting lights, soft furnishings, and the look of blinding love on Rafael's face.

The door was opened for us, and shut for us, too. He carried me to a bed, his eyes never leaving my face. "My woman," he growled. "Mine."

"Yes. I'm yours."

He kissed me. Deep, and powerful, his lips ground against mine, his tongue teasing and exploring, savoring every inch of my mouth. He kissed me and it felt like I'd never been kissed before, the feeling was so overwhelming. I came up for air, because I needed to breathe, and God, it felt delicious to fill my lungs, I felt the connection to my breath and my body, and to the earth, and to Rafael lying on top of me, touching my skin.

The connection. That's what it was. I was entirely connected to the earth now; I wasn't half and half, caught in between, suspended in mid-air, neither one thing or the other. I was grounded, whole in my humanness. Rafael reveled in it, touching me, helping me discover that connection.

I stroked his cheek, tracing the line of his jaw to his lips, and rubbed my thumb over them. With a glint in his eyes, he lightly bit the tip of my thumb and laughed, swooping down to kiss my collarbone, his tongue trailing lightly down, sighing in pure pleasure of the taste of me.

The connection pulsed at the base of my spine almost violently; I arched my back and moaned. Muladhara chakra, the root chakra… Kundalini awakening… I knew all the theory, but I'd never felt it, and now it was exploding within me. I could almost see the red light glowing from between my legs, a new power blossoming within me. Rafael's eyes were dark and hungry, they roamed around my body, savoring my skin, wanting more, pulling at my buttons and tugging at my zips until there was more bare skin to kiss.

I needed more of him, too. I pulled off his shirt as easily as if it were made of paper, my need giving me an animal strength. The smooth muscles of his chest felt like a blessing under my fingers, a benediction. I inhaled him, kissing the nape of his neck and running my hands down his flat stomach, feeling every inch of him. He groaned out loud as my fingertips dipped down and lightly brushed his huge, throbbing cock, straining against his pants. He flexed; his biceps bulged, and I almost passed out from the sensation that pulsed from my core.

The connection. It was magnificent, overpowering, sublime. I wanted more.

Like a genie had granted my wish, his pants were suddenly gone, and so were mine, we were both naked, nothing between us, nothing holding us back. We came together like fighters, clashing hard, he ground his body against mine, oh God, he was so hard, I needed to feel *that* connection too. Desperately, I grabbed him, that hard length filling my hands, and guided him, positioning him in the perfect place, then, I waited, trembling in anticipation.

He looked down at me, savoring the moment. "Imogen," he murmured, eyes drowning in lust. "I love you." He thrust into me, and I let out a moan of such intense pleasure that it must have shaken the heavens. He cried out too, the sensation overpowering, too much, and still, not enough. Slowly, so slowly, he withdrew, and thrust into me again, my back arched, meeting him, both drowning in him and swallowing him completely. The connection pulsed, crashing like a wave within me, within *us*, as he pulled back, and filled me completely, over and over again, keeping the tempo steady like a master conductor controls an orchestra. Rafael, the maestro of pleasure, kept me on the edge like that, right on the edge of orgasm, in the place where pleasure and pain threaten to overwhelm you completely.

His grip on me tightened; the tempo didn't change, slowly out, hard in, he teased me, but he was about to explode, too. "Please," I begged him. "Please." I wanted to feel him come.

He withdrew, his eyes locked on me, eyes drowning in passion. He gazed down at me and growled. "Mine."

I whimpered. "Yours. I'm yours."

Thrust. Oh, God…

I exploded.

Rafael's mouth fell on my neck, and he bit me.

CHAPTER 23

$\mathcal{W}$e lay helpless, side by side, for a long time. Bodies slick with sweat, perfumed with the earthy musky scent of sex, crumpled together like discarded toys.

I felt insanely good. Better than I'd ever felt in my entire life. I never wanted to move ever again, in case I disrupted the feeling of being perfectly, completely satisfied.

"Kill me now," I mumbled. "I want to go out on a high."

Rafael laughed. "Don't joke, my darling. You're human. You *can* be killed."

"Then I'd die happy." I shuffled closer, loving the way his skin slid on mine.

"You'd miss out on us doing it again."

I paused. "You make a good point." Just when I couldn't feel any more pleasure, another layer settled on top of me. The idea that I could do *that* with Rafael, over and over again, as many times as we wanted. *Yessss.*

I stretched out, feeling my tendons pop and muscles roll deliciously. Everything was going to be okay. Tomorrow, we'd get Leroy free, and take him back to Emerald Valley. My dad would remember who Sariel was, and we'd be able to give him back to the Ancient. And if we couldn't do that, Leroy and Marigold would figure out a way to force him back through the portal or something.

Rafael and I would get married. We'd be happy. I had so much faith in the future.

A knock at the door pierced my bubble of bliss.

Rafael sighed, and got up, taking a robe from the closet and wrapping it around himself before opening the door. Boris stood in the doorway, his posture tense. "My King, we have a problem."

I shuffled off the bed and started pulling my shirt back on. "What's wrong?" We had many problems, too many to keep track of, actually. Despite my hopes and dreams, there was still a whole mountain of things to overcome before we could savor our peace.

Suddenly, I was stupidly grateful for the tiny fragment of pure bliss that we'd snatched, away from all our troubles. "Is it Emerald Valley? Has there been another earthquake?"

Boris looked over at me. "No, the tremors have lessened since we left the valley. They're continuing regularly, but not with the force of the last one that took down part of the east ridge."

"That's good news," I sighed in relief. At least we had a stay of execution from the Ancient shaking the valley apart.

"What is the problem?" Rafael asked him.

Boris glanced back at me. "Our lawyers have delivered the emancipation papers to Leroy's mother," he said, his gruff voice quiet. "She is… enraged."

I scrambled off the bed, electrified. "Oh, fuck."

"Our team on the ground was concerned for Leroy's safety, so they broke down the door. They are standing guard in between them. His mother is… quite distressed."

Rafael had pulled his clothes on at lightning speed. He

held out his hand to me. I jammed my legs in my jeans and buttoned them, rushing forward to meet him at the same time.

The bubble of bliss was gone. "I shouldn't have left him," I whimpered, stabbing at the lobby button of the elevator. "We should have forced him to come with us."

"You wouldn't have forced him," Rafael murmured back.

"Gah. No, I wouldn't have." I chewed on the skin around my fingernail. "I left him because he needed to stay with her for the end. He needed this closure."

Rafael squeezed my hand. "Yes."

It didn't make me feel any better. Nervously, I bit my nails and gazed out the window.

"He'll be okay," Rafael told me. "She won't be able to hurt him. He has so much magic to protect himself, he'd have a shield up."

Boris drove like a maniac. The hotel was only a stone's throw from Leroy's apartment, another blistering display of the divide between rich and poor. On one street, luxury boutiques spat out well-dressed people, their faces surgically carved to a cold perfection. On the next, three people lay asleep underneath a cardboard shelter in front of a crumbling facade of a building with the stench of urine hanging heavy in the air.

We pulled up right outside Leroy's apartment and tumbled out. Hand in hand, we burst into the lobby and ran up the cold concrete steps.

I could hear Glenda screaming from several floors away. "How dare you do this to me? After everything I've done! After everything I've gone through!"

I pushed harder.

"Do you know how hard it has been for me? Do you know how much it *hurt?* The torture of getting clean? I did it for you! And this is how you repay me?"

We reached the second floor, then the third, and burst into the hallway. There was a crash coming from the apartment. She was trashing the place. I heard Leroy answer her in a low, steady tone, and she screeched back in reply.

"I've done it all for you! I've given up everything for you! I gave up my whole life when I got pregnant with you! I took a beating from O'Kelly when he found out I was too far gone to get rid of you, he beat me out of his stable, did you know that? And I couldn't go back! He wouldn't *have* me back," she screamed.

I held back a snarl. For a long time, Leroy played with the idea in his head that his mother only did terrible things because of her addiction. We'd talked about it, gently and carefully, together as well as with his therapist, and he admitted that there were long periods in which his mother had been sober, but still beat him and occasionally pimped him out for grocery money. She told him it was his duty, since she couldn't work the streets anymore, he would have to. At *eleven years old*.

Addiction can do terrible things to people, and I'd seen redemption before. But Leroy's mom didn't have the crushing lows of remorse when she'd done something awful to him. She never did. Slowly, with the help of therapy, Leroy realized this.

She'd never taken responsibility for her actions. Every single time, she rewrote history, lied to herself and everyone else, and blamed anything she could. She'd never once apologized for hurting him.

Now, I could hear her blaming him for everything she'd done, and it made me want to kill her.

"I've got no money because of you," she screamed. "I've been waiting by the phone for a whole year to find out if you were okay. I went through withdrawals for you – I thought it would kill me! For you! And this is how you repay me?"

We rushed down the hallway, past a couple of Rafael's vamps, straight through the open door.

The place was a mess. She'd overturned the chairs and tables, and smashed plates on the floor. Fragments of paper fluttered on every surface – she'd ripped the emancipation papers into tiny pieces and thrown them in the air. Now, pacing like a hyena, slavering, spitting, with abuse leaking from her like a burst sewage pipe, she raged in the kitchen, back and forth, throwing cups and smashing bowls on the floor.

Leroy stood by the wall next to the T.V, glass lying scattered by his feet. A chill ran through me; she'd thrown something heavy at him, and it had smashed the TV. With a low growl, I stalked forward and planted myself in front of him. The security vamps melted away, standing back.

Glenda whirled around and screamed when she saw me. "You! You fucking *bitch!* This is all your fault. You've poisoned him against me." She stomped towards me, her bony face spitting mad, hands clawed, murder in her eyes.

Rafael reached out and grabbed her by the back of the neck. She let out a strangled yelp as her forward motion was arrested. Hissing and spitting, she clawed out at Rafael like a feral cat.

Cold with fury, he shook her sharply, just once. "You will listen to him," he growled.

She didn't stop. She struggled in his grip, yellowed eyes narrowed, and she spat at me. "Fucking bitch. You fucking bitch. You stole him from me."

"He's not a thing, Glenda," I said coolly. "He's not an object. He's not a tool. He's a person."

"He's mine," she shrieked, struggling in Rafael's grip. "He's my son. He'll do what I tell him."

"No." My voice snapped like a gunshot. With an enormous effort, I clenched my fists, shoving the urge to punch her until her head broke off completely. It was odd; I was completely human now, but I had never felt so powerful in my whole life. I took one step closer – just one, and raised one eyebrow. "The only thing you will do now is *listen to him.*"

She laughed scornfully, still writhing helplessly. "You don't get to tell me what to do. No one gets to tell me what to do!" She tore at Rafael's hands and arched her back, trying to break free, but he held her tight. "Leroy will listen to *me*. He's my kid. Mine, you hear me? He will listen to me." She spat at me; a big mouthful of saliva sprayed on the stained thread-bare carpet at her feet. "Leroy," she snapped. "Get rid of these people. Tell them to leave. Now. They're not here for us, baby. They're only here to try and destroy us, to try and break us up. I'm here for you, Leroy. I'm your mom. I need you."

There was a beat of silence. Leroy was behind me; I didn't dare turn around. I needed to be strong for him, and if I was to look at him, I might bundle him up and run away with him forever.

He needed this. He needed to see the awful, cold hard truth.

Glenda's mouth curled up in a smirk at Leroy's silence. "And then you can tell your social workers to forget about the emancipation, okay? Things have been tough, I know. It's been hard on both of us."

"Both of us?" Leroy's voice was tiny.

"Yeah. Of course." She thrust her chin up. "It's been so hard getting clean, Leroy. But I did it for you."

"You did it for me?"

"Of course!" Her face split into a wide grin. "Aren't you proud of me?"

"Agent King told me you got locked up, and had to go to court ordered rehab. They forced you to get clean."

"I'm still clean now, though, sweetheart!" Her voice was wheedling. "All I could think of was how much I needed you back in my life, so I stayed clean."

"Do you have a job?"

She peered at him. "No. Why?"

"How will you take care of me?"

"We'll take care of each other, son. We've got each other." She gave him the most insincere smile I'd ever seen in my life.

There was a loaded silence. Leroy broke it. "Why did you sell me?"

"I never sold you," she gave a scornful laugh. "You don't remember things right."

"You sold me lots of times."

"You're only a little kid, Leroy. You must have gotten confused." She shrugged. "Sometimes I got someone to look after you when I couldn't, you know that, baby. When I was sick." Her ratty face wrinkled up in a pout. "It's a sickness, you know. I'm sick. I needed help, so I got people to help me."

"You sold me." His voice was empty, dispassionate. "You pimped me out."

"I never did! It's not my fault."

"You offered me to men in the subway, a month before you sold me to that counselor. Do you remember telling that fat businessman that he could do what he wanted, but not to bruise my face?" He paused, letting his words hit like a punch. "I had a welfare check the next day, and you didn't want the social worker to ask any questions."

Glenda's frantic movements slowed. A wary look came into her eyes. "No. That didn't happen, baby. You're remembering it wrong."

Behind me, Leroy took a step closer. A hard edge crept into his voice. "He took a photo of me, you know. Doing... things... to him."

Glenda froze. Her eyes narrowed.

"Agent King told me that they busted that guy for child porn a few months back. He still had the photo of me. He's already given a statement. I'll testify, too." He paused. His tone lowered, heavy and final.

"At my emancipation hearing."

Her eyes bulged. She looked at him, standing behind me, breathing heavily, nostrils flaring. Her jaw ground from side to side. No words came out of her.

There was nothing more explosive than a narcissist caught in a lie. They never believed they were lying, of course, they were always right. Someone else was always to blame, they were the victim, they'd never done anything wrong. When they were caught out, it was hard for their brain to process reality slapping them in the face.

Leroy took another step closer to me, and took my hand. "Imogen saved my life. She saved me from the blood witch you sold me to, for starters, but then she saved *me*. She saved my soul. She took me exactly as I am – broken to pieces – and she put me back again so I was stronger than ever."

Glenda stared at him. My heart thumped so hard I thought it might leap out of my chest.

"Imogen showed me that it wasn't my fault, what happened to me, and she showed me exactly how powerful I really was. She taught me that my past made me who I was. It tempered me, like steel. It didn't matter that I was broken." He hesitated, taking a deep breath. "But it does matter that you were the one who broke me."

Glenda's face crumbled. Her shoulders slumped. All the fight suddenly went out of her. She sagged in Rafael's grip, and he let her go. She stood there, not moving, her mouth open, frozen in a parody of a helpless scream.

"Imogen's suffered too. Like you. You've suffered, I get that. I understand that. Life hasn't been fair to you, just like life hasn't been fair to Imogen. The difference between you and her is that Imogen would walk through fire to save me."

I glanced down at him, and squeezed his hand. He was right. I'd give anything to make sure Leroy was safe. I smiled down at him. "You're worth it, you know. You're worth more than anything in the world."

He grinned back at me. "I know. You made me believe it. I love you, Immy."

"I love you too, buddy," I whispered back.

There was a long moment of silence. Glenda slumped forward, putting her hands on the back of the ratty brown sofa. Rafael stepped back, letting her crumble. She mouthed helplessly, her face twitching, like watching a computer over-loaded with commands stutter and freeze, about to explode.

"Let's go," I tugged Leroy's hand. "Let's go home."

He nodded.

Rafael came to my side, and Leroy turned his back on his mother, still slumped over the couch. Rafael took his other hand and pulled him towards the door.

I shot Glenda one last look. Her expression changed the second Leroy turned his back – her face twisted in outrage; a pure-black venomous hatred blazed in her eyes. Lightning fast, her hands plunged down the back of the sofa, behind the cushions.

I turned my back on her.

There was a rustling noise, then, an ominous click. Adrenaline flooded through me, electrifying my whole body; I whirled back around. Glenda had a gun, and it was pointed right at me.

CHAPTER 24

The bang was deafening.

Leroy reacted first; whirling around, letting go of my hand, he shouted once and threw out a net of bright blue light. Rafael snarled, let go of Leroy's hand and flew towards Glenda with bloody murder in his eyes. It was too late, though.

The bullet reached me first.

It smashed into my chest, penetrating the flesh, plowing straight into my body unimpeded by the hard bones of my ribcage, sending fragments of rib scattering into the surrounding tissue. It popped my lung like a giant balloon and triggered a cascade of blood within me, coming to rest only inches away from my heart. I felt the smack when the bullet hit me, it drove me back a step. I felt it all, each tiny little bone chip and lung explosion. I looked down at the blood soaking my shirt, gushing from the tiny hole in my chest. Then, I felt nothing.

"No!" Leroy screamed.

I blinked at him. "It's okay..." I said.

It always was okay. I always healed. I didn't feel any pain.

Rafael had ripped the gun out of Glenda's hand and crushed the barrel in his fingers. She backed away into the kitchen, suddenly wildly aware that he wasn't human. But as soon as she was disarmed he ignored her, and ran back to me. Boris took his place, looming over Glenda, baring his fangs and growling at her as she cowered on the floor in the kitchen, screaming in mortal terror.

Leroy's expression was wild; he patted me gently, eyes wide and frightened. "Immy... Immy, no..."

"It's okay," I repeated. I felt cold, though.

Rafael's hands pressed against me, holding my chest, applying pressure, as he screamed orders at his team. I glanced up at him, confused. "What..?"

It didn't hurt. I didn't feel anything, except for the cold. It was a strange feeling – a bitter, empty numbness. It was weird; last time I'd been shot, the pain had almost ripped me in two.

My legs wobbled, then decided to ignore whatever unconscious thoughts I directed towards them to keep me standing. Rafael caught me as I collapsed, and lay me gently on the ground, pleading with me to hold on. *Hold on.* His desperation seemed a little over the top.

I gazed up at him, remembering. "Oh."

That's right. I was human. I'd been shot in the chest.

I was going to die.

Leroy knelt next to me, holding my hand, squeezing, his eyes frantic and pleading. He knew. He could feel it. My beautiful, strong, talented kid. We'd come so far together. I didn't want to leave him. Rafael, on my other side, put pressure on the bullet wound, holding me together. I didn't want to leave him, either. I'd only just discovered all the facets of love – romantic love, passionate love, maternal love, sisterly love.

My lips trembled. I needed to speak, but my punctured

lung couldn't give me the air I needed. I had enough, though. Just enough to give voice to the words from my heart. "I don't want to die," I whispered.

My brain laughed back at me manically. I'd gone almost three-hundred thousand years trying to die. Deliberately seeking out ways to end this long, long lifetime, and within two hours of becoming mortal, I was dying.

Leroy and Rafael knelt over me, squeezing my hand, stroking my face, pleading and begging for me to hold on.

I couldn't do it, though. I wanted to. I wanted to live. But I'd been shot enough times to know that my wound was fatal to a human body. I was losing too much blood; my internal organs were destroyed, and my lifeforce was leaving me.

My immortal life was over. This was my mortal death.

A tear leaked out from my eye. My vision was tunneling; all I could see was Leroy and Rafael, hunched over me.

I had no more breath in my body. No more life. I desperately wanted to stay.

Death had come for me. *Finally*.

THE END

HA HA. JUST KIDDING

CHAPTER 25

A delicious smell tickled my senses, prodding my brain into alertness. It smelt amazing, fresh and sweet, with a hint of sultry smokiness and excitement, just like candy apples at a Beltane night fair. My eyes twitched, letting my nose savor the scent before full consciousness sank in.

Yum. What *was* that?

I blinked, desperate to see.

Ouch. Too bright. I pinched my eyes closed again. Wherever I was, the light was way too bright.

Hmm. I was dead, right? Was this Heaven? Maybe. The bright light was a little cliché…

That delicious smell drifted over me again in a light, cool gust of air. With it came a sound; a sigh, a rough, male noise loaded with intense, passionate relief. The noise made my heart swell within my chest.

Finally, my brain connected with the rest of my body. My toes twitched first, then my calves, my hamstrings flexed, supple and feeling refreshed, wired with a strange new energy. My tummy squirmed as if a million butterflies had taken flight inside of me. My chest felt whole, not punctured at all by searing metal. My lungs were intact. I followed the path of my breath from my nostrils, all the way to the bottom of my diaphragm, feeling my whole system zing with energy. I was hungry, excited, buzzing with emotion.

My eyes twitched again. A shard of light pierced my brain, and I squeezed my eyes shut. Too bright. A noise escaped my lips, a little squeak.

Something squeezed my hand; firm, dry and familiar. Oh, God, that felt so good. I wish I could have opened my eyes to see him. I knew it was him, too. Trust Rafael to follow me into Death's chilly embrace.

He read my mind, as he often did. I scented a whiff of glass and metal, and felt an object slip on my face, resting on my nose, with little arms sliding over my ears. "My love," he whispered to me. "There. You can open your eyes now."

"Rafael?" I blinked again, the sunglasses held back the worst of the glare now, but the brightness was still overwhelming. "Oh."

He pulled me upright, too impatient to wait for my eyes to adjust, he took my face in his hands and buried his lips in mine, and he kissed me deeply. I forgot my confusion, the overwhelming light beyond my sunglasses, the zinging, hard-metal feeling inside my body, and I kissed him back.

I could have kissed him forever, except something was tickling at the back of my mind. A danger lurking in the background, ruining this precious moment. I could feel it in the atoms in the air around me, charged as if a lightning storm raged around me. I could taste it in the air; a hint of smoke and the dry dust of rockfall.

I pulled back. "I'm not dead."

"No, my love."

"So I wasn't truly mortal after all." I furrowed my brow. "Weird. But good, I guess. I didn't want to die, after all. Who would have thought it?" I squinted, trying to let in enough light through the cracks in my eyelids so I could finally focus. "So... Where are we?" I breathed out. My lungs felt cool, but the breath... It was oddly warm.

"Back in Emerald Valley." Rafael's voice was low, cautious.

I frowned. "Where is Leroy? Is he okay?"

"He is fine. He's here too. Outside."

I patted the bed underneath me. It felt firm, and familiar. "I'm at Jamieson's, aren't I? In the surgery, right?"

Rafael squeezed my hand. "Yes. We brought you back here."

"Right." I blinked gently. I still couldn't open my eyes enough to see properly. "So, where is Jamieson?"

"He's... outside."

Something was weird. Everything was weird, in fact. My skin felt amazing, tingly and strong and sensitive, but hot, like I'd just lain down to sunbathe in the hot sun, in Barcelona, in midsummer. "Why do my eyes hurt so much?"

"It is daytime, my love," he said quietly. "Morning. You are Awakened for the first time."

I felt him put a capital A on Awakened. I took a sharp breath in, as understanding slammed into me.

"Oh." I clutched his hand. "I *did* die, didn't I?"

There was a long, long pause. I felt his hesitation. "In a manner of speaking."

I pulled him closer. "Rafael..."

"Yes, my love?"

"Am I..." I swallowed. "Am I a vampire?"

He hesitated.

I ground my jaw. "Goddamn it, Rafael! You *turned* me?"

His lips were close to my ear. "I couldn't lose you," he murmured. "I'm sorry, Imogen. I know how you crave death, but I was selfish, and only thought of myself." He pressed his forehead to mine. "I'm sorry. I couldn't lose you."

"Bah," I slapped him pathetically on the chest. "I'm not worried about that. I'm glad I'm still here. I didn't want to die in the end, anyway." I lightly slapped his cheek. "But you turned me! That's dangerous! It's too much blood... You could have died!"

He laughed, relief saturating his tone. "You *were* dying. You did die, in fact – your heart stopped. Both Leroy and I were desperate to save you. I received his permission to try and trigger the metamorphosis. I wasn't sure it was going to work, but Leroy gave you CPR while I opened a vein and poured my blood into you, right there on the floor of Glenda's living room."

"Gross."

He chuckled. "Luckily, I had already bitten you three times," he said, and I felt his smile. "The pathogen was already in your system."

My cheeks grew warm. I remembered every single time he'd bitten me. Each time had felt like a promise.

A vampire. I was a newborn vampire. The concept was too insane for me to comprehend. I'd never let myself hope that I could be mortal, let alone changed into a third, inconceivable option.

He rubbed his lips over mine. "You're not mad?"

"Not at all," I mumbled back. "This is kind of the best of both worlds. I'm not immortal anymore, but I'm harder to kill." I exhaled heavily, feeling how the oxygen sat differently within my body.

It was so strange. I'd barely gotten used to the feeling of humanness; the earthly bond, that lusty roughness, the unfiltered sensations. It felt like I was one with the earth, closer to the root of all creation. Now, instead of dirt, I felt like raw metal pulled from the ground. Tougher and stronger, but made from the earth nevertheless. I flexed my fingers, feeling a steel strength in my grip, and I blinked, trying to make my eyes focus. "How long is it going to take for my eyes to adjust?"

"It depends." A chill sank into his tone. His initial relief at having me wake up had disappeared. His tone slid towards despair.

Something was still very, very wrong.

I sat bolt-upright. "Oh, shit. The Ancient. The valley! Oh, God, Raf! What's going on? The Ancient – is he still here?"

He clutched my arms, holding me. "It's okay. It's going to be okay. Just... just stay here."

"What do you mean?" I struggled lightly in his grip. "What do you mean, stay here?" The chill from his voice hit me, ice slid down my spine. "Rafael... what is going on?"

He held me tightly. "The Ancient triggered another earthquake this morning, when we landed," he said quietly. "It broke apart the southern ridge; it's on the verge of collapse. If he shakes the earth even one more time, even just a tremor, it will destroy the whole valley. The valley floor will level, and the portal will be buried."

I swallowed. I cracked open my eyes, forcing myself to bear the harsh light that penetrated my eyes even with the dark sunglasses on. I needed to see him.

Slowly, his face came into focus. His dark eyes devoured me, screaming words of desperation even with his lush lips stilled. The muscle in his jaw twitched. I'd never seen this expression on his face before. Fear.

"Rafael..." I was suddenly very, very scared. "What are you doing?"

"Leroy and Marigold are opening the pocket dimension," he said softly. "Right now."

"No," I whispered. "No, they can't." They can't be anywhere near him. He is a monster.

"We don't have a choice. He could trigger the end of this world. You *will* be safe," Rafael's voice vibrated with his promise. "I am taking no chances. I will make sure the Ancient cannot get to you. I have eight security teams surrounding this building, combat squads, heavily armed and ready to protect you. Beyond that, just outside, I have Brick and Sonja, along with Queen Samara and her army, and Queen Amelia, with… well, she's just got Pepe with her," he added, trailing off.

"No," I whispered. My lips felt numb. They were all in danger.

"And beyond that, Backman and her shifters, Debbie the lion, and Cassandra, as well as the older children. Sebastian is camped out just outside the door, in fact. He seems determined to redeem himself by protecting you."

Oh, God…

His brow furrowed. "Brandon is at the window of the pocket dimension. He never left it. I assume he is trying to protect you, too." He leaned closer, dark eyes boring into mine. "We're shielding you," he said quietly. "All of us. We will make sure the Ancient cannot get to you. You will be safe."

I stared back at him, my eyes adjusting slowly. They seemed to prefer the endless warm darkness of his gaze than anything else. There was so much love there, so much determination. He'd risked his life to save me, and he was doing it again.

They all were.

I couldn't let them. I had to put a stop to this.

Taking a deep breath, I sighed it out again. "Okay," I said.

Rafael tilted his head. "Okay?"

I nodded. "Yes. I suppose we have no choice."

"Good," he said vehemently. He chuckled once, lightly. "I was worried I would have to restrain you."

"Me? Nah?" I said, sitting up. "This sun is a bitch, though. I can't see properly. I might need some more shade so I can look at you." I pointed to the corner of the surgery, where I knew that Jamieson had an Akubra hat on a hat stand, a souvenir from his last trip to Uluru. "Pass me that hat, would you?"

"You will be sensitive to the sun for a while," he said softly, leaving my side to pick up the hat. In the blink of an eye he was back, gently placing the Akubra on my head. "A year or so, perhaps."

I swung my legs around until I was in a sitting position, hanging over the bed. "My skin feels too warm," I said, rubbing my arms. "Do you have any sunscreen?"

He nodded. "All my team carry it with them. I'll just get some." He walked towards the front door.

I waited until he'd reached the hallway. Then, I jumped off the bed, and ran.

CHAPTER 26

*R*afael shouted behind me.

My heart cried out, distraught that I had to do this to him, but I kept running. Straight out the back door, blissfully left wide open, letting in that blazing white early morning sunshine. I was faster than ever; my speed was not diminished at all by my little sojourn into humanity. Vampiric speed suited me just fine. Too bad I wouldn't get to savor it. I shot straight past both Bravo and Charlie security teams, ignoring their outraged shouts.

The sun burned my skin a little, but I ignored it easily. The pain was nothing, a mere irritation, although in my desperate rush towards the town square I sent up a prayer of gratitude to my mother, who blessed me with melanin so that I might survive this dash towards my final death.

I couldn't let anyone else suffer for this. I wouldn't put hundreds of bodies in between myself and my destroyer. I had to face the Ancient now. Alone.

The town square came into view. I blazed past Debbie, roaring at the boundary line where the sidewalk meets the grass, Cassandra, slithering alongside her. I spotted Backman in front of the statue of Sir Humphrey.

My heart squeezed. She was in human form, blissfully upright, spine perfectly healed. I could go to my final death knowing she would be okay.

On either side of her, Leroy and Marigold stood, arms up, outstretched, shouting the final Words of the spell into the wind. The pocket dimension was about to come down. I was right on time.

I ran into the town square at the precise moment the dimension pulsed, flared with lavender light, then drifted away in the breeze, revealing the Ancient.

He stood on the grass, head raised, eyes glowing bright-white, an enormous figure of demented, glorious torment.

His eyes turned towards me. He knew I was coming. He could feel me.

Leroy followed his gaze, and saw me. The look of devastation on his face almost broke my heart in two, but I had to do this. I came to an abrupt stop on the grass, twenty feet away.

The Ancient's face twisted with burning hatred, as he locked his eyes on me. I took a deep breath in, lifted my chin, and I faced my doom.

Leroy stepped in front of me. I pushed him out of the way. "No," I snarled through gritted teeth. "Go away."

"Never," he grunted, scuttling back in front of me. I slapped at the back of his head, pushing him away again.

Suddenly, my vision was blocked by Backman's broad shoulders. She'd stepped in front of me, too. I growled, and moved to the side so I could see the face of my final death approaching.

The Ancient's expression flickered from outrage, to confusion, then back again. His gaze hardened, his loathing of me overcame everything else, and he bared his teeth. He took one step towards me, then hesitated again. Something drew his attention away briefly; his head twitched involuntarily, trying to turn almost against his will. There was nothing behind him though, just Brandon, still sitting exactly where he'd been the last time I'd seen him, with Claude perched right next to him. Except now, Brandon's face didn't hold his usual bored, arrogant expression. He was open-mouthed, wide-eyed, transfixed in absolute wonder at the glorious, terrible creature that stalked towards me.

The Ancient shook himself, refocused, and took another step closer.

Except Marigold had stepped in front of me now, and her and Backman were having a very gentle wrestling match, both trying to push the other out of the way. The Ancient's eyes narrowed. His focus snapped from me, his gaze burning hot with hatred, then melting to a look of confusion when he saw the people around me, fighting to protect me.

To be fair, it was kind of new. No one had ever put themselves between the Ancient and me before.

Then, Rafael was in front of me, arms outstretched, shepherding me behind him.

The great beast hesitated again, studying the scene in front of him. There was no clear line of sight to me anymore; bodies shielded me, the bodies of everyone I loved. There was a long, loaded moment of silence, as he watched them wrestle for space in front of me.

He was confused.

He couldn't comprehend it. Just like I hadn't been able to understand it when my love for Leroy had triggered my humanity to devour my star nature, the Ancient couldn't understand the emotions that drove us. He couldn't comprehend the connection we felt to each other. The love and the pain. The desire and the intense exasperation. The pride, the jealousy, the rage, and the intense adoration. The full spectrum of human emotion.

He didn't understand it.

Finally, he opened his mouth, his voice cold and terrible. "They can't save you," he lifted his chin. "They will die if they interfere. And I cannot suffer your presence one moment longer."

I met his white-hot gaze easily. "Oooh. You can't *suffer* my *presence?* How come?" I arched my brow. "Are you a little wimpy pussy-boy who can't handle my existence?" I pulled a face. "Boo hoo. Poor angry little monster-man. Why don't you write me a bad review on YouTube? Give me some downvotes. Pop on your fedora and brush the Dorito crumbs from your shirt and angrily berate me for existing, why don't you?" *Come on. Let's get this over with.*

His eyes flared wide at my insults. "Monster? *You* are the monster. An abomination."

"Yeah… Except I'm not," I shrugged, feigning nonchalance even as my muscles tensed. I had to time this right. I had to step past Rafael, around Backman and Marigold, and jump over Leroy, and there would be nothing between us. "I'm just an ordinary vamp, now, you know. I've had a couple of big days."

His hard gaze wavered. He stared at me, confused. "How is this…" He snarled once, suddenly impatient. "What is this…" He clenched his fists, his jaw ground, as he battled with his emotions.

I was confused, too. He wasn't behaving as he normally did. I didn't expect him to hesitate; he never had before.

Just then, I realized. He'd never been confused. He'd always been so sure of himself. I was a monster, a mix of two things that should never have been. I was a thief, who stole his precious Sariel. I had to be punished by being ripped into shreds.

That conviction was being tested, and he was confused.

He was feeling a human emotion. He didn't like it.

Suddenly, he shook himself and flexed his shoulders, snapping out blazing white wings made of pure light. It was far too bright; I had to turn my head away, but his voice thrilled through me like a sonic boom. "Regardless. It does not matter what you are anymore. It matters what you have done. You are a *thief*."

"Because I stole the night stars and put them in my eyes?" I batted my eyelashes. "Because I stole your heart away?" I edged sideways, getting my feet ready to run around Backman. "Because I stole all the delicious jelly in the world and put it in my ass?" I laughed. "Okay, that one was terrible, I know. But I don't think you're ready for this jelly."

Rafael, never taking his eyes off the Ancient, let out a tiny sigh. "We're facing the apocalypse and possibly our final death, and you are making *the* worst jokes in the world…"

"Kiss my bootylicious butt, Raf."

Leroy groaned. "What the hell is wrong with you?"

"Drill bug," Backman rumbled. "That was the worst joke I've ever heard."

"It was great! Just like my booty."

"ENOUGH!"

The Ancient's roar was like an explosion, a bomb detonating, a noise that penetrated all the realms around us. I froze, feeling the air around me shake. I squeezed my eyes shut for a second. *Please don't trigger an earthquake.*

I didn't dare breathe. None of us moved.

He lowered his head, eyes blazing white in his terrible face. "Leave her," he growled. He moved again, one step closer.

My family moved closer to me, squashing me with their bodies. "Never," Marigold thrust her chin up.

His eyes shot sparks at us. "Then you will die with her."

This was it. He took another step closer, and reached out with his hands.

Suddenly, another body stepped in between us.

Jamieson. My father.

"No," I whispered, my lips numb.

The Ancient's murderous, blazing eyes were wrenched away from me, and fell on my father. The effect was instantaneous, explosive. He reared back, eyes wide, he was astonished; absolutely flabbergasted. I watched as an intense array of emotions washed over his face, pouring out of him and smashing into us; shock, heartache, pain, passion, and finally… hope.

"Sariel," he breathed out. His eyebrows pinched together, his expression pleading. "Sariel… is that really you?"

Jamieson lifted his chin, staring back at the Ancient. A long moment of silence stretched between them. Finally, my father smiled, that beautiful, wise smile, and he nodded. "It's me, Saman," he said. "It's me, brother."

"Sariel…" The Ancient's lips trembled, his eyes blinking bright-gold instead of a rage-filled white light. "I've missed you so much."

"I know, brother."

"You've been gone an eternity." Golden tears welled up in the Ancient's eyes and rushed down his cheeks. "I've missed you."

Jamieson stepped forward, walking right up to the Ancient – Saman – and took his hand. "I'm sorry I left you."

"You left? You weren't stolen?" Suddenly the creature that had stalked me for millennia looked just like a lost little boy.

I took a sharp breath in. Saman. I knew that name.

Holy shit. Holy actual shit.

Now that they were together, it made perfect sense. It *all* made sense. Sariel, the fallen watcher. A story as old as time, the tale of the angel who fell in love with the daughters of men. I'd heard the story before, many times, never once understanding it, never thinking for a second that it was real.

That was my father. Sariel, the fallen watcher. *The angel.*

And Saman, the Rising Sun. The one who stayed behind and shook the heavens with his cries.

They were angels. My father had been an *angel.*

I watched, open mouthed, as my father patted the avenging angel on the arm gently. "No, Saman. I wasn't stolen. I fell in love with this world, and I stayed here."

Saman's eyes flared wide, a sob escaped his lips. "I thought you were stolen. I thought the creatures here took you and consumed you."

Jamieson sighed deeply and shook his head. "No, brother. I was only consumed by love."

"Love?" The Ancient tilted his head. "I understand love, brother. I love you. I love creation. I watched creation and loved it, just like we were supposed to. But then, you were gone."

"I hurt you," Jamieson said softly. "I'm so sorry, Saman, my brother. I watched creation and loved it, just like you, but I loved it so much I became part of it."

Saman's chin trembled. "I've missed you so much." He clutched at his chest. "This feeling... this feeling..."

My father placed his hand over Saman's, resting over his heart, and he nodded at his brother. "Relief," he said, smiling up at the terrifying creature. "It's relief. There's lots of emotions here on this plane of existence," he added sagely. "You should try feeling some. It's quite lovely."

"Ah-hem." I cleared my throat.

Saman and Sariel turned towards me. Saman frowned, and glared at me. "Abomination," he muttered.

My father nudged him reprovingly. "Hush. That's my daughter."

His eyes bulged. He took a step back. "Daughter?"

"A unique creation, conceived as my angelic nature drifted away," Jamieson said, smiling gently at him. "I loved her mother. It was her love that helped me transform myself into the human I am now."

Saman tilted his head. "Why would you want to do that?"

"Because I *wanted* to, brother. This existence is exciting, pleasurable, painful and intensely beautiful," he said. "I have cycled through endless incarnations, and I have every intention of cycling through more. It's fun, Saman. This life is fun."

He pouted. "Fun?"

"Yes. You should try it."

His voice lowered. "I would not know how."

"You've been to this realm many times now," Jamieson said. "Is there nothing that has intrigued you? Nothing that you would like to explore further?"

"I was too busy trying to destroy the one who I thought consumed you," Saman muttered, frowning deeply. "I had no time for frivolities."

"Well, what about now? Is there an emotion you wish to pursue? Something you wish to explore?"

Saman's huge shoulders slumped. God, he was magnificent. He frowned so deeply his eyebrows almost met in the middle. "There was something..."

"What was it?"

"A strange sensation, when I was in this prison dimension," he said slowly. "Someone was watching me. Waiting for me. There was a bubbly feeling... an expectation..." He shook his head. "I cannot explain it. The feeling was so intriguing that I must confess, I did not return to our celestial realm because I was curious as to what this feeling was. Also, I wanted to destroy the abomina–"

Jamieson gave him a sharp look.

Saman's eyes flicked towards me. "*Daughter*," he finished.

An odd expression came over his face, and he shifted on his feet uncomfortably. "Sorry about that, by the way," he called over. "A misunderstanding."

I bared my teeth at him. "I'm going to fuck you up, asshole."

"Language, darling," Jamieson chided.

"I'm going to fuck you up, *Uncle*." I amended.

He chuckled. "That's better.

"You cannot blame me," Saman rubbed his chest again. "I have been in tortured agony, every time you displayed your angelic nature. It called to me; it spoke of my missing brother." His face crumbled again. "And every time I came, he wasn't here. I've been so *lost*."

I gritted my teeth. As awful as it was, I understood what he was saying. He lost his brother, part of himself, and he had no idea what had happened to him.

"Told you," Marigold muttered beside me. "I did, didn't I? I said so ages ago. I told you that the Ancient ripped you apart because you were causing him pain. It all makes sense," she breathed out, grinning. "It's why my demon bio dad thought you were one of them. Haagenti was their brother, too, once upon a time. They were all angels."

Saman's mouth twisted at the mention of the demon. "That scoundrel," he muttered. "But at least I knew where Haagenti had gone, along with the rest of our troublemaking siblings. They went Down." He looked at Jamieson again, the expression on his face almost heartbreaking. "I didn't know where you were," he said sadly.

"I'm here now, brother." My father opened his arms, and Saman stooped down to hug him.

We watched, dumbstruck, as the glorious angel embraced the little old man. After a long, long time, he stepped back and wiped the tears from his cheeks. "Can I visit you?" he asked, looking down on Jamieson. "I can stay in his dimension for three days at a time in my current form. May I stay for a time?"

"Of course you may visit, brother," Jamieson punched him lightly on the arm. He had to go on his tiptoes to reach.

Saman let out a long slow breath, and lifted his gaze to the horizon. "I must confess I am somewhat intrigued by your interest in this world. The humans are somewhat attractive, I'll admit," he mused. "Although their beauty does not compare to ours. The landscape, I suppose, is quite marvelous," he said, turning in a circle, surveying the town square slowly. "I suppose I have been used to surveying it collectively, rather than appreciating each part for itself. Grass, for example," he mused, looking down. "Each blade is a singular delight. Collectively, it overwhelms. It is intriguing." He frowned, and turned again, facing away from us. "I wonder if there—"

He stopped abruptly, choking on his words, as his eyes fell on Brandon, sitting cross-legged on the grass behind him.

There was a long, long loaded silence, heavy with the weight of anticipation. Then, very slowly, his eyes wide and wild, Saman knelt down on the grass next to Brandon, and reached out to him with a trembling hand.

EPILOGUE

I stepped out onto the balcony at the country club to take a peek at the crowd gathering below. Twilight had come and gone; the full blackness of night had fallen upon us like a velvet blanket sprinkled with shining diamond stars. I'd been hoping the night would bring me comfort, but the crowd below set my skin tingling with goosebumps.

I didn't know vampires could get goosebumps, but here I was, shivering like a little scaredy-cat, hiding on my balcony.

I'd gone my whole life being scared. In the last few days, it had been turned upside down and inside out. This felt like the end. One more scary thing, then I could sink into my new existence, savoring my bliss.

I looked down on the lawn and swallowed. There were so many people. Ambassadors and dignitaries, movie stars, heads of state, billionaires, CEO's and generals. And that was just the humans. The vampire courts were all here too, Queen Samara was here with her entourage, as well as Queen Amelia, with Pepe perched proudly on her shoulder.

My new vampire sight focused easily on each person, zooming in and inspecting each one carefully.

Leroy stood on the stage, looking like a young teen heart-throb dressed all in black. My heart ached when I saw him. I was *so* proud. He'd gone back to L.A. briefly, back to court, and testified against his mother.

He told them everything. Not only had he been granted emancipation, but Glenda was now in jail awaiting trial for a laundry list of crimes.

I had no idea if she was capable of redemption now. I didn't really care. She was nothing to me. I wasn't even that mad about her shooting me. My only focus was on Leroy, and how brave he'd been. He'd said goodbye to his past, to the monster who bore him and then broke him, and he'd risen like the phoenix from the ashes.

Now, he waited for me on the platform, grinning from ear to ear. He was happy. It was all I ever wanted. He was so glorious, it almost hurt to look at him.

My eyes flickered over the rest of the crowd.

There was Backman and Marigold, sitting up the front, Backman resplendent in her tuxedo, Marigold radiant in a white gown that bulged a little over her belly. Her twins had started to kick each other yesterday. She let me feel her stomach, and I cried when I felt it.

Brick and Sonja sat next to them. Sonja, like me, had been overwhelmed with emotion these past few days. It seemed that my transformation to vampire had triggered some sort of Barbie doll magic moment for her. She'd just gotten used to the idea that her King – her deity – would be marrying someone who was not a vampire, and I had to undo all that processing by becoming a vampire after all.

She was overloaded with happiness. Brick held her carefully, as if she were a delicate piece of china, and kissed her gently on the temple.

Just across from them, my uncle, the angel Saman, sat in the aisle seat. He'd shrunk himself down to human proportions, stuffed his body into a sharply tailored tuxedo, and was staring in awe at Brandon sitting next to him.

He hadn't taken his eyes off Brandon in three whole days.

I was still slightly shell-shocked from how things had turned out; my head whirled when I thought about the last few days. It seemed like one minute, I was a suicidal immortal woman, blundering through my existence, alone, depressed and angry, occasionally being ripped to shreds by some incomprehensibly wrathful celestial creature. And the next minute, I had a family, and friends, and a lover – a fiancé – who I couldn't get enough of.

And the *next* minute, I was a vampire, no longer immortal but quite hard to kill. I'd finally found my father, and the wrathful celestial creature actually turned out to be my uncle, who was now sitting there on a fold-out chair making goo-goo eyes at the handsome werewolf who used to be obsessed with me.

It all made sense. My angelic nature, Saman's blistering wrath, the fact that he'd appeared several times as a giant wheel covered in eyeballs... Hindsight was twenty-twenty, but even I could slap myself for being so oblivious about everything.

The mind boggled. I suppose I wasn't the only one who had been stupid. Saman was an idiot, too. And now, he was punch-drunk with love.

"Are you ready, darling?" My father shuffled onto the balcony beside me and gazed out towards the lawn. "Ooh. That's an overwhelming sight, isn't it?"

"It's a lot," I admitted, swallowing roughly. "Do you have any ketamine on you?"

He laughed. "Not today, I'm afraid. Here." He passed me a glass of champagne. "This should help."

I took a swig, and winced. I used to like champagne, but nothing compared to the taste of fresh human blood. It worked, though. The alcohol hit my bloodstream and buzzed through my system, distracting me from my nerves. I took another deep swig, and passed Jamieson the glass back.

He gazed down at the crowd. "I see my brother hasn't snapped out of it yet," he chuckled. "Look at him. Oh, I did miss him, the poor giant idiot."

I smiled at him. "I'm glad you remembered that he was your brother. Kinda last-minute, though."

"Me too," he grinned back. "I couldn't bear to have my own brother rip my daughter apart all over a simple misunderstanding."

I winced. "Honestly, I'm going to have to get some sort of payback over that."

"Oh, Saman has an eternity of suffering to look forward to. Look at him," he pointed. "An angel, fallen in love with a human. He'll never know a moment's peace again." He sighed happily. "Did you know, the very first time I saw your mother, I didn't take my eyes off her for a whole week. She was *that* beautiful." He turned, and met my eyes. "You are so much like her."

"I wish she was here," I whispered. Tears welled up in my eyes.

"She is," he rubbed my cheek. "That's the beautiful thing about this existence, my daughter. No one ever truly leaves us. We're all connected, you know. All of us. Every little thing in the universe is one and the same, and we'll never be apart."

The crowd below us grew quiet, snatching my attention away. I looked down.

Rafael was here. My heart pounded in my chest when I saw him. He walked, straight backed, broad shouldered, intensely powerful, directly up to the stage. He shook Leroy's hand, turned around, and caught my eye.

He smiled up at me.

I gazed at him, dumbfounded. Blissfully, overwhelmingly punch-drunk with love.

THE END FOR REAL THIS TIME.

THANK YOU

From the bottom of my heart, thank you so much. To everyone that emailed me or messaged me to tell me that they loved the series, everyone that left a lovely review, and everyone that preordered each book... please know that my heart exploded with joy every time.

If there was something you hated, or you spotted a typo, please send me an email here info@laurettahignett.com and let me know. I'm human, unfortunately, (and so is my editor!)

If you *did* enjoy it, I'd love it if you could leave me a review on Amazon here. As an indie author, every little bit helps.

But wait, there's more! Sandy Becker is getting her own series. **Oops, I Ate A Vengeance Demon** - Book one in my new series **Foils and Fury** – will be out October 14th. Get it here!

Check out the blurb here:

Getting possessed by a demon wasn't on my to-do list. I was just too busy.

I had a 50 hour work week, a hellraiser of a toddler, debilitating morning sickness and a husband who thought his only job was taking out the trash. I was at breaking point.

I don't remember being possessed, or attacking Terry, or my local priest pulling the demon out of me and trapping her in a banana (with the help of a stranger, a badass girl who apparently wrangled supernatural creatures for a living.)

But the aftermath was wild. Terry promised he'd try harder, and give me more support.

He lied. And I broke.

So... I ate the banana. I absorbed the vengeance demon.

She's a part of me now, sharing my body; we're like two people in a car. Most of the time, I'm driving. Sometimes, I let her take the wheel.

She's the rage of wronged women; the vengeance of the vulnerable, wild justice for the oppressed. She can hear bad thoughts, she can sense evil intentions. She can tell when someone wants to abuse their power, and she whispers their secrets to me.

She also eats the internal organs of evil people... which is a little awkward, since I'm a vegetarian.

Her methods might be a little blunt. And bloodthirsty. But she's definitely got my back, and I need her help right now.

My best friend is being blackmailed. Someone's gotten hold of Chloe's nudes, and is threatening to send them to her whole contact list. Together, me and my vengeance demon need to find who did this, and help bring him to justice.

Hopefully, my kind of justice. The kind involving the police and a courtroom. Not the kind where I'm picking gristle and sinew out of my teeth for a week.

But you never know...

In the meantime, take a stroll through my backlist, see if there's anything you like.

Revelations Series

A cursed woman, destined to bring about the apocalypse.
The religious sect, determined to kill her.
The demon who wants to save her.
"It's Good Omens with a Twilight feel"

ACKNOWLEDGMENTS

Special thanks to my editor Natalie Nolly, who puts up with my bullshit on a daily basis.

Also to Laina Mason, the best cheerleader and best friend a girl could have.

Thank you also to Chris Rowan for the last-minute eyeballs and helpful French swearwords.

All my undying love goes to Heather G Harris, an incredible author and the woman who single-handedly destroyed my imposter syndrome.

Printed in Great Britain
by Amazon

17597380R10144